A CLEFT OF STARS

GEOFFREY JENKINS was born in Port Elizabeth, South Africa and educated in the Transvaal, where he wrote his first book – a local history – at the age of seventeen. After leaving school he worked as a sub-editor in Rhodesia, later becoming a newspaperman in both Britain and South Africa.

His first novel, *A Twist of Sand*, was published in 1959 and immediately became a best-seller; it was later filmed. Since then he has written seven more successful novels which have sold over five million copies in 23 different languages.

Geoffrey Jenkins is now working on a new adventure story and, with his wife Eve Palmer – also an author – *The Companion Guide to South Africa*. They live near Pretoria.

Other books by Geoffrey Jenkins

GEOFFREY JENKINS

A Cleft of
Stars

Authors Choice Press
New York Bloomington

A Cleft of Stars

iUniverse books may be ordered through booksellers or by contacting:

Authors Choice Press
an imprint of iUniverse

iUniverse
1663 Liberty Drive
Bloomington, IN 47403
www.iuniverse.com
1-800-Authors (1-800-288-4677)

ISBN: 978-1-4401-7713-2 (pbk)

Printed in the United States of America

iUniverse rev. date: 9/18/09

AUTHOR'S FOREWORD

In 1905 the biggest diamond the world has ever known was found at the Premier Mine near Pretoria, South Africa. It was the 3106-carat Cullinan which, later cut into several major stones, now forms the centrepiece of the British Crown Jewels.

The actual discovery of the diamond as I have described it in this novel is fictional but my central theme of the mystery surrounding the great gem is real. It is, in fact, vouched for by no less an authority on diamonds than De Beers.

The Hill (also known as Mapungubwe) is likewise an actual place in South Africa where during the 1930s discoveries of ancient treasure were made which have been without rival in Africa since the excavation of Tutankhamen.

Pretoria, 1973

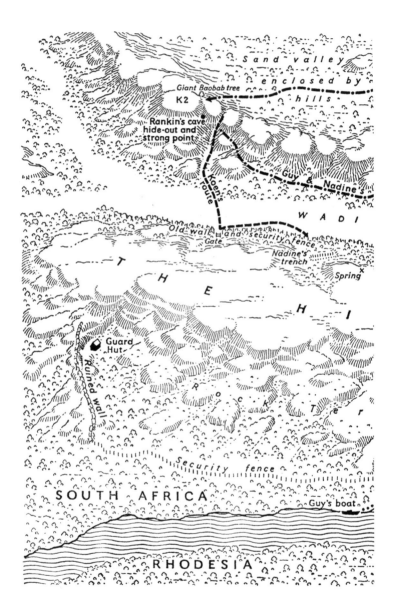

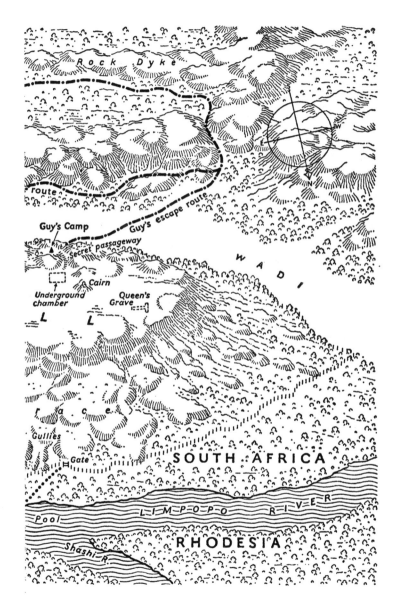

Rock Dyke

route

Guy's escape route

Guy's Camp

secret passageway

Underground chamber

Cairn

Queen's Grave

L L

W A D I

T e r r a c e

Gullies

Gate

SOUTH AFRICA

L I M P O P O   R I V E R

Pool

RHODESIA

Shashi R.

CHAPTER ONE

' "There were indications that the Cullinan was only part of a much larger diamond," ' read Nadine.

Whether it was my deep-down aversion to diamonds which shut my ears to Nadine's words or the noticeable jerk of the little man sitting next to me which sidetracked my attention, I cannot at this distance of time remember. But I do know that I date the extraordinary events which followed from that moment, and her words as the beginning of that life-in-death voyage which remains as strange as any undertaken on great waters. I feel, too, that having had it on my mind for a quarter of a century (since shortly after World War II) I can now commit it all to paper. Because with the building of the great dam the King's secret is now doubly safe, under hundreds of feet of water. Previously there was always the chance that some freak of nature might have removed the millions of tons of silt under which it lies buried. Who knows, had I revealed it before, the value of the gem itself might have sparked off an enterprise for its recovery.

None of this was in our minds that rather dreary day, and the place was as far from high adventure as it is possible to imagine.

It was a Friday afternoon, visitors' day at the Pretoria Central Prison. Friends and relatives were allowed to chat to inmates through a barrier of steel mesh. Warders and hard lights were everywhere. Prisoners were brought in batches of about twenty at a time and allowed about ten minutes' conversation. Nadine never missed a Friday.

I was serving an eighteen months' sentence for illicit diamond buying; only six endless months had gone by before that outwardly unimportant Friday. I was also not to know then that Nadine's words were to trigger off my bitterness at being framed, to crystallize it and to take on a strong – and fateful – purpose.

'Guy darling, you're not listening.'

I pulled my wandering attention back to her and tried to

9

smile. She looked very lovely, even under the hard lights, with her crown of black hair, her deep green eyes and classic features. The place was hot with summer and the relentless lights but she looked cool in a lime-green, sleeveless dress. When she moved a waft of her Guerlain came across to me, momentarily damping the all-present smell of prison disinfectant.

At first it had been fairly easy, on her weekly visits, for her to keep me in touch with the world outside. As the months passed, however, prison life seemed more and more to shut her out. I think she felt my interest slipping for in the previous weeks she had undertaken to bring and read to me small newspaper items or extracts from scientific papers she thought might interest me. Any physical contact was forbidden; I could not even touch her hand.

The little man blurted out, 'If he isn't, miss, then I am.'

We both turned on him in astonishment. He had a fixed smile and a Charlie Chaplin moustache. The artificial grin nevertheless did not hide his interest. He leaned towards us sideways on his bar-type wooden stool. The plump, brassy blonde he had been talking to gave us a hostile brush-off stare and turned away.

'Again, miss – the whole of wot you was reading out.'

Nadine may have thought the little cock-sparrow was a cellmate of mine. In fact, he was next door, but we'd never spoken to one another. She picked up the paper again, partly to hide her embarrassment.

'Wot's that? It ain't a newspaper.' He spoke rapidly, insistently.

She glanced from him to me, unsure whether or not to go on.

Before she could reply he added, 'It sounds like one, though. And you read lovely, miss.'

I didn't know what to say. He'd put the skids under our conversation.

'It's a photocopy of an item from an old copy of the *Transvaal Leader*,' Nadine replied. 'I happened on it when I was looking up something in the university library's files . . . I . . . simply thought it might interest you, Guy. That's why I had it copied and brought it along.'

The little man peered at the date.

'August 1909,' said Nadine.

The little man glanced furtively at the nearest warder. His hissed, almost savage whisper was in contrast to the bright, set smile.

'Get on with it – get *on* with it, for Chrissake!'

Nadine resumed uncertainly, stumbling over an occasional word or phrase. One could almost feel his vibrations.

' "The Cullinan Diamond was found at the Premier Mine near Pretoria in January 1905 and it was then agreed by experts that only a portion of what must have been the original stone had been discovered. Proof of this comes from the fact that the stone exhibited a cleavage plane and only two natural planes – in other words, it had been cut before-hand. A report is now in widespread circulation in the Transvaal that a larger portion of the great diamond must exist . . ." '

'Sorry, ma'am. No reading of unauthorized material to prisoners.'

A warder placed himself between our intent listener and myself.

'That a newspaper?' he asked.

The little man tried wheedling. 'Come off it, officer. It's a very old one – 1909. No harm in that, is there?'

The warder tapped him lightly and almost affectionately on the shoulder with his baton.

'Newspapers is newspapers, Charlie. Nothing about dates in the regulations. Old or new, it's just the same. Must be vetted first by the Super.'

Nadine was confused. 'I didn't think such an old report mattered either. I'm sorry. It's not important. I've something else here too but it's been cleared.'

She held up a current newspaper cutting which had been pasted up on a sheet of notepaper. It carried the Superintendent's stamp.

'Okay,' said the guard.

Charlie's eyes darted from me to Nadine. 'Keep that other one for me when I come out, miss.'

The warder laughed and clapped him again. 'In and out, that's our Charlie. We quite miss his ugly little mug when he's away too – eh Charlie?'

Charlie's smile remained ingratiating but his eyes told a

11

different story. The warder went.

There was an awkward pause. His blonde companion muttered something angrily about not wasting her time on people who didn't appreciate her company.

There were shadows in Nadine's eyes and a flat note of reproach in her voice.

'Do you want to hear, Guy?'

'Yes, of course. You know I do.'

I thought it sounded slick and insincere the minute I'd said it. Nadine's eyes dropped to and rested on the engagement ring I had given her. It was a strange design, a copy of one which had excited archaeologists. The original, they said, could have been Coptic or Assyrian – Babylonian, even. It was as beautiful and unusual as Nadine herself.

A silence fell between us. Nadine didn't look up when finally she began.

'It's about Ted Hill – from last night's paper. Someone has been digging there without a licence. Treasure-hunters, it says.' Her voice trembled. 'Up on the summit, near the queen's grave . . .' She looked at me and her eyes blurred. 'Oh, Guy! *Our* Hill! The queen's grave!'

The wire barrier might have been a mile instead of a fraction of an inch thick for all the comfort I could offer her. I waited uncomfortably while she recovered her composure.

Then she went on, summarizing the report in her own words. Again I sensed the little man's intense interest. The brassy blonde flounced off her stool and made for the door.

'So they're going to have the place patrolled every now and again to keep check.'

'I feel sorry for whoever gets the job in that wilderness,' I remarked.

Charlie craned forward, one hand familiarly on my arm and the other propping his chin on a wooden ledge where the mesh ended. He forced himself into the conversation.

'The Hill, eh?'

From the way he echoed her we both realized that he was probing though there were odd overtones about it. It was improbable that he had ever been to The Hill.

'The authorities intend blocking the natural entrances to The Hill with barbed wire and gates,' Nadine continued. 'They think that the irregular patrols should be enough to keep away the riff-raff.'

'Well . . .' I began doubtfully.

Nadine glanced at her watch. The warders had begun to collect at the far end of the room. Visiting time was over.

'There's a lot more,' she added quickly. 'The guard for the patrol will be flown first to an emergency landing strip in the bush some miles from The Hill and he'll hike from there. They hope this will create the element of surprise. It doesn't say how long he'll stay at a time . . . there's also a hut to be built for the guard on the river terrace – you remember, Guy, on the opposite side of The Hill from where I found the statuette . . .' Her eyes held mine. They were full of unsaid, unsayable things.

The warder's voice cut across the room, a jocular roar in imitation of a publican's. 'Time, gentlemen, please!'

Charlie spat it out, too low for Nadine to hear. 'Shit on him! Couldn't he have waited a moment longer?'

'Time, gentlemen, *if* you please!'

Our eyes locked hastily in unspoken goodbyes, and then Nadine was gone.

The prisoners formed into double file to march out. I found Charlie next to me. He started to whisper something, but a warder overheard.

'Shut up, Charlie! You had plenty of time to say it to your tart even if you couldn't do it.'

Charlie's smile remained, but his eyes were venomous.

'Bowker!' the senior warder called to me. 'Get your fat arse into the library. Super's orders. He wants some books fixed. Take someone with you to help.'

Almost automatically I chose Charlie.

'Okay,' said the warder, 'but if it were diamonds you were fixing, Charlie Furstenberg would be your man.'

There was a half-hearted cackle from the other prisoners. The man called out our names from a paper and ticked them off.

'Furstenberg, Charlie. Bowker – Christ, how's this for a laugh! William Guybon Atherstone! Where'd you get that lot from, Bowker?'

'I was too young to be consulted at the time of my christening,' I came back.

'Another crack like that and you'll go into solitary instead of enjoying yourself in the library,' the warder snapped. 'Super's darling,' he added in a mock-Oxford accent, 'just because he's had the benefits of a university education, unlike us other poor buggers. Anyway, we don't steal to make our way . . .'

'Keep your mouth shut!' hissed Charlie. 'Don't reply!'

I stared at the neck of the man ahead of me, biting back my retort. A minute ticked by and I did not rise.

'March!' the guard ordered finally. 'Bowker and Furstenberg, sharp left!'

The library had indeed proved itself a haven for me. I spent a lot of time there and had virtually the free run of the place. Control was nominal. I was recataloguing it and had reorganized the system of issuing books. I was also rebinding a number of damaged volumes.

Charlie and I checked in. I led him to an alcove where a pile of books awaited repair.

I jerked my head towards the visitors' room. 'What was that all about? What the hell are you playing at?'

'Keep your voice down, chum. Do you want some stool pigeon to squeal to the Super?'

I was angry, off-balance. 'See here, Furstenberg . . .'

The smile was fixed. 'Everyone calls me Charlie.'

'Charlie, then. First you muscle in on an old report half a century old, as excited as if you'd just been given the Cullinan itself for a present, then you have the brass to do the same thing a second time. None of it is your bloody business; is that clear?'

I couldn't read what was going on behind his foxy black eyes. He didn't react to my hectoring tone.

'That's a fine girl you've got there, Guy. You didn't appreciate her today.'

'My girl is my affair also.'

'There ain't many dolls who'd take the trouble to look up bits of old newspapers for a bloke who's down on his luck.'

I splashed some glue savagely on the spine of a book. Charlie watched me quizzically.

'Maybe you don't know it, but I'm allergic to diamonds,' I retorted. 'The Cullinan in particular. My father found it. If he hadn't, I wouldn't be in this mess today.'

Suddenly I caught a glimpse of another Charlie. For a

14

moment he dropped his cheap slangy way of speaking. 'IDB is like extra-marital intercourse – it's widely practised but officially frowned upon.' Then the grinning mask was firmly back in place. 'And it's hell when you're found out. We're both taking the rap for the same thing.'

'I was framed,' I retorted.

'There's no room for you fartin' amateurs in this game,' he said roughly. 'Leave it to us professionals. I slip up now and then and land inside but that's an occupational hazard. You should keep out of this, mate.'

Bitterness mixed with my anger. 'I was framed,' I repeated. 'Framed by a bastard whom I tried to help. And as if that weren't enough, it was the same bastard who found the Cullinan with my father.'

I can still see Charlie's long look. 'Rankin!' he said slowly. 'John Rankin!'

He perched himself on the edge of the work table and stared at me with the bright grin stencilled on his swarthy face.

At length he said, 'So Rankin shopped you! Now there's a zip-lip sonofabitch for you! Never been inside himself, they say. A big operator. Anyone who crossed his path would get hurt.'

'A big operator,' I repeated. 'How do you know that?'

'One hears things around in the trade.'

'I wish I'd heard things around concerning what became of Rankin. We searched the country for him before my trial. Key witness. Not a sign. Vanished. Not a trace, not a single damn trace.'

Charlie slid off the table and pretended to be helping me for the benefit of the warder sitting out of earshot by the door.

'Classic Rankin pattern,' he replied. 'It's happened before.'

'I simply tried to help him . . . Hell, what's the use of moaning at this stage? I'm here for another year anyway.'

'Like to tell me about it?'

Charlie's suggestion was sympathetic, perfectly timed. I didn't know then there could be a double-cross within a double-cross. Nor did I know Charlie. It helped me to talk. I entered his shabby confessional.

'I had a way-out sort of job,' I told him. 'I started a rock museum in Johannesburg – you've seen those old rocks which are etched with the outlines of wild animals. I became interested in them at university . . .'

'There are lots of them down on the diggings near Lichtenburg,' remarked Charlie.

'Lichtenburg!' I burst out. 'I'll never forget Lichtenburg . . '.

There had been a concentration of my rocks on the edge of what once had been the site of one of the world's great diamond rushes – at Lichtenburg, in the Western Transvaal. It was winter when I arrived. The veld looked like a gigantic graveyard of earth mounds from abandoned, worked-out claims. An icy wind whipped the dust off them. I spotted a hut made of old grain sacks and a surly Hottentot working a trommel, or diamond washing machine, nearby. I asked my way. The man gestured to the hut. A voice called to enter.

Lying inside a sleeping-bag on the floor and covered with a dirty, stinking kaross was – Rankin.

I had remembered him from my boyhood as a tall, restless, wiry man with a shock of dark hair. Now his face under its tan was gaunt with pneumonia and hunger, but if he hadn't been as tough as an old boot and in remarkable physical shape for his age he would have been dead. The interior was grim: a paraffin box for a bedside table; and on it a guttered candle, a tiny solid-meths stove, a mug and a bottle of brandy.

I offered to take him to hospital but he refused. I then tried money – it would have been strange to have put a few dollars into hands which had once held an untold fortune in the shape of the Cullinan – but he refused that too. He said he had resources in the form of diamonds but he couldn't trust the Hottentot to take them to a diamond dealer called Cohen who ran a shop some miles away. He and Cohen had had close dealings in the past. Would I oblige?

I did – and walked straight into a police trap.

Cohen was a police stooge. When I was arrested I told my story about Rankin. Cohen swore he had never heard of him. I took the detectives next day to Rankin's claim. There wasn't a sign of him or the Hottentot, who had accompanied me to Cohen's and obviously tipped Rankin off. Even my lawyer refused to credit that Rankin had ever existed. I never got to the bottom of the Cohen-Rankin set-up. All I knew was that I took the rap.

It was an open-and-shut, sordid little case. The magistrate, in sentencing me to eighteen months' imprisonment in Pretoria,

16

moralized on young adventurers with get-rich-quick ideas. Nadine came at once to the dreary little town. Throughout the trial her faith in me never wavered. She was the only person who believed my story about Rankin. After my conviction she tried to persuade me to forget him. Her heart, she said, was big enough to bridge eighteen months in prison because she had pledged it for a lifetime. She often spoke of plans for our new life together when I came out of jail.

It was Charlie's remark when I had finished this account which sowed the first seed of revenge.

'You're going after Rankin when you come out, surely?'

My inner turmoil and frustration edged my answer. 'What's the use? Nadine spent a small fortune trying to locate him before the trial. There wasn't a clue – not a single, solitary trace.'

'She's quite a girl, that,' said Charlie. 'Plenty of lolly?'

'Her father's Harold Raikes, the gold mining tycoon.'

Charlie whistled. 'Well then, you've nothing to worry about. In your place, I'd forget about Rankin.'

'He didn't think much of me before this business anyway. Collecting rocks wasn't his idea of a job fit for the man who was to marry his only daughter. He made that more than plain. Now he hates my guts for what happened.'

Charlie slipped a renovated book under a big screw-press.

I was too engrossed in the tale of my misfortune to notice the over-casual note in his question. I also felt better inclined towards him after having got Rankin off my chest.

'What's this place, The Hill?'

'It's a sort of ancient ruined fortress way up in the Northern Transvaal – beyond the back of beyond. Slap on the banks of the Limpopo River on the Rhodesian border. No one knows who built it, or when.'

'What's so special about it that it needs a guard?'

'There was a big treasure strike there in the 'thirties,' I explained. 'There could be a lot more. The government clamped down and sealed off the area – forbidden territory. It looks, though, as if someone is trying a little private enterprise from what Nadine had to say. There were a couple of scientific expeditions but they came to an end with the war. There's only been one since. They cost a packet.'

'What's your interest in The Hill?' he persisted. 'Or hers?'

17

A warning note sounded at the back of my mind. I'd told Charlie Furstenberg enough – perhaps too much – about myself.

I shrugged it off. 'Scientific. Both of us.'

But he eyed me narrowly and persisted.

'Say, if you knew where Rankin was, would you go after him?'

I was taken aback by this continued questioning. Until then I had never seriously considered either revenge on Rankin or forcing an admission of my innocence out of him. He was simply the target of my hatred, as disembodied as a malign ghost. Charlie's question therefore only sounded academic.

'Naturally. I told you. I've got a big score to settle.'

Charlie started to fiddle with a book, his eyes down. Probably I would not have seen the trap in them if he had looked directly at me, they were so dark and inscrutable.

His voice was very soft. I thought I was hearing things.

'Rankin's at The Hill.'

I have no recollection of grabbing him by the front of his khaki overall and lifting him bodily so that his face was level with my own.

'Let me go, you fool!' he snapped, keeping his voice down. 'They'll see! Let go – do you want to spoil everything?'

I released him but my hands were shaking so I couldn't hold the book-binding tools steady when I pretended to start working again.

At last I found my voice. 'Who says so?'

Charlie shrugged. 'The grapevine. It's reliable. He's there all right.'

'But how . . . !'

'Rankin's holed up there, I tell you. If you both know the layout of the place it should be easy enough to find him.'

A tidal wave of emotions, unformed plans and hopes swept across my mind. They included Rankin, The Hill, Nadine, my release date, Charlie, the future. I simply stood and looked stupidly at the piles of battered books on the table.

Charlie said, 'Get a grip of yourself, man. So – are you going after him?'

I was too overwrought to notice his insistence.

'Yes! Yes! Just let me get my hands on him!'

There was an odd, almost reminiscent note in his response.

'*Mazel un b'rachah* then!'

'What does that mean, for Pete's sake?'

He was very quiet. 'Good luck and prosperity. We used to say it to clinch a bargain at the Diamond Dealers' Club in New York. It's Yiddish. Traditional. Binding. Members never break their word. Or hardly ever.'

For a moment the set smile vanished as a curtain opened on the past, revealing a hard, almost cruel face.

I said softly, 'You've come a long way on the back of that little devil called IDB, Charlie.'

In a flash the fixed smile was back and his reply held no overtones.

'It's the way the cookie crumbles, boy.' He looked at me keenly. 'You've got a lot to think over. My guess is that you won't sleep tonight.'

Nor did I.

In the small hours, from Charlie's cell next to mine, came the words of a song, sung too softly to reach beyond my own ears:

> *Winkel, winkel, little store,*
> *How I wonder more and more,*
> *Whether with the mine so nigh,*
> *You deal in diamonds on the sly.*

I made a vow to go back to The Hill, alone.

CHAPTER TWO

My resolve brought me no inner peace: on the contrary, it did the opposite. A restless fret took over from my previous static bitterness and I started counting the days until my release. My frame of mind, sharpened often to explosion-point against my fellow-prisoners, was aggravated by my decision that Nadine could have no hand in my confrontation with Rankin. How this was to be engineered cost me as many nights' sleep as my plans to waylay Rankin himself. At times the weight of the problem seemed as heavy as The Hill's own bulk. This was especially so after I had seen Nadine on her Friday visits. For she was so bound up with The Hill that it seemed inconceivable to exclude her.

Nadine and I had gone to The Hill together as students on the first post-war scientific expedition in 1947. The place had, as I had told Charlie, lain undisturbed for years. Its natural population of wild animals had soared during the war period when ammunition for hunting was unobtainable. What few communications had existed in the way of tracks had been destroyed by floods or sandstorms.

The Hill has no counterpart in Africa. It is a kind of land-locked Gibraltar across a strategic communications route where two great rivers and a natural north-south migration highway meet. It is situated about sixty miles west of the South African border town of Messina, where one of the world's richest copper mines is located. The town lies in the heart of a broad belt of semi desert which spans a one hundred and fifty mile wide strip of territory from the Zoutpansberg mountains of the Northern Transvaal to the southern reaches of Rhodesia. To the north and south is pleasant savannah country. Sandwiched between is a sandy area of burning heat half the size of Scotland studded with eroded, mesa-like hills, or koppies as they are known in South Africa. It is primarily the home of the grotesque baobab trees whose bulbous, purple-hued trunks reel across the arid landscape like an army of drunken Falstaffs, blown and dropsied with stored water. Archaeological evidence shows that as recently as a thousand years ago the climate of this part of Southern Africa was vastly different from what it is today and that it supported great populations.

The two main rivers of this land, the Limpopo and the Shashi, meet about half a mile from The Hill to form the common international boundary between South Africa, Rhodesia and Botswana. The British military column which annexed Rhodesia to Queen Victoria's Empire marched past nearby towards the end of the nineteenth century. For ten centuries before that the traffic had been in the opposite direction. Hordes of Negroid peoples emigrated southwards from Central to Southern Africa. Geography channelled these migrating legions into a natural funnel. Astride the mouth of that funnel stands The Hill. Its natural merits as a fortress – unscalable cliffs hundreds of feet high, a summit surrounded by natural walls of stone – were strengthened by

20

man into a stronghold impregnable to all but twentieth-century weapons. Like Gibraltar dominating the Mediterranean approaches, The Hill sits square across the double river approaches; it also possesses its own independent water supply against siege in the form of a spring on the summit. To all this is added one asset of incalculable military value to its defenders: there was, and still remains, only one narrow secret stairway through the rock to the top. This was formed at some forgotten time in the past by a huge block of rock weighing thousands of tons shattering near the summit (probably under the intense summer heat) and 'calving' or slipping sideways to open up a cleft. It is so narrow and steep that only one man at a time can make his way up. The entrance at ground level has been concealed for centuries by a huge wild fig of a rare species. It was named after General Smuts, South Africa's great soldier-statesman. With these assets, no Horatio holding the bridge had a finer strategic advantage than The Hill offered one regiment of determined men on its flat table top. Who occupied this Gibraltar held Southern Africa. Without The Hill's word, none dared pass.

Militarily and geographically, therefore, The Hill is without an equal. This would not account for it alone being named *The* Hill. It is certainly raw, savage, forbidding, cruel – characteristically African – but the Dark Continent has a thousand mountains nobler and ten thousand hills more eye-catching than the rough-cut slab of untidy sandstone. Why then its special title: The Hill?

It is the supernatural which elevates it to this claim – a curse so old and deep-rooted that The Hill is regarded by natives as the ultimate taboo. To merely look at it, they maintain, means death. Consequently a large area round about it has been left uninhabited for centuries. Far away from it, if the dreaded name The Hill is mentioned, natives will turn their backs in its direction. They believe it is sacred to the great ancestral spirits who lodged their treasures in its fastnesses. Nothing is known of its past, except legend, since Africa has no indigenous written history. No other hill holds so many unexplained secrets; the dark crumbling rocks, recesses and ruined fortifications, built and laid out with almost uncannily modern skill, seem to draw a cloak of mystery about themselves. There is a palpable air of dread and death. One almost

21

expects to see the strongpoints on the skyline come alive with the soldiers of a vanished master-race manning it against phantom hordes sweeping in from the north.

It took nearly a century of European occupation of the Transvaal before the taboo, the remoteness, the malaria, wild animals and the intolerable heat which had isolated The Hill were overcome. In the early 1930s a terrified native broke the age-old curse and showed a farmer-prospector the secret route to the summit. There had been a cloudburst a day or two before, and gold lay exposed. Frenzied scratching with hunting knives revealed the first evidence of Africa's strangest and richest treasure trove since Tutankhamen. The men had happened on a royal grave which was later to yield a golden crown and regalia, a golden model rhino idol and countless gold beads. Priceless lesser articles also came to light, such as superb pottery related to vanished Middle East civilizations, striking large beads with a similar background, and Chinese porcelain of the late Sung period (twelfth to fourteenth centuries AD). Outside Egypt, no hoard like it has been discovered in Africa, before or since.

One of the treasure-finders was a student from Pretoria University. He and his father, recognizing the uniqueness of the discovery, turned over its secret to the institution. The state stepped in and further treasure-hunting was banned. Part of The Hill was excavated scientifically before the outbreak of World War II put an end to the operations. Before this, however, the experts were startled to find evidence of ancient religious practices, including 'beast burials' and funerary urns, which have no parallel on the Dark Continent south of the Sahara. The skill of the goldwork and purity of the metal is hard to match even in the space age. A ceremonial cemetery points to the fact that this sophisticated master-race, which held Africa at bay from a position chosen with unerring military insight, passed away peacefully and not by conquest. Long after they had disappeared, their curse held The Hill shut fast.

Nadine and I, fellow-students in archaeology at the Witwatersrand University, joined the first post-war expedition to The Hill with enthusiasm. I was in my middle twenties, a late starter because of the war, most of which I spent in a German POW camp; and she about five years younger. I had been too busy with my studies to take much notice of the dark-haired girl who was rumoured to be the richest in the university, daughter of Harold Raikes the magnate, a household word in the Golden City.

Our convoy of three Land-Rovers had rendezvoused at Messina and had then struck westwards, parallel to the Limpopo, to reach our destination. It was a rough, tough trip and one vehicle was damaged. There was a great deal of preliminary work to be done before the excavations proper could start. Much of the previous scientific work had been lost because the pits and trenches had been choked with soil. In any event, pre-war expeditions had concentrated mainly on the north-western tip of The Hill's tabletop summit where the queen's grave and its treasures had been discovered. This was clearly only a part of the occupation area. Dr Drummond, the professor who had led the expedition, believed that the whole summit and a surrounding walled area at ground level had formed a unit as a fortress-city. He decided to start operations within the containing wall on the ground, concentrating on two places: the foot of the secret stairway, and at another about 150 yards away also against the cliffs. This latter was named Mahobe's in honour of a long-dead chieftainess of the nearest tribe.

Nadine was to me no more than one of a group during the early stages of the expedition. Perhaps her beauty and wealth made her a little remote. Then, one afternoon when most of us were working at the secret stairway site, there was a sudden shout from Nadine at Mahobe's. Our 'dig' was considered to have better prospects than Mahobe's, which was more or less a shot in the dark. It was not an excited whoop but there was something in her voice which had us all at her trench in a flash.

Nadine was on her knees in the excavation, bare-headed, her dark hair flecked with the dust which coated everything at the slightest breeze. She wore a pair of faded fawn jeans and a golden-yellow shirt, open at the throat. I stopped short. I stared, not at the priceless thing she held, but at her face. Maybe the fire of the malaria already burning in my veins – for which I was shipped away prematurely before I really got to know The Hill – sharpened my perception of Nadine.

She knelt in the trench, in a curious votive attitude, facing

The Hill and cradling the statuette she had found, as though in some strange way identifying with its age-old mystery. She did not look up at us but simply crouched there with the thing in her arms. All the millenia of Africa seemed to be epitomized in that vignette of the sinister Hill and the lovely girl bowed in the dust at its foot. Suddenly, too, I was acutely aware of the unusualness of her face: there appeared to be some Eastern Mediterranean derivation in its dark loveliness, but the classic line was broken by the high, almost Slavic cheekbones, the generous mouth and straight, full eyebrows. She was looking at the figurine, calmly and impassively, with an air of detachment from her surroundings.

The spell was broken by a noisy barrage of questions, excitement and congratulations. Nadine stood up and passed the figure, still partly hidden in a lump of earth to Dr Drummond. With a loud exclamation he took it from her while the others crowded around. Nadine still stood waist-deep in the trench: I went to her and offered a hand to pull her up. I then saw what was in her eyes. It was only for a few seconds that we stood so, her foot braced for the jump, our hands and eyes locked. I hauled her up – a little too vigorously perhaps – for at the top she was slightly off balance and lurched against me. She steadied herself after a longer pause than was necessary. She stared at me curiously, searchingly, the sea-green of the fine eyes still hazed from their mute communion with the unknown. She then joined Dr Drummond, who was pouring out excited, expert praise. I stood back from the group.

Dr Drummond declared she must have found some place of ritualistic worship. Work was called off for the day to clean up and examine Nadine's find. We gathered in high anticipation in the big marquee which served as a mess room and the professor prepared to extract the statuette from its matrix, as the envelope of earth is called. The late afternoon brought no relief from the heat. It came in waves through the shimmering canvas. My ears started to ring and I felt nauseated. Nadine helped Dr Drummond deftly with drills, probes and brushes. As the figure became progressively exposed Dr Drummond became more excited. It was a female figure, carved from a material which resembled ivory. The head was revealed first, showing clear, fine features, a rather prominent nose and

24

high forehead. The breasts were capped with gold leaf of wafer thinness. Dr Drummond exclaimed that the metal was as thin and apparently as pure as any modern process could achieve. More earth was cleared and we saw the navel similarly capped in gold. As the matrix was brushed off further to expose the waist, however, no more of the precious metal came to light. Then the last concealing fragment of earth fell away, showing buttocks which had none of the gross enlargement called steatopygia which is the sign of a primitive race. It was a slim body fashioned in perfect physiological detail.

A hush fell upon the onlookers and Dr Drummond handed the figure to Nadine. He began drawing some comparison with emphasis on sex worship among the Hamitic peoples of the Mediterranean coastline. In the heat haze the group seemed far away, as if I were looking at them through the wrong end of a telescope. The oppressiveness bore down upon me; the buzzing in my ears grew. I did not know that malaria was at work. I was able to focus only by screwing up my eyes. I swayed on my feet, waves of hot and cold sweat sweeping across me. The nearest thing to it I had known was air-sickness.

I remember trying to concentrate on Nadine's face when she started to speak. Her words were drowned by a roar in my ears . . .

I clawed at the trestle table to save myself, but my hands seemed to have no power. I slid to the ground.

They told me at the hospital that my delirium lasted five days while the fever ran its course. Each time I rose to semi-consciousness I fought to catch Nadine's words. My fogged brain conjured her up clothed in gold, a priestess sacrificing before an altar shaped like The Hill; I saw her kneeling and begged her to lift her eyes to mine but she would not; I saw her drop the priestess's robe and stand naked except for golden points like the statuette's at her breasts and navel. She came towards me . . .

I broke through to consciousness in a torrent of sweat.

Nadine was sitting by my bed in the white ward.

It is easy to fall in love after a war which has torn apart the lives of half the world and one comes young and new to the task of remaking it. The Hill and its age-old mystery lay close to both our hearts. My own work – the study of the art

25

of a people who left to posterity their genius in the form of beautifully engraved boulders with wild animal designs – was related.

We fell in love.

We both sensed rather than felt the first tug of the tide that day in the little hospital at Messina. She told me how my sudden collapse had caused consternation among the expedition. It had been impossible to consider driving me through the bush tracks in the dark. Next morning, still delirious, I'd been taken by two of the party by Land-Rover to the hospital.

Nadine sat by the bed and eyed me thoughtfully.

'That was the moment when all our troubles began.'

My brain felt as agile as a hipped dinosaur. I hadn't begun to consider how she herself came to be at the town instead of The Hill. I experienced a sense of warm elation that she was there, and it was enough at that stage.

She smiled. 'You've been missing from the world for nearly a week. It didn't stop because of that, you know.'

I did not want to be lumped into the general category of troubles. Moreover, I was limp and edgy. 'One can't help contracting malaria either.'

'Well, we can be sure that *it* wasn't visited upon you.'

'What on earth do you mean?'

Her eyes were very clear and a little puzzled.

'All our other problems – well, we weren't so sure about them.'

I was not responding properly. My soggy brain took in the fact that she wasn't wearing bush clothes, which meant she must have stayed in town overnight and changed specially to come to visit me. The cool white cotton dress enhanced her dark hair.

'Guy, do you believe what they say about The Hill?' she went on before I could answer.

My fever days had been too blanked with superheated images to want any more gropings now that I was conscious again. It was good to see her next to me, warm and real. Other things didn't seem important.

'The taboo, I suppose?'

'Ye . . . es. When you live, eat and sleep right next to The Hill – no, I can't really explain what I mean. It's more a feeling than anything else. It's not simply an ordinary hill. I'm

26

sorry I'm putting it badly but . . . but there's something there. Something.'

'When I made the preliminary reconnaissance ahead of the expedition itself I couldn't raise help within thirty miles once the natives heard we were bound for The Hill,' I replied. 'As far as I am concerned there's nothing to it. You get these extraordinary psychological upsurges of the primitive all over Africa. For instance, there's a tribe living near this very town which claims you can rid yourself of a headache merely by walking along a path the witch doctor indicates and rubbing it off on the bushes.'

She blurted out unexpectedly as if she could not keep back the news any longer. 'We've abandoned the expedition.'

'What!'

I felt acutely let down in a double sense. Oddly, the more telling reason was that I had imagined all along that she had taken the trouble to make the rough trip from The Hill specially to see me. Her real motive seemed much more matter-of-fact.

'Don't tell me your statuette is an image of the powers of darkness and that it's brought down a curse on the expedition like that of Tutankhamen!'

She flushed slightly. 'Let me tell you. When the fuss of getting you away safely to hospital was over we set to work again. But we found we couldn't. All the survey pegs marking the trenches had been uprooted and scattered about.'

'Probably baboons,' I asserted. 'Gardner had the same problem in '36. They're very inquisitive creatures and The Hill swarms with them. They've got a big colony up near the spring on the summit. They won't meddle with pegs if you paint 'em with pitch, however. The heat keeps it sticky and coats their paws, which they hate. I put a drum of it among the stores for that very purpose.'

'We did exactly that,' Nadine answered steadily. 'Next day the same thing happened. Everything was higgledy-piggledy, an awful mess. It took us half a day simply to re-mark the digging sites. Then the following day: repeat performance.'

'If The Hill's taboo is no more sinister than a baboon's curiosity, you've nothing to fear.'

'The convincing way you say that indicates how deeply you believe it, Guy. I think I share your views.'

The ensuing pause in our conversation was full of under-currents.

'Well,' I ventured a little uncertainly under her steady gaze, 'You tell me, then. You made the big discovery. Maybe there's even another gold hoard there.'

She shook her head and the thick hair fell halfway across her cheek. I resented the hairdresser's gloss that had replaced the dust at The Hill. It affected me as a further sense of sell-out.

'I'm not a treasure-seeker. Guy, can't you see what I'm trying to tell *you*? The Hill . . .'

I was too unhappy about the expedition's ending, perhaps still too ill to appreciate that her emotions were ahead of her words.

Again she gave me a long considering look. Then she resumed matter-of-factly. 'The first night after you'd gone the two remaining Land-Rovers were parked against the cliff face between the two main digging sites. We'd put them there during the day for the sake of the shade. About midnight we were all awakened by a tremendous crash. A huge boulder had fallen off The Hill on top of them.'

'It happens all the time,' I replied a little impatiently. 'Sandstone decays in the summer and in winter when it cools chunks crumble and fall off. That's what happened in a big way when the secret stairway was formed long ago.'

'I know, I know! Every one of the strange happenings I'm about to tell you about has a double interpretation. First, then, the jeeps were a write-off. Dr Drummond was furious – and disturbed too. Next morning he and Jock Stewart decided to climb to the summit via the secret "stairway" to see if they could spot what had caused the boulder to break away. It would have been crazy to have attempted to climb in the dark immediately after the incident. Since the two vehicles were paid for by public subscription there had to be some sort of acceptable explanation of how all that money came to be lost. Dr Drummond was also concerned about something else on the table top . . . he hinted at a possible new site but gave no details.

'Jock told us afterwards that about two-thirds of the way up the "stairway" the professor had been leading. He was perhaps 150 feet from the bottom. You haven't been up yet, have you Guy? Let me explain: the passageway narrows and there's a nasty corner you have to squeeze round. The person below loses sight of anyone ahead. The Prof was negotiating this tricky section and was out of Jock's view. Suddenly Jock heard a choking sound. He went up as fast as he could and found Dr Drummond hanging from a wire noose round his neck. Luckily he'd thrown up his arm as he fell. That saved him and stopped the slipknot from strangling him. The wire was six feet long – the same as a gallows drop – and it was brand-new.

'Now Jock knows all about emergency drill; he's done plenty of rock work. That's why Dr Drummond chose him in the first place to go along. He found that the loop had cut into the Prof's neck and had dislocated his right shoulder.'

'Why should a poacher lay a snare there?' I interrupted. 'The climb's far too difficult for any but the smallest game to venture up it to the spring.'

Nadine went on quietly without replying directly to my question. 'Listen. Jock had almost freed Dr Drummond when he himself slipped. He dropped until his right leg broke his fall by lodging across the bad narrow section. You could say he was lucky, in a way. If he hadn't stuck there would have been nothing to prevent him falling to the bottom. He'd have been killed, for sure. As it was, his leg was smashed in two places and there's a lot of damage to the knee. He'll never climb again. He's in the next ward here in the hospital.'

'It could happen to anyone,' I rejoined, trying to dispel the sinister undertone in what she was saying. 'Jock probably became careless in his hurry to help the Prof.'

She thrust her tongue against her front teeth so that it forced open her lips slightly.

'Jock said he didn't slip. He was pushed.'

'Never! There's not a soul there! The Hill's been deserted from the time the last scientific expedition left just before war broke out. Our party's the first since: you know that as well as I do.'

'Yes, Guy, I know it only too well. It gives force to what I'm saying. All excavations came to a complete stop then, of course. We patched up their injuries and waited for your jeep to return. That same night Bob and Dave decided to move the spare petrol away from the cliff area in case of another rockfall. They made a dump about half a mile away from the camp out in the open and heaped sand over the jerricans so that there would be no danger of sparks from the camp fires. It's fantastic, I know, but the dump blew up like an outsize Guy Fawkes display.'

I sat incredulous.

'Yes,' she repeated. 'Somehow or other sealed and buried jerricans managed to ignite. Like the rockfall business, it also took place in the middle of the night. The explosions were like bombs. The cans leapt high into the air trailing flames – one after another they went up. It was really pretty spectacular, if we hadn't all been so scared.'

'What,' I asked grimly, 'was given as the cause of that?'

'The heat. Spontaneous combustion. Sympathetic explosions.'

'Rubbish! Petrol in sealed cans doesn't catch fire by spontaneous combustion! Anyway, it's cooler at night than during the day if you care to put that explanation to the test.'

'We were looking round for some sort of rational answer and it was good enough at the time for a crowd of really frightened people. The spirit had been completely knocked out of the venture by then and Dr Drummond had to take an on-the-spot decision on his own responsibility about what to do because there was no way of getting in touch with the authorities – you know yourself the nearest phone is sixty miles away. He couldn't afford either to take any risks in that heat with Jock's injury. He followed the only course he could and called off the expedition. We were all only too relieved about it and glad to leave. When your jeep returned we managed to find enough fuel in the tanks of the wrecked ones for it and made our way here to Messina. It was appallingly overcrowded and Jock suffered hell with his leg over the rough sections. Dr Drummond has already left to go back home and report.'

The end of the expedition was the beginning of our love; The Hill with its associations could not have been other than part of it. This was strengthened by Nadine's wish to have her engagement ring copied from the queen's taken from the royal grave on the tabletop. I obtained official permission for

30

this with considerable difficulty. In spite of her father's opposition, we intended to marry.

Then, the day in Cohen's store when I handed over Rankin's diamonds and faced a police revolver, our world collapsed.

How I would put the pieces together again I planned a thousand times during my remaining year in prison after Charlie Furstenberg had divulged that Rankin was at The Hill. My pent-up feelings took the form of frustrated energy which I channelled into reconstructing the jail library in its entirety. Shortly after our conversation Charlie was moved to a 'privileged' section of the prison and later put to work in the jail hospital. There was no reason why the little Jew should have been given such special consideration. I saw him only once or twice more in the distance during my imprisonment. We never had the chance to talk again.

Oddly enough, it was my library work which supplied the solution to the problem of concealing from Nadine my mission to find Rankin. About a month before I was due out the Superintendent informed me that I had been given a remission of a week off my sentence in recognition of it.

Nadine came as usual on the last visitors' day, unaware of my remission. She was radiant, full of plans for our future. 'Only a week and I shall come and fetch you home,' were her parting words.

A few hours later I was released. I made my way furtively to Johannesburg, saw my old professor briefly, picked up a few belongings – and a rifle.

I headed for The Hill.

CHAPTER THREE

The tool cut the barbed wire, and again I was in the presence of the hill which is death to look upon.

Not a bird sang, not an insect moved.

The wire sprang back to the nearest post, the barbs throwing up little spurts of dust as they plucked at the burning sand. To my tensed senses there was some doubt whether I had

31

actually heard the faint noise of the wire's *ting* or whether it was tinnitus, an imaginary sound which isolation evokes in the desert, having no reality except in the ear of the hearer.

By cutting the wire I had crossed my Rubicon and was committed to the critical stage of my pursuit of Rankin. I had forced a way into the prohibited area of The Hill and our confrontation would have to take place somewhere among the sunstruck tumble of rocks and hills which I could see as I raised my eyes cautiously to the level of the wide sandstone terrace on which The Hill stands along the river front. The terrace – a platform of rock half a mile long – rises abruptly about thirty feet out of a soft incline which is, in fact, the river's maximum bed at floor level. In normal times it is no more than a broad belt of sand studded with stunted palms and small trees. In The Hill's hey-day this steep platform served as its outer line of defence against attack from the river quarter. Centuries of erosion, however, had fashioned two or three sizeable gullies into gateways through the defences. These access points had now been blocked by rolls of military-style barbed wire where they opened on to the river bed and higher up at terrace-level by an eight-strand security fence with a workmanlike overhang at the top to prevent climbing. Furthermore, the head of each of these entry-points was reinforced by a padlocked barbed-wire gate. Whoever had done the job knew what he was about. Two high stone walls, still in a state of fair repair, completed the process of sealing off the place on either flank.

These were the reported precautions Nadine had read out to me that day in prison. It would not be impossible to break into the fortress enclosure but it needed time and resourcefulness. My commando training had enabled me to work through the outlying rolls of barbed wire – a long, exacting crawl – but I had been stumped by the security fence and gate. Then I remembered a curious old instrument in my pocket called a diamond pencil. It was one of the things I had brought with me in my hasty departure. It was a diamond-cutter's tool which had belonged to my grandfather and had a direct association with the Cullinan, for he had lent it to the famous Joseph Asscher of Amsterdam to make the initial cut in the great gem. It was an odd-looking thing with a bronze hexagonal shaft which had been worn smooth, as if by many hands in the past. In its tip was set a diamond to cut other diamonds. Called technically a 'sharp' my diamond pencil looked like an ordinary pencil made of metal, slightly thicker where the fingers gripped it, tapering towards both ends. Before the invention of the modern polariscope, which 'sees' into the heart of a diamond, cutting depended entirely on skill. A diamond has a hidden natural grain which must be established. A groove is cut along the surface of this plane with a diamond pencil, which then receives the cleaving knife. If diamond would cut diamond, I reasoned, diamond would cut the barbed wire obstructing me now.

It did.

I ducked down from my quick survey of the terrace. My face came close to a tuft of grass and I could see every dead, bleached bristle and the pitiful cluster of rain-starved, torpedo-shaped seeds. I tried to clamp my body against the fiery ground, out of The Hill's line of vision, behind a *kanniedood* ('never-die') tree. Its trunk made a natural post for the fence.

My heart was fluttering like a bird's. Somewhere ahead was the guard's hut Nadine had also mentioned and somewhere too might be the guard himself. He would be armed and was not likely to regard as friendly an intruder who had just broken in through his fence, gun in hand.

I lay low, half expecting at any moment a challenge or even a shot.

My pulse pounded and sweat dripped on to the grass patch – probably the only moisture that had come its way in years. Close-to I saw how the wire had sliced into the trunk and its acid sap had rusted the bright metal. The black-and-grey striped bark curled and peeled off in papery strips. The leafless thing may have been alive, or as dead as thousands of other trees in the drought-devastated countryside.

I lay with my arms forward to present the smallest target. I eased my grip on the shaft of the diamond pencil, deliberately clenching and unclenching my fingers as if the small movement could also do something for the tension which lay across my stomach like a steel band. I tried taking several long controlled breaths to quiet my nerves; then I watched in astonishment the nails of my thumb and forefinger – made brittle by the heat and moistureless air – split down to the quick.

After five minutes I could take the sun's torture on my back no longer. Where my chest and stomach lay against the gritty earth were soaked patches through my khaki shirt. Despite the risk of being spotted, I realized I would have to shift soon. Even the shadow from the *kanniedood* trunk, like a sundial's black bar against the glowing sand, took on an attraction which was out of all proportion to its slight shade. I squirmed, still not chancing a full bodily movement, which caused the cartridges in my shirt pocket to dig into me. They were overhot but I dismissed a fear that they might explode against my chest. However, they did make me speculate whether the barrel of my old Mannlicher (it had once been my father's) might be so distorted by the heat that I couldn't have hit Rankin at thirty yards had he appeared in front of me like a genie out of the dancing mirage.

I sat up, my mouth dry. I chewed and sucked at an astringent mopani tree leaf I had picked on my way from the river. It is the favourite food of elephants and the butterfly-shaped leaf is a thirst-beater for humans and animals alike. I decided to ease myself under the cut wire and reconnoitre cautiously towards the base of The Hill.

Now that I was confronted by The Hill itself, the plans which I had made round Rankin, both in prison and on my way up-river from Messina, seemed incomplete and somewhat unworkable. Perhaps my keenness to get at him had clouded my recollection of the detailed geography of the place, or even its size. Charlie had said 'Rankin is at The Hill' as if he were to be found simply in occupation of it. When I looked now at the mass rising up before my eyes I realized that I had been over-optimistic about tracking him down quickly. The cliffs of the fortress reared up a couple of hundred feet sheer from the broad terrace. From my low angle the table-top of the north-western summit where the queen's grave lay was invisible. Compared with this flat section the rest of the surface of the summit was more broken, being pierced here and there with great jags of rock. My view of The Hill was the same as its old enemies had had, and the receiving end wasn't pleasant. There was also a strange air of watchfulness which I could not define.

At the back of The Hill I could see a broad wadi of sand – an ancient watercourse perhaps – about a mile wide. Here our expedition had camped. The wadi separated The Hill from a great circle of hills beyond to the south, a broken complex about five miles in circumference and two across. Intersecting this to the halfway mark, like a sawn-off wagon wheel spoke, was a broad dyke of rock. These hills were generally lower than the fortress itself, although one directly across the wadi had a peak almost as high as the tabletop.

The first move in my plan of campaign was to find out whether the area was in the process of being policed by irregular patrols and, if so, how strong they were. I guessed that only one man might be involved. I'd come to this conclusion after questioning Nadine in prison as discreetly as possible after I'd made my decision. Her inquiries to the authorities had run slap up against a security screen but the fact that a light plane was being used to ferry the patrol to the bush airstrip some miles away seemed to point to a single guard, or at the most two. Before starting my search for Rankin I wanted to be sure it did not founder on the patrol. I had allowed for this contingency and had decided that if guards were active I would by-pass The Hill by river and lie low until they had been withdrawn.

I raised my head again and scanned the terrace. However, I could not spot the patrol hut, which I thought must be situated somewhere close to The Hill's cliffs facing my way among big boulders.

A shout from the river behind me sent my heart racing. It sounded raucous and inhuman in the oppressive vacuum of silence. I hastily sought somewhere to hide. The *kanniedood* trunk was inside the fence itself and was too slender for concealment. The nearest real cover was a tattered clump of chest-high elephant palm about fifty yards back along my route, beyond the rolls of barbed wire. My only path was forward through the cut wire which meant rising into full sight on the terrace.

The seconds I spent wavering seemed like hours. I glanced anxiously back to the pool where the two great rivers met and then – in spite of again hearing the unnatural shout – my heart changed into lower gear; for on the surface of the water I saw a tell-tale line of froth. The cry wasn't human, but a fish-eagle's. The clear harsh call, which precedes its dive-bomber swoop from high cloud, is one of the great sights of river-sea estuaries in Southern Africa. But here on the dried-up river the drought had debased the noble hunter to a carrion scavenger quarrelling with crocodiles for one stinking piece of mudfish or winkling putrid crabs from lairs become their graves as the water receded.

I wiped my sweating hands on my gritty shirt front. The bird's cry underlined the fact that if I hesitated where I was I could be trapped without the opportunity to escape. My immediate target was plain – the partly ruined defence wall to my left running along the eastern edge of the terrace. Its drop was not so sheer as the one facing the river and therefore I reckoned it would be possible to negotiate it. If I could get behind the wall on a narrow shelf between it and the drop I could approach the guard hut unseen and discover whether it was occupied or not. My further plans depended on that. The alternative route that remained was simply across the broad terrace itself, bare as a billiard table.

There was about a hundred yards of open ground from my gully to the wall. It was flat like the rest of the terrace but intersected by a number of small runnels – smaller versions of the wire-blocked gullies – which would provide some slight cover.

I acted on my decision: leading with my left shoulder I rolled on to the cut fence, holding the rifle tucked against my chest. On the naked terrace I lay still while all eternity seemed to hold its breath. Then I jerked to a low crouch and made a shambling sort of crawl to the nearest gully and threw myself in. I hid there until the sun forced me on to the next hollow.

Again and again I repeated the performance until at length I found myself gasping behind the safety of the eight-foot wall near its extremity where it had collapsed. To work around it was easy enough and, except for the first twenty yards or so where it lipped the drop, the going was easy for (as I had surmised) the terrace flattened out and shelved towards the river bed. This was probably the reason why a protecting wall had been built there in the first place.

I hung back for a moment, reluctant to leave the river which had served me well so far. I had camouflaged the odd boat I had travelled in up river under a palm clump by the big pool and a double-check now showed me it was completely hidden from view. My shoestring budget had precluded a

Land-Rover but in Messina I had seen for sale this curious craft which had been used for catching tiger-fish on the river. Its hull was a cut-out aluminium float from a wartime Catalina flying-boat and it was propelled by an ageing outboard motor. The boat's shallow draught was ideal for my purpose, for the higher I ascended the river the worse it became until finally it was reduced to a series of stagnant hippo pools interconnected by shallow channels twisting through moats of burning sand. At length, at the Limpopo's junction with the Shashi, the water became a soupy devil's brew stinking of dead fish and crocodiles, surrounded by a fringe of un-savoury mud.

I shook off my unwillingness to cut my lines of communica-tion and set off along the wall, I edged along cautiously hoping to find a spy hole. The structure was built of un-mortared tabular blocks set stringer-wise but there was no coursing or bonding as in modern building practice. Portions of the upper surface had fallen away here and there. It con-tinued true towards my target, the guard's hut in the north-eastern sector of The Hill on the corner opposite the queen's grave. It looked as if eventually the wall ended slap against the cliff face.

It was slow going at first because of the drop within a foot or two of the outer face but within range of the cliffs this ledge broadened in keeping with the shelving terrain and I picked up speed, moving at a tight crouch, gun in hand. I decided to load only when I could see my objective, for fear that a chance fall might loose off a shot and give me away. Nearer the cliffs and therefore nearer the hut the wall became more solid: it would have taken a modern tank or bulldozer to break through.

It was imperative I should see what lay on the other side. I went on to where a huge boulder had been used to form part of the wall, in the hope that I might be able to climb it. It was unnecessary, however, for where the blocks joined the boulder there were several rainwater drainage holes at the height of my head.

I started to get my eye to one of them but it was blocked with rubble and dirt. I reached to clear it with my fingers but drew back in alarm at the feel of something alive. There was a movement and hiss like a tyre deflating and a puff-adder's head emerged. I dodged out of range of its strike with a shudder at the sight of the beautiful mother-of-pearl palate gleaming behind the deadly fangs.

There were more drainage holes where the wall continued on the other side of the boulder and this time I took the precaution of cleaning one out with my rifle butt before trying to look. I loaded the Mannlicher silently with one round – it had no magazine – and rested it ready to hand against the wall.

The guard's hut was only a biscuit's toss away on the other side. It was a rough affair built of *kanniedood* poles with a sloping thatched roof and several windows. A radio aerial was strung from a long pole on the roof to a nearby cliff and a big barrel-shaped water tank stood near by with a ladder against it.

I watched and waited, but there was no sign of life or movement.

It seemed significant that a window at the back (presumably the kitchen) was open, which meant that the hut was in current occupation. In the shadow of the wall I was cool and I could afford to let the moves come from the other side. After half an hour I decided that it was safe. Apart from checking the place I was also tempted by thoughts of a long drink from the tank. My mopani leaf had been chewed tasteless.

I spat it out and started to climb the wall. It was smooth and difficult and I flinched at the thought of another puff-adder since I had to search blindly for grips in the open stone joints each time I handed myself up a stage farther.

When I reached the top, still nothing moved at the hut. There was only that open window as a giveaway. Watching it, I dropped down carefully, silently, ducking for a minute behind a fallen rock halfway to the back door. I made a final sprint from its cover and flattened myself against the hut's wall by the open window.

Then I risked a glance into the room beyond. There were plates and a cup on a crude deal table and a cut loaf of bread, but no human occupant. An inner door was shut; the outside door locked.

I was overcome by a sense of unease and suspicion. The kitchen set-up looked like a trap.

I disengaged the Mannlicher's safety catch and made my

way, inch by inch, towards the front.

It was the smell which brought me to a halt: not the fishy stench of the river, but a fetid, animal odour which reached into the pit of my stomach and knotted my muscles.

I knelt down, scarcely breathing, and by feel alone double-checked the rifle's safety catch while I cased every point of the compass. I snicked back the flap of my shirt pocket containing the shells in order to be able to reload quickly.

Then something thumped softly on the inside of the wooden wall close to my face.

I started my spring for the front door as the thought crashed home that the murderer was only an inch or two away through the planks.

He came out carrying the dead man's head.

I cannoned headlong into him, tripped and hurtled over his back, firing from the hip as a purely reflex action.

The brute lay kicking. It was not on the dying hyena, however, that my sickened gaze fastened.

A man's head, the lower jaw missing, with stray pieces of skin and hair adhering to the face and scalp, rolled away from the animal's snapping, frothing jaws.

Between the eyes was a bullet-hole and the back had been smashed wide by a soft-nosed bullet.

CHAPTER FOUR

I hauled myself up by the verandah post, winded and sick from the heavy fall. I stared transfixed at the sight of tobacco-stained teeth projecting from beneath a fragment of lip on the skull; as I did so terror mounted like a quick-burning fuse from the sphincter muscles of my anus into my stomach. Blind panic exploded like a grenade and I jerked away into a wild career across the open terrace – away, away, anything to be away from the awful silence of that bizarre execution and the thought of the murderer's sights on my own back.

I ran zig-zagging from the imaginary gun until I was brought to a halt by the security fence. I clawed my way along it and threw myself more by instinct than reason through the gap

I had cut, and hid my head below the level of the terrace, out of sight of the watchful eyes with which my supercharged imagination invested The Hill.

Gradually my breath returned, and with it my sanity. The sun on my hatless head and the unbroken stillness bore in upon me the futility of my crazy sprint. The wild oscillations of irrational fear steadied round the deadpoint. I got a grip on myself and tried to make some sort of assessment, and to force myself to go back to the hut.

It was essential to establish the identity of the dead man: Rankin or a guard. If it was Rankin, my whole plan was shot and then all I could do would be to return, tail between legs, to Nadine – if she would still have me after my walkout. For the first time since leaving I began to have doubts. The hardships of the river had enabled me to push consideration of my shabby trick out of mind but now I had to face it squarely. The end had to justify the means and if Rankin was dead I had lost the end – and possibly Nadine as well.

If the skull was the guard's, there was only one person likely to have murdered him: Rankin. The thought gave me a measure of grim inverted satisfaction: I had often wondered, during my stay in jail, whether time had passed me by and I would arrive at The Hill to find Rankin gone. But if the murderer was Rankin, I was in deadly danger and I would have to watch every step I made. If he was capable of killing an official guard, he was capable of anything. But why hadn't he disposed of the body? Or – the thought brought a taste of sourness into my gullet – had I interrupted the disposal process: hyenas?

What I needed now was a gun and a lot of vigilance. The mere fact that the hyena had been busy inside the hut indicated that the killer could not be around and therefore it would be safe to go back.

What then had I run away *from*? I had seen dead men before, in the war. True, the skull was a ghastly sight, but if it was Rankin's, so what? I had little sympathy to spare for him. If it was the guard's; he was a stranger. What then had sparked off my terror?

I felt the rising surge in my bowels as I forced myself back on to the terrace. The Hill? Whichever way one looked one's eyes always came back to it; sprawled shimmering, ugly, gigantic across the view. The hard sunlight seemed to magnify rather than decrease its mystery. It was inevitable, too, that my concentration should focus on the tabletop with its royal grave. It seemed to echo the accusation: you double-crossed Nadine.

I started back towards the hut, walking straight and fast. If I went on thinking in this way, in this isolation, I'd be crazy within a few days. The Hill, I told myself, was nothing more than an unusual koppie at a strategic river junction. The mystery of the lost origin of a group of unknown invaders who had fortified it had been blown up to become a riddle into which one could read anything.

I strode up to the skull and I blenched. I temporized about examining it by first retrieving my hat and rifle. I felt again the tiny ripple of fear-activated muscle in my buttocks and to counteract it I took out a shell for the Mannlicher. The bolt action was looser than it should have been but I put this down to the bang it had had when it fell, and to its age. While I loaded I found myself eyeing every corner of the surroundings but once I had a bullet in the breech I felt better. I then made my way to the verandah. I needed a wall at my back as a precaution against ambush while I took stock of the situation. First, I decided to force myself to examine the skull. However, when I started towards it and had only reached the edge of the verandah, there was such a stench of decaying flesh that suddenly I found myself hanging on to a post, vomiting violently. When the fit had passed I went to the water tank and had a long drink. I came to the conclusion then that it would be better to postpone my examination of the hut and the victim until I could face the ordeal: perhaps in the cool of late afternoon. I still couldn't bring myself to approach the skull so I fetched the ladder and shinned up the roof for the long bamboo pole supporting the radio aerial, which I then used to spear and edge the skull inside the hut. Then I shut the door and window.

The ladder gave me another idea: laid over the rolls of barbed wire below the security fence it would give easy access to the river from the terrace and back again. Acting on this, I carried it on my shoulder across the bare stretch of terrace with a feeling of trailing my coat to unseen enemies; as if to tempt them further, I rested at intervals with my back deliberately turned to The Hill. I took my time, too, at the gate and painstakingly sawed with the diamond pencil through several more strands of wire, to make a sizeable gap. In the end I had a quick, safe route open.

It was my need for a rational approach which also crystallized my decision to make camp at The Hill itself. I made my choice of site as much with my heart as with my head. I plumped for a circle of big rocks near the foot of the secret stairway, not far from the trench where our love had taken fire. This site, I reasoned, commanded the fortress's most vital strategic point and if Rankin were holed up on the summit he could not by-pass it. Footpaths dating from the time of the expedition all converged there. Also, being on the side of The Hill away from the river, I could hide myself and avoid discovery from that quarter. And the soaring cliffs gave welcome shade. The actual entrance to the secret stairway was about twenty-five feet above the ground and concealed by the big old fig tree whose roots, hanging down from the cliffside, formed a grassy cage. It could be a useful hide-out if the need arose.

I unloaded the boat and started on the first of two journeys to hump my few possessions to the place. The exposed solitary walk across the terrace in the hard light, with nerves strung high and rifle at the ready, reminded me of the classic confrontation in a Western where the good guy and the bad guy shoot it out in the empty street. The more the range closed towards The Hill the tenser I became. But there was no shot, no sound even, except that of my heels on the rock. I skirted the cliffs under the tabletop (I was now at the opposite extremity of the fortress from the hut) and made full use of the cover afforded by the scatter of great boulders which had fallen from the cliffs. Once I had rounded the point there were more sheltering boulders on the wadi side. I picked my way cautiously through these and it was with a sense of anticlimax that I reached the foot of the stairway. There was not a sign of human occupation and the sandy tracks were devoid of any but animal spoor. I dumped the gunny-sack containing my things and made my second journey to the boat via the hut and filled a jerrican with water from the tank. To get there I walked clean across the broad front of The Hill facing the river. Afterwards I relaxed, for if I was to be shot at, that would have been the time. The return to my camping-place was without incident.

It took most of the afternoon to make the trips. Perhaps their uneventfulness lulled me into putting off the issue of examining the skull and mortuary-like interior of the hut until the next day. They certainly convinced me it would be quite safe to light a small fire that night (behind the protecting screen of rocks where it wouldn't be seen) as a precaution against wild animals, and I spent until dusk gathering wood. I found a dead leadwood tree whose long-burning timber – known to veldmen as 'hard-coal' – would last for hours without attention and keep prowling hyenas at bay while I slept. It also has the useful characteristic of burning with sudden sparks and flares, probably from old insect nests deep in the heartwood.

Night fell.

I hung about until it was completely dark but I didn't feel safe to settle down until I had carried out a test to see if my fire could be spotted – just in case. The night was hot but it would be cheerless sitting alone in the blackness; nevertheless, I determined to do so if necessary. I took the rifle and went to the outer limit of The Hill's fortifications facing the wadi – in other words, the sector between the fortress itself and the adjoining ring of hills to the south. The drop from the terrace into the wadi's sandy bed was less than that on the river front: some twenty feet, I guessed. Also, the fortified wall was in a worse state of repair and there seemed to be more rolls of barbed wire here.

I found that the ring of boulders round my fire hid it completely from that particular angle. Satisfied, I then worked round in a semi-circle towards Nadine's trench, checking further. Suddenly there was a movement on the ground ahead. For a moment my eyes conjured up a man crawling towards me, head up. I swung my sights on to the object; when I made out what it was I grinned with relief. A starving armadillo scuffed at the iron-hard ground and what I had taken for a head was no more threatening than a baby riding on its mother's back, tail entwined with hers. Somehow the touching sight evoked a surge of deep longing for Nadine.

From her trench the glow of the fire could be seen clearly through a gap in the boulders (they were about ten feet high) but I decided I would risk keeping it alight because the moon would soon be rising in this direction and if I kept my eyes open I must spot anyone approaching a long way off.

I thought again of Nadine and swore a quiet oath to myself that I would find Rankin at whatever cost and see again in her eyes what I had first seen here.

Then I walked quickly back to the fire and poured myself a stiff shot of brandy. As the rough stuff went down a maniacal scream, tapering off to a long choking gurgle, itself more horrible than the first, cut through the night. I cursed the hyena and wished I had a spare shot to scare it away with. I had come to The Hill with only ten rounds: I'd bought them with the couple of pounds I had managed to scrounge off the Prisoners' Friend when I left jail. I consciously damped my rising feelings against Rankin and the purpose of the bullets. I had bummed the money, not to kill Rankin with them, but to give me teeth for my purpose: to get him to confess. And I meant to go within an inch of his life if necessary, to extract that information.

I took another uneasy gulp of my drink as a further drawn-out burst of hyena hysteria bounced from cliff to cliff. The sound then seemed to gain a second wind and began reverberating from the circle of koppies opposite. An answer, which was not an echo, came from the far side of The Hill. It was probably another brute, devouring the one I had shot at the hut. A bright star – I thought it was Vega – hung above the tabletop. I began to tell myself that if I was right then there were scavengers that night in the sky too, for Vega is in the constellation of the Vulture – but I shook off the fancy impatiently. The emptiness and the curious air of watchfulness of the old fortress were beginning to get on my nerves.

It appeared I couldn't get away from hyenas. After leaving jail I had used them as a bait to extract an official letter from my former professor, Dr Sands; saying that my purpose in visiting The Hill area was to collect fossilized hyena droppings. These droppings, thousands of years old and containing fragments of bone which are often those of extinct creatures, are valuable and meaningful to science, filling in small gaps about what creatures once roamed Southern Africa. The letter was a bluff, of course, so that if I were picked up by the guards I could talk my way out of trouble on the grounds that I had a legitimate purpose. Dr Sands was the only person who had any idea of my whereabouts.

Some baboons on the summit began barking, adding to the hyenas' racket. Restless and uneasy, I poured myself another drink. The atmosphere of the place was like walking into a wet blanket hanging on a line: there was no resistance and yet it enveloped one completely. I began to regret that I had not settled the identity of the dead man.

All at once the hyena and baboons stopped. The silence was heavy enough to cut. I left the fire, drink in one hand and rifle in the other, and crunching overloudly across the broken scraps of ancient pottery, walked towards the tell-tale opening facing Nadine's trench. The heavens were now full of stars and the Milky Way lay suspended like a cosmic vapour jet trail; the Southern Cross hung like a vast Insignia of the Garter on a black velvet royal sleeve. The Hill's mass loomed high against the star-line. Subconsciously I registered that something was amiss. I put the drink aside and went outside my camp circle, pressing myself against one of the boulders.

Then I saw what had silenced the animals. Where the moon should have been rising silver there was an ugly red glow in the sky above The Hill from the direction of the guard hut.

It was on fire.

I was about to race towards it when I stopped in my tracks. Instead I slid silently to the ground against the rough sandstone.

The rocks relayed the sinister whisper of metal as a rifle bolt went home.

The night seemed to hold its breath and I froze at the foot of the rock. The sound of metal had been very near: the rocks acted as a sounding-board. Whoever was after me probably hadn't reckoned on that. He must have approached from the blind side from which one couldn't see the fire. The fact that he had loaded his rifle so near my camp meant that he was not prepared to find anyone about. Now, however, he must realize that I was very close.

Alongside the burning hut's red glow the moon began to rise. If I didn't act fast it would spotlight me but not the gunman hidden on the shadowed side of the camp circle. I was at a further disadvantage because one of the rocks was split in such a way as to make a natural loophole for him to fire

45

through while remaining invisible. From my present position it would be impossible to get a shot at him first.

Spurred on by the growing lightness of the rising moon I cast about for an escape route. When I turned cautiously towards The Hill the solution came to me. The moonlight which exposed me where I now crouched could be my salvation. The geological formation of the cliffs, known as *holkrans sandsteen,* spelled out my line of escape. Meaning literally 'hollowed-out sandstone', this particular type of rock weathers exactly as the name suggests, forming a natural hollow at the base capped by an overhang. Every cliff has in fact its own cave shelter at its base. This now offered me a secure funkhole right under the gunman's eye. Between me and safety, however, lay a few exposed yards.

I hadn't even finished my snap assessment of the situation before an unearthly cry, like a Gaelic death-keen, cascaded down the rocks from The Hill's summit. My finger tightened automatically on the trigger and I guessed that my pursuer's must have done the same. The half-human cry of a starving baboon – in daylight I had caught a glimpse of pathetic and emaciated specimens – was taken up by its companions until it became a general chorus.

I saw it as a further opportunity, and under cover of the noise I cautiously rolled over and over towards the cliff with the rifle hard against me until I was about halfway up an intervening slope. I was ready to change position for the subsequent down-grade leading to the cliff shelter when the baboon cries cut off. I was left sprawled, face downwards, not daring to move, at the point of maximum exposure.

I lay still.

I did not spot the whip-like tail and clutching claws until they were within six inches of my face. A four-inch scorpion reached out inquiringly and its pincers caressed my cheek. They felt closer, more inquisitively, and I could not suppress a shiver. The sting whipped to the ready in a tight arc while I held my breath to deaden all movement, for I knew that when it struck I would not be able to resist the agony, which would jerk my head back and the movement would be seen. I tried as the seconds raced by to think how long a man can hold his breath; then there was a thudding flurry of hands and feet over, past and around my prostrate body. Startled

46

chakking exploded and hairy bodies skidded and jumped over me. One opportunist black paw snatched up the poised scorpion. A cloud of dust rose like a smokescreen from the startled baboon troop, whose last members had not paused before I launched myself under its cover and in a moment I was safe in deep shadow under the rocky lip.

I felt safer still after half an hour had passed. But the situation was simply a stalemate: if neither of us gave himself away we could go on until morning when the advantage would be his with a full magazine against my single shot at a time which was all the Mannlicher was capable of. I had to take the initiative somehow and confirm beyond doubt that the gunman was Rankin. It certainly wasn't the guard, to destroy his own hut.

Everything: the apparent carelessness about advertising his presence by making a bonfire of the place; and his emergency loading hard by my own fire, pointed to the fact that he had not seen my comings and goings during the afternoon. Yet, against this was the plain evidence that the hyena at the hut had been shot recently and that whoever had done so could not be far away. Perhaps, on further thought, he had decided that the need to cremate the guard's remains outweighed all other considerations.

Whatever the answer, the fact that I had heard him loading his rifle showed that he had been taken by surprise and meant business. It also added a more dangerous dimension to our contest: it became not merely Rankin (whom I felt sure it was) versus Guy Bowker; but a trigger-happy maniac ready to silence any unknown stranger who came to The Hill.

I decided to end the impasse and make for the fig tree's root cage at the mouth of the secret entrance before the moon became much stronger. I was confident I could manage this without being seen. It was a short uphill climb through rubble; and several fissures at the foot of the cliff face would also afford cover. From behind the screen I would have a view of the camp fire.

I blackened my face, arms, clothes and gun with some unpleasant-smelling dust from the shelter floor. My sweat made it stick. I inched upwards towards my objective with long halts in the safe places, keeping the rifle clear of the rocks for fear of a tell-tale clink. The short distance was an eternity: every moment I expected a shot from below.

Then I crawled through the lattice-work of roots, some as fine as grass, and peered down on my camp site.

There was no sign of anyone. It all seemed so peaceful: the friendly glow with an occasional spurt of typical leadwood sparks, my binoculars hanging from a nicked rock, my drink where I had put it down.

After an hour of tight vigilance a doubt crept into my mind. Had I indeed heard a rifle bolt – might it not have been a rock cracking? A cicada ground out a weary parody of his rain-days. In the far distance a jackal complained; it was answered by a short jittery laugh from a hyena which broke off short as if the brute suspected my tense watch. From afar came the distant chuffer of a lion. The red glow of the blaze was gone from the sky and the moon was white.

Suddenly, as if by magic, a figure crouched by the fire, rifle at the ready, bush hat hard down over his eyes. It was so quick I did not see where he came from. As quickly, my rifle barrel was through the screen and my sights were trained on his head. He wasn't looking in my direction, though, but at the signs of my occupation. I could see from the set of his shoulders how tense he was. His back was half-turned, his face obscured. If I had any doubts about his purpose or qualms about gunning down an unsuspecting victim, his next action dispelled them. He took a handful of ash and rubbed it over his rifle barrel, breech, magazine and trigger guard – all the bright metal parts.

More than anything, I wanted to see his face. However, he moved swiftly across to kneel by the gunny-sack which stood out orange-yellow against the ground. He ignored it but his gaze went all round the compass, including the opening through which I had emerged. I watched his left hand, almost of its own independent will, finger the garish coloured mesh, while the wild animal it served kept tight watch. His other hand was curled round the rifle trigger. Those epicene hands were the hands of a craftsman and they frightened me as they touched and explored my things, passing on all there was to know to the spring-taut, unmoving body.

Then he turned towards me, cocking his head as if at some sound, and I had my answer. There was no mistaking Rankin's high forehead and slightly predatory look. The V of my sight stood clear against the middle of his forehead and I held his life in my trigger finger. But I dropped my aim past his head, along his back down to his leg. I wanted him winged, able to confess.

I fired.

The old gun exploded in my face.

There was a crash and stunning flash within inches of my eyes and at the same time I was hurled out of the root cage by a blow on the forehead by the back-firing bolt. As I crashed unconscious among the rocks I thought I heard the smack and ricochet of two rapid-fire shots from Rankin.

I could not have been out for more than a few minutes; my fogged instincts on rising to consciousness told me that if I wanted to stay alive I must stay absolutely motionless despite the awful waves of nausea and flashes before my eyes.

I lay sprawled half-in and half-out of a rocky cleft not more than eighteen inches deep and twice as long as a man. It had an upward incline; my head was downwards. The root cage was about ten feet above and to one side.

I eased myself into a slightly better position and then cushioned my face in my arms biting down the nausea induced by pain and the smell of my own burnt hair and eyelashes. The head-down angle of my body didn't help either. Nor could I focus properly: the cordite seemed to have seared my eyes and blood dripped into them from the gash in my forehead which the bolt had made.

If I continued to lie where I was, I reasoned muzzily, Rankin might be persuaded that I was indeed dead and come to look for my body. Which wouldn't help me; he'd spot me as soon as he came near the root cage. If he chose to wait – and I had already had experience of his patience – I'd be bound to give myself away sooner or later and he would flush me out. It might be as late as next day, when I wouldn't even have the cover of darkness. Somehow or other I had to break out of the trap. I tried to look at the problem coolly, detachedly, but I was too tense and a solution eluded me. The higher the moon rose the slighter would my chances become.

The only way out seemed to be the secret passageway but it would be impossible to reach its entrance in the root cage undetected. In any case, even should I gain the summit of The Hill, Rankin could starve me out without firing a shot.

I worried at the problem from every angle. I decided eventually that it might help if I knew more or less where Rankin was. I slid forward a few inches and lifted my eyes cautiously above my hiding-place. The camp was the same: utterly peaceful, nothing disturbed – and no Rankin. I presumed that he must have returned to his previous loophole. From it he commanded the fire, the cage and the approaches to the secret stairway. As I watched the fire gave a sudden flare but it was not bright enough to penetrate to where I felt sure Rankin lay hidden.

I explored every possibility of a solution again but nothing emerged. When the fire flared again I peered harder, hoping that in spite of my bad vision I would spot something. It was a bigger flare this time and the sparks reached high.

The answer came as it subsided and I tried to project myself into Rankin's skin and think what I would do in his situation. The flare must have momentarily dazzled his night-sight and blotted out his picture of my cliff-side. Given one big burst of sparks again it might be possible for me to get clear unseen. The fire had been burning for hours, however, and how could I predict when a flare was coming? As if in reply, it sparked again: a miserable, tiny jet which was no cover at all.

I was about to put the slim chance aside and rethink the whole problem from a new angle when it occurred to me that if *I* could make the fire flare I could pick my own moment to escape in the general direction of the wadi, away entirely from The Hill. Every possible method to achieve this, both practical and impractical, chased through my head. Somewhere, I felt, there must be an answer. Now that I had almost decided on my course of action it was foolish to risk exposure again. I started to creep back quietly in order to offer the lowest profile possible. The clip of shells in my pocket dug into me. At once I knew the answer: tossed into the fire, the clip would explode and blow sparks and embers in every direction, blinding Rankin. It would also constitute a noisy diversion. Rankin would hardly expect a fusillade of shots within a few feet of his face.

I was excited at the prospect and fingered the clip but held myself back. The two critical factors would be when to toss the five shells into the fire and my aim, which would have to be perfect. There would be no second chance. I would also have to wait for one of the fire's periodic flares so that Rankin would remain unsuspecting when it landed and kicked up sparks. About the faint thud the clip would make in falling I could do nothing.

Grasping the clip, I slithered back into my previous position overlooking the fire. I had barely eased over on my left side to give my throwing arm free play when the fire flared. I was relieved that the pay-off came so soon. I was shaking and sweating. A long wait would have wrecked my efforts.

I lobbed the clip at the fire and ducked down hard.

I didn't hear it drop. There was nothing but the continuing pregnant silence.

I lay immobile, trembling with anticipation, wondering how long the cartridges would take to explode. I dared not consider a miss. When I could take the strain no longer I peeped from my hide-out. The fireside picture was the same. I felt then that it must have gone wide of the mark and I started to fine-comb the camping-site for it with my wretched eyesight.

Without warning the fire erupted like a grenade-burst. There were five shells in the clip; I do not know how many separate reports I heard before I catapulted myself from the funkhole and ran at a tight crouch down the slope towards a path which led behind the rocks to safety. Then followed two heavier crashes in quick succession and Rankin's bullets whined and sang off the cliffs. There was a third, but no ricochet, and I realized that he was firing into the root cage and not in my direction.

I stubbed my foot, tripped, and fell heavily. Breathless, I got to my feet and found myself on the pathway with a great boulder between myself and Rankin. I sped away, keeping it between him and me while more shots crashed and echoed as he pumped shells into my hiding-place of a few minutes before. The ground levelled off and I raced into the open in the moonlight. Rankin remained within range still, however. I sprinted and jinked in case he saw me but another burst of firing told me he was concentrating on The Hill.

Then I struck the old wall which marked the outer line of fortifications and was over it almost before I remembered the twenty-foot drop to the wadi below. I found foot and hand-holds and started to work my way down like a fly on a wall. But I slipped and fell, landing awkwardly and heavily in the

51

sand. Had it been ordinary ground I might have broken a limb; as it was, the breath was knocked out of me for the second time that evening.

I lay gasping and before I had recovered properly I high-tailed across the wadi into the circle of hills beyond. I followed a shallow ravine to the top and found an agglomeration of rocky outcrops which were perfect cover.

The firing ceased and across my sandy moat of safety The Hill reared pallid under the moonlight.

CHAPTER FIVE

I was parched and my tongue felt like leather. I also wanted water to clean up the sticky mess of blood and grit on my forehead. During my escape blood had run from the cut into my injured right eye and now, as I lay quietly among the sheltering rocks, it began to congeal, further hindering my vision. I was badly bruised where the bolt had struck me. My physical discomfort, however, was not as great as my anguish of mind. I cursed that old rifle for letting me down at the moment when everything was going my way.

I got to my feet, wondering where I should begin to search for water. The present area was clearly useless. The broken summit, though ideal cover in the cool of night, would become an intolerable furnace by day. I rejected a passing thought of making a wide detour of the fortress and returning to my boat. It seemed too much like throwing in the towel before the fight had begun and I was determined to remain within striking distance of Rankin while I concocted a fresh plan. The faraway glow of my fire was visible from my elevated position and I knew Rankin must be nearby. My task was to find some safe shelter where I could keep watch and later get my hands on him. The focus of my attention was The Hill and would remain so while he was anywhere near it.

I probed for water-bearing plants among the rocks – ghostly in the moonlight which now illumined the circle of hills. I was on a smallish peak at the western extremity while below me, stretching eastwards for a couple of miles, was a wide valley wholly ringed by the chain of hills. From my position on the rim I faced the inside of the bowl. The hills were of a more or less uniform height all round the compass except for one prominent square-cut crag which rose out of the northern group facing the wadi and, of course, across its sand, The Hill. It was the most noteworthy peak in the area with the exception of The Hill itself. Our scientific party had christened it simply K2 but there had been no opportunity to explore it. The moonlight softened the raw terrain and scabbed remains of bush but I knew what a death-trap it could be if I were caught there without water.

This thought gave urgency to my search, and I renewed it anxiously. At chest-height, out of reach of animals, I spotted a sickly flower above a crown of fronds. It was what I sought – a *kaffirtulp* or hypoxis – indicating a water-filled bulb which was just visible between rocks. With the diamond pencil I stripped away the envelope of husks and gulped down the sticky orange-yellow liquid which made a good, if somewhat flat, drink. I used damp segments of the bulb to clean my face.

I felt better and concentrated on Rankin. I still held one ace: he did not know it was Guy Bowker who was on his trail. If he had seen and recognized me he would have realized without doubt that I had come for a reckoning and, rather than showing aggression, might have vanished as completely as he had done from the diggings.

From the direction of The Hill came a thud and the magnified echo of a single shot which brought me satisfactory knowledge that my man was still in place – firing at shadows maybe, or at the movement of an animal.

Then I sighted the kind of hide-out I was seeking when the moon silhouetted a giant baobab on top of the distant crag of K2. The span of the biggest I had ever seen before was sixty feet and I guessed this one was as big. Its branches were patterned like a surrealist finger-spread against the moon. Not only would the water-filled monster provide a sentry-box if it were hollow (many of them are) but it would also solve my water problem. The tree would be cool and safe, with an unlimited supply of water-laden pith tasting slightly like acid drops.

I set off without further ado to climb K2. The going on

the downslope into the valley was easy enough but once at the bottom it became heavy in thick sand. Because of this, I soon revised my time schedule for reaching the baobab: I reckoned now it would take a couple of hours.

I tried to lighten the slog by devising an accompaniment of words to my stomping steps. It came easily enough and I grinned to myself: *Damn all Diamonds! Damn all Diamonds!* My boots quickly filled with sand and held me back but I didn't want to shed them for fear of snakes. After the initial few hundred yards I had to pause to catch my breath.

When I started off again I felt as if my mind were drifting away from the physical self plodding along. I found myself reciting a childhood verse of my father's which I had known disrespectfully as the Dismal Diamond Ditty:

> *The Evil Eye shall have no power to harm*
> *Him that shall wear the Diamond as a charm;*
> *No monarch shall attempt to thwart his will*
> *And e'en the gods his wishes shall fulfil.*

I started to march in rhythm with the jingle. Perhaps the liquid I had drunk contained some mild hypnotic; perhaps it was lack of sleep and reaction which dredged the words from the recesses of my brain.

I took five strides onwards and I found myself reverting to the first line like a cracked gramophone record: *'The Evil Eye . . .'*

The harmless game suddenly went sour on me. Christ, how I hated diamonds!

My own name – William Guybon Atherstone Bowker – which had aroused the prison officer's derision, was in itself a proclamation of my father's diamond mania. I had been named in honour of the expert who, a century earlier, had identified the first 'shining stone' and had set South Africa on the road to becoming more famous for diamonds than the legendary Golconda of the East. The diamond had been found by a youth on the banks of the Orange River before anyone suspected that South Africa contained the world's largest diamond fields; it had been merely a child's plaything before being spotted by an acute trader.

Remembering this bit of history turned my mental spotlight on to my father, discoverer of the great Cullinan. Not only had diamonds been my father's life but he had bent the lives of his wife and son to them too. Appropriately, he had married the daughter of one of Amsterdam's leading diamond cutters; Erasmus had assisted Asscher at the cutting of the Cullinan. He had also lent him for the task the diamond pencil now reposing in my pocket. Perhaps my mother's long background of diamonds enabled her to accept my father's burning passion for them, but for my part it provoked a reaction so strong that by the time I was a teenager I loathed and rejected anything and everything connected with the things.

Early in 1905 my father and Rankin together had found the Cullinan, the size of a man's fist and weighing a pound and a quarter, at the Premier Mine near Pretoria. From the moment of its discovery the gem was an embarrassment, by virtue of both its size and its value. The unlikely manner of its discovery added further glamour: my father and Rankin had spotted what they thought was a chunk of broken bottle sticking out of an open-cast face; they had prised it out with a screwdriver.

The two men had sold the diamond to the mine for a sum which was rumoured to be about half a million sterling – an immense fortune at that time – which they had split between them. They were fêted and honoured and a thousand tributes showered upon them. But the diamond was so big that a buyer couldn't be found for it. So it was sent on a kind of shop-window tour of all the cities in South Africa; but still no purchaser came forward. Later the Transvaal government of the day had a brainwave. It bought the diamond and had it presented by the mine owner, Thomas Cullinan, to King Edward VII as a gift for his sixty-sixth birthday late in 1907. Cullinan was knighted and the diamond named after him. The great gem was still uncut and King Edward turned to the man who often before had served the British Royal Family well, Asscher of Amsterdam. But Asscher was not to be hurried over cutting the stone and studied it for months before undertaking the nerve-racking task the following year, when it was divided into nine major stones, all of which today either form part of the British Royal Regalia or are personal jewels of the Royal Family.

I could remember every detail of the day I was taken as a child, in an atmosphere of awe and reverence, to the Tower of London to see the main stone of the Cullinan, the Star of Africa, set in the head of the Sovereign's Sceptre. Charles II's gold, richly-jewelled Sceptre was refurbished with the Cullinan at the command of King Edward. I, like the other onlookers, goggled through the armour-plated glass at the great drop-shaped thing – over two and a quarter inches long and nearly one and a quarter wide – blazing under electric light. Our guide went on to say that the Cullinan's second largest portion was set in the Imperial State Crown next to the Black Prince's Ruby which Henry V had worn at Agincourt and the Sapphire of Edward the Confessor . . .

Suddenly my father's hand had crushed mine in a fierce grip. I turned in astonishment to see him staring at the great jewel as if in a trance. He whispered, 'Where that comes from there must be plenty more.' I yelled; as much in fright at his blank eyes as at his grip.

Now my reverie was cut short by the distant clap of another shot and its long echo among the hills – and I was back in the present, being hunted by my father's own partner. Bastard! I thought rancorously, I'm glad you're still imagining things! I wished I could see The Hill, which was largely hidden from my view by the intervening range. I had managed to labour through the sand to about the halfway mark in the valley and I felt exhausted; but the baobab beckoned from the top of K2 like the lattice-sight of an ack-ack gun against the skyline.

I was tempted to rest but the sound of the shot drove me on in another burst of energy. However, I soon started to flag: the sand seemed even thicker. Once again I found the child-hood doggerel rising as if of its own accord into my tired mind: '*Him that shall wear the Diamond as a charm . . .*' My mind's eye turned inward, back to my father: he had always insisted that I should write diamond with a capital D because the Roman poet who had composed the ditty had done so. It was also a mark of respect for diamonds. Capital D or no capital D, I reminded myself cynically, it hadn't helped him, even with the biggest diamond in the world to his credit, to charm away the Evil Eye. Mystery surrounded his death: he was variously supposed to have been shot by a gang in London when on a visit to float a syndicate, or run down in a fake street accident.

Shortly after his death my mother and I had left South

Africa to settle with Erasmus in Amsterdam and I went to school in England. Erasmus had always shut up like a clam when I had questioned him about my father's end. The most I could extract from him was the tribute that 'he was the world's greatest diamond-finder'. In many other respects, too, I came to the conclusion that Erasmus knew a great deal more about my father than he cared to admit.

When it came to talking about the Cullinan gem itself, however, Erasmus was much more forthcoming. He lived in the same street as the maestro Asscher who had made his reputation a couple of years before the discovery of the Cullinan by cutting the Excelsior, also from a South African mine, which, until the Cullinan itself, had been the largest diamond ever discovered. The street was as famous for diamonds as Antwerps' Pelikaanstraat for in it had also lived Coster and Voorsanger, who had re-cut the Koh-I-noor for Queen Victoria. Erasmus, a pupil of Asscher's, had been present at the cleaving of the Cullinan and had lent him the ancient diamond pencil for the job.

I had heard this story in detail many times from my grandfather: after his long study of the hidden planes of the Cullinan, Asscher was ready at last on a cold February day in 1908. He had made his final checks and had marked in with Indian ink those places which were invisible to all eyes but his.

It was a day of high drama in the freezing grey Dutch city. A police cordon was thrown around Asscher's factory. Everyone approaching was searched. A doctor and a special nurse stood by Asscher. The great man was tight with strain. He was examined by the doctor and his blood pressure found to be as high as a fighter pilot's in a dogfight.

To mark the solemnity of the occasion, Asscher wore a black waistcoat. He rolled his shirtsleeves to the elbow like a fencer and knotted his white overall in a big bow at the back of his neck.

He took the great diamond which he had set firmly beforehand in a shellac mixture at the end of a little solder cup, or 'dop' as it is known. Before attempting the groove which would guide the knife along the cleavage plane, Asscher paused. He, more than anyone else, knew the consequences of an error of judgment: the diamond would shatter at the

57

stroke of the cut and only a handful of powder would remain of one of the great wonders of the world.

For a moment the master craftsman held my grandfather's diamond pencil high, poised for the first cut. Unlike its twentieth-century counterpart (called a 'sharp') its diamond cutting tip could not be revolved to change its angle for deeper or finer cuts. It was for 'sentimental reasons', said my grandfather, that Asscher had used the old tool. He never elaborated this remark.

Then Asscher gave a little sigh and leant forward and began the incision at the top of the hidden plane. There was no sound except the rasp of diamond upon diamond. A frost of diamond dust formed as the groove deepened. Asscher ran a finger along this 'millionaire's ice', sweeping it away into a tin box below.

He then placed the cleaving knife with its specially tempered blade in the groove, holding it between his left thumb and forefinger, while his other fingers rested loosely across the 'dop'. A wooden mallet or short steel rod is used as a striker. Asscher chose the rod.

Like a marksman who fears to dwell too long on his aim, Asscher struck.

Two fragments fell into the box below – but they were not diamond. The ultra-hard steel blade had shattered. The Cullinan sat in its 'dop' – unmarked.

As if in a trance Asscher reached for the second cleaver. He fitted it into the slot. For the second time he raised the short rod above his head. A muscle twitched from the point of his chin along the line of his jaw to his left ear. The rod fell. There was a firm, sensitive click.

The Cullinan dropped in two main halves and four fragments into the tin box, and Asscher to the floor in a dead faint.

One shot – followed by two in quick succession from the direction of The Hill – jerked me back to the hard realities of my present situation: a tough, breath-robbing slog; thirst; clutching sand; and a killer at large. I had long since lost the benefits of my *kaffirtulp* drink. My forehead throbbed and my right-eye vision was hazed. I was worn out and in no shape to encounter Rankin. I was almost grateful to him for blasting off periodically but the fact that nearly an hour had

58

elapsed since his previous shot showed the extent of his tenacity. The baobab now started to look invitingly near but I had some way still to cover through sand before I would hit the first hard slopes of K2.

I set off, flagging, on this final leg, each sand-filled boot a penance. Again I could not prevent thoughts of diamonds from pushing their way to the forefront of my mind: Rankin's diamonds had pitchforked me into my present crisis and my father's diamonds had shaped my life. It was no exaggeration to say that he had tried to mould me like one of his own blasted diamond facets. My education which, because of the family's continual travelling, had largely come from him, had all been diamond-orientated. To him (and therefore to me) the heroes of history were the heroes of diamonds, the lines of my geography the courses of diamond-bearing kimberlite pipes, my mathematics the intricacies of metric carat measurement. Even my study of languages had been tainted with the jargon-smatterings of the diamond races – Yiddish, Hindustani, Persian and Arabic. Because twelve of the world's fifty major diamonds are South African, my father had indoctrinated me about South Africa. Its history, however, had no meaning for him before 1867 when two youths found a *blink-klip* on the banks of the Orange River near a one-horse village called Hopetown. It was inevitable that we should have made a sentimental journey to the place. There remain to this day on the window of a local store scratch marks which were made to test a diamond which was to rocket to world acclaim as the 83-carat Star of South Africa, and begin the country's diamond rush.

My father carried his infatuation so far as to force me to study Alexander the Great's campaigns – not as campaigns but because he maintained that diamond mining had originated with Alexander the Great when he had ordered his soldiers to recover gems from a snake-guarded pit. The ingenious conqueror had used lanoline-soaked sheepskins to which the diamonds stuck. The modern vibrating-table with its grease-covered terraces over which diamond concentrate is sluiced was, in my father's eyes, merely a sophisticated development of Alexander's 330 BC idea.

My father's death came almost as a relief from this sort of thing and formal schooling in England made a welcome con-

59

trast. I did a lot of yachting and joined the Royal Navy at the outbreak of war. I was captured during a cross-Channel Combined Operations strike and spent the rest of the war in a POW camp. My mother was shot by the Gestapo in Amsterdam: I never heard why.

I shook my head like a punch-drunk boxer and cleared away the intruding cloud of memories. The ground began to rise and become harder – K2 at last. I got rid of the sand from my boots and paused before the final effort of the ascent. From where I crouched only the tabletop of The Hill lay open to my view, rather lovely but with that enduring air of watchfulness mysterious in its own way, like Nadine with the queen's ring. It brought to mind a final kickback of my night's diamond recollections: my father had an affectation of calling an engagement ring a Tower Ring because out-of-favour Royal Favourites used the rings lovingly bestowed upon them to scratch messages before execution on the walls and windows of the Tower of London. I intended to find our love again in its own special context – damn all diamonds!

I pulled on my boots and started up the steep slope out of the bowl towards the rim, keeping below the skyline to avoid detection by Rankin. The wadi separating K2 from The Hill was deserted and the pinpoint of light from my fire had disappeared. There had been no shots for a long time; I took this at face value only because my mind and body were too fagged to make any effort beyond the last burst to reach the baobab. I arrived at a plateau on the top and trudged the few remaining yards to my target. Its massive trunk had (as I had hoped) a cool hollow in which I would be safe. I crawled thankfully into it and with the diamond pencil sliced a segment of pithy bark to suck and quench my thirst. The thin, acid sweetness tasted better than any drink I'd ever known.

I propped myself up against the cool wall of the interior, meaning to keep watch for Rankin. But my eyes grew heavier and my right one more painful until I could keep them open no longer. So I yielded and stretched out on the ground: the last thing I remembered was Charlie Furstenberg's doggerel:

'*Winkel, winkel, little store . . .*'

I slept.

CHAPTER SIX

The buzzing in my ears woke me.

I came to with a start of guilt at having overslept, perhaps at having slept at all. It was broad daylight outside the shelter and I caught the sound of a faint, disappearing drone. My right eye was swollen and full of pus; my leg muscles stiff and aching. I became aware of my physical discomforts but it was the humming which made me wide awake and tense. My snap diagnosis, as I became fully conscious, made me feel sick and depressed. I had heard that faint sound once before when I had collapsed during the scientific expedition and I knew that it portended an attack of malaria.

Before getting round to considering its effects on my campaign against Rankin, I concentrated on its immediate implications which were negative and ominous: illness made me a sitting duck for him. Thirst and inevitable delirium could drive me out into the open once the attack got under way. There either Rankin or heat-stroke would get me.

I sat up quickly, determined to try and sidetrack those consequences as much as I could before my senses started to slip away. In a kind of panic I got out the diamond pencil and started to hack myself a supply of the baobab's acid-sweet pith as an insurance against the days ahead, at the same time cramming my mouth with it and chewing to obtain as much liquid as I could. I also gathered together flaked bark, leaves and other veld rubbish into a corner to make a rough sick-bed for myself. I tried to focus my thoughts on the attractive smell of my den's concealed moisture as a kind of mental gimmick to keep myself hidden and not venture out when I became irrational. Whatever happened, I drummed into myself over and over, I must remain inside the hump-backed walls and low gnarled roof.

My testing-time came quicker than I expected when the hum returned, still distant but deep inside my head.

I went to the entrance and spat out the chewed pith, meaning to recharge my mouth immediately with a fresh supply. As my head emerged so did the sound grow and I realized with a surge of thankfulness that it was nothing to do with me but that it came from overhead in the sky – a plane.

For a moment I forgot all about Rankin and made my way beyond the tree's thick shade to try and spot the aircraft. Its echo struck back from the koppies and the way it waxed and waned led me to think it must be circling out of sight on the river side of The Hill.

I was automatically suspicious of its movements, a carry-over from my first instinct, after emerging from jail, to duck at the sight of a policeman. There were several harmless explanations of the plane's presence: it might be on a cross-border flight to Rhodesia and was simply checking its bearings on the most prominent landmark in the area; or it might be a sportsman taking an innocent look-see on his way to a shooting safari in neighbouring Botswana.

On the other hand, it could be the official plane returning to pick up the guard whose body I had seen. If so, once again Rankin became the key to my innocence. If I were picked up near The Hill's forbidden area in suspicious circumstances, how could I prove that I had not been involved in the burning of the hut, the ashes of which no doubt contained a charred skull? Circumstantial evidence alone was strong enough to bring me to trial – for murder this time.

I was not able to pinpoint the sound because of the hills' double echo, so I left the baobab altogether and went a few yards to the edge of the rock outcrop where K2 fell several hundred feet in a steep slope to the wadi below. It afforded me a grand view and almost at once I sighted the bright flash of a spinning airscrew in the strange hard light away to the north, near the confluence of the Shashi and Limpopo rivers; in other words, by the pool near which I had hidden my boat.

I felt exposed and naked on the coverless cliff-top despite the fact that the pilot could not possibly see me, and I sank to one knee to watch the plane's movements. It was very low, making towards The Hill. After a few minutes it crossed the confluence. Then it swung wide in order to avoid The Hill and headed towards the valley between the fortress and K2 whose floor consisted of the wadi. At the same time the machine dropped very low – no more than sixty feet, I judged.

This ruled out my first thought of a bearings check or casual joyride. The pilot was risking his neck now flying through the valley with its updraughts of superheated air. What made me doubly sure that it was a guard-plane was the fact that I identified it as a Tiger Moth of the type the Air Force had used as trainers during the war and had later sold. It was just the sort of light, highly manœuvrable machine for a bush landing-strip.

The plane ducked and dropped and for a moment I thought it was about to sideslip into a jagged mass of rocks which seemed mere feet below the wheels. But it pulled clear and began an erratic course over my camping-site. At that height the pilot could not fail to spot the remains of my fire and other things scattered about. He banked, as if scrutinizing them closely, then edged in perilously close to the cliffs. He completed a tight circle and retraced his flight-path, slowing almost to stalling speed. Then two heads craned out peering down at what lay below. I kept low and motionless; when the plane turned back yet again after passing over the tabletop I became convinced that the pilots were carrying out a methodical search of The Hill and its surroundings. Whatever their reason, I decided I'd be wise to keep well out of sight.

I dismissed the only possible reason which might involve me, namely, that Dr Sands had revealed to someone my presence at The Hill. But it seemed scarcely likely that my collecting hyena fossils was considered important enough to warrant a plane search.

As I watched, the plane, its business with The Hill apparently finished, headed towards the western hills, the hills from which I'd started towards K2 the previous night.

I knew I should get back at once into my hide-out, but curiosity overcame my caution for a moment and I decided to see quickly if anything below me on K2 could have attracted the plane.

I craned over the drop and below me in a kind of natural strongpoint projecting from the steeply sloping face I saw Rankin, aiming his rifle at the aircraft.

My first thought was that he had cleaned my fire's ash off his barrel – there was a helio-shot of light off it which dazzled me momentarily.

My second was an irrational, revenge-fired satisfaction that

63

despite my lack of weapons, I was at last close to the man whom above anyone else I wanted.

The third was that he must be mad: the night before he had tried to kill me though he thought I was a stranger, and now he was about to open up on an innocent aircraft.

'You bloody unspeakable bastard Rankin!' I said softly, as if already I had my hands on him.

I started to quiver and found my shirt drenched with sweat when I realized that to get where he was Rankin must have passed close by my tree shelter during the night. In fact, after he had fired the last shot I had heard from The Hill he and I must have been on a collision course, he crossing the mile-wide wadi towards K2 and I heading towards the tree on its top from inside the bowl of hills. It had only been the intervening rim with its chain of small peaks which had prevented our seeing one another in the bright moonlight. I blessed the quirk of chance which had taken me to the tree, enabling me once again to look down upon my prey; bush-hatted, tense-shouldered, the same predatory stance of man and gun I'd seen and recoiled from in the light of my fire.

I lay prone, with as little as possible of my head showing against the skyline in case he should glance my way, though all his attention seemed to be on the plane fussing over the defiles where I had been the night before.

He would have been a sitting duck for me if I had had a gun of any sort, even a small pistol. He was kneeling, with his rifle resting on a stone breastwork, following the machine with his sights. The plane was following a west-east course above the line of the wadi; K2 faced towards The Hill at right angles to its route, in other words due north. Rankin's command-post – created by a natural fall of sandstone but fortified by man – was about twenty feet wide and five deep. It dominated the whole wadi area. A partially ruined wall across the cliff slope ended short of a barred entrance.

I decided to rush this entrance while Rankin was pre-occupied with the plane and slid full-length into a V-shaped cleft which led down to the old wall. But it petered out about halfway to my objective and I clung precariously to the rotten rock at full stretch until it gave way and I was pitched onwards in a kind of short-step toddling glissade with my knees hunched up to my chest. In the final few feet, however, my heels started to slide from under me and I jack-knifed upright into an out-of-control run, my arms windmilling.

This constituted a gesture to the searching aircraft; as the pilot spotted me he at once gunned his engine.

I lurched on and hit the wall with a bone-jarring thud but had sense enough to drag myself through a gap to the far side out of Rankin's sight. I knew that if I didn't act right away the plane would be overhead and lay itself wide open to Rankin's gun. So I worked my way painfully along the wall on my knees with the haphazard idea of getting at Rankin.

Where the wall ended I looked out: the rock within six inches of my face seemed to dissolve and I yelled as much from shock as surprise when fragments of hot lead sprayed the side of my neck. The plane was so near now that I didn't even hear the shot above its roar.

In a flash I flung myself at the doorway across an exposed gap, where a single mis-step would have sent me crashing to my death below. I leapt at the stone coping above the barricaded entrance and my momentum sent me up the overhang with my feet scrabbling for holds in minute fissures.

And all of a sudden I was over and seemed to look straight into a roaring propeller, a goggled face and the walled enclosure with Rankin kneeling rifle to shoulder. The range was down to point-blank; there was nothing I could do any more. The engine drowned the sound of Rankin's shot but I knew that he had fired: from the bitter smell of cordite and the slight tilt one wing gave as the plane swept over, so low that I could have stood up and grabbed its wheels as it passed.

Rankin had got it.

He knew, however, that he had missed me for I saw him lay out within quick reach of his hand a nickel-plated derringer: a short-range pistol with twin heavy-calibre barrels.

The plane's slipstream tore the bush hat from his head but there was no need for me to confirm my identification.

'Rankin! You bloody murdering bastard!'

My words were swamped by a tearing crash as the plane hit the side of K2.

I launched myself at him feet first with the idea of mule-kicking him in the chest but he moved with remarkable speed and fired the derringer. The heavy-duty slug tore into the heel of my right boot; it was like being hit by an iron bar. As a result only my left boot struck him, ineffectually, and as I crashed to the ground against the breastwork a second shot screamed off it near my shoulder without touching me. With a surge of alarm I realized that I was up against a man who, though in his sixties, was iron-hard from a tough life and was quite capable of hammering me in a straight fight.

I half got to my feet as he came on at me, holding the derringer low. There was a sharp click and a flick-knife blade shot out under the weapon's lower barrel. I jerked upright and for a split second we faced one another.

Then with my right hand I whipped the diamond pencil from my pocket.

I saw recognition start into his eyes at the sight and he swerved as I feinted at his belly with it, laying himself wide open, as I intended, for my real *coup de grâce*.

He saw murder in my eyes.

'Rankin!' I scarcely heard my own whisper.

'They were *cut* diamonds!'

Anything he had said or done then would have been too late to save him from my karate elbow-chop to the heart. It travelled only the distance of my elbow's arc and I felt his rib-cage splinter.

He gave a shallow cough and stood swaying in slow motion even after the light of consciousness had gone from his eyes. I caught him by the shirt front before he fell, and laid him down.

My immediate concern was for the occupants of the plane because at any moment I expected to see the wreck go up in flames. The pilot had almost cleared the top of K2, but not quite. There was a cloud of dust among the torn scrub and what looked like smoke.

It required a great effort of will to master the reaction after the fight and force myself across the dangerous unprotected gap near the command-post's entrance. Then I sprinted to the crash. I was goaded by the fear of fire although when I reached it there was more dust than smoke – and no sign of life. The tail section had been ripped off and lay about thirty yards behind the main wreck. Littering the crash path were small branches which had been torn off by the wing struts. Finally the wings and landing wheels had come adrift; the fuselage lay with the airscrew tangled round a boulder.

I went first to free the figure I could see slumped against the windscreen of the rear cockpit. This was difficult to reach because the wreck had finished up as high as my head across a group of rocks. So I mounted the fuselage at the smashed tail end and wormed my way forward. When I reached the cockpit I bent forward and loosed the safety straps, still unable to see who it was. In doing so my arm partly brushed aside the flying helmet.

The long black hair fell heavily, tiredly almost, across the plane's yellow paintwork.

I reached over and turned ·the face, my heart pounding.

It was Nadine.

CHAPTER SEVEN

Something inside me should have turned over at the sight of her but it didn't. I simply regarded her with a curious crunch of negative emotions, scarcely considering that she might be injured or even dead. We had never quarrelled, Nadine and I, so I found it difficult at first to define the resentment I experienced at her presence. The object of my anger accordingly was not so much herself but small things about her – I found her smart navy-and-yellow zipfronted jacket ridiculous, with its five-inch broad stripes across the breast and waist; I asked myself why the hell she had to wear the fancy vinyl hood I had knocked askew instead of a common-or-garden leather flying helmet.

I didn't realize that what I was experiencing was a deep-down sidekick from my showdown with Rankin and that my anger was really against myself for having half killed him and, for all I knew, robbed myself of the chance of getting him to confess. Nor did I find Nadine's arrival like a shot bird falling into my lap as touching as it might have been. I had planned to return to her and make amends by presenting her with a clean, slate in regard to myself; and the fact that she had broken in on the first act while a lot of loose ends still lay around left me frustrated and annoyed. Nothing had worked out as I had intended: the situation seemed to have taken

control, not I. I mentally castigated Dr Sands for an inter-
fering if well-intentioned, two-timing old busybody. Without
his directions, Nadine couldn't possibly have located me so
soon in the huge territory.

I drew her goggles back to her hairline. Her eyes remained
closed, her head and shoulders lolling slackly. I had always
loved above all her expression of serenity. Even in her
moments of deepest emotion it had never left her. Now I
looked on a face which was the same, yet different. There
was pain in it and a slight puffiness about the cheeks and lips
on the left side under the nostril. With dawning astonishment
I realized that I had been the cause of it. The knowledge
didn't soften my resentment; just heightened the tumult of my
emotions.

I began to haul her out of the cockpit but stopped halfway
at the thought that she might have internal injuries. There was
no sign of blood but still she made no sound. A further hasty
check revealed nothing. Then I manhandled her on to my
shoulders and stumbled towards the rear of the plane, out of
reach of a possible explosion. There was a growing smell of
burning rubber, hot oil and fuel. The hard gloss of the vinyl
jacket prevented my feeling any contact with her body. Where
the softness of her breasts should have rested against my
shoulder there was merely the insentient plastic. It was as
though the slack body had never known desire for mine. It
all seemed part of the strange impersonality of the scene.

Once we were well clear of any possible blast I put Nadine
down and propped her up against a boulder. I unfastened a
press stud above her right temple and got rid of the cap and
goggles. Her long hair fell down and framed the stark white
face, softening its contours. I made a hurried examination of
her head but could find no injury. When I tried to free the
awkward zip of her polo collar I found my fingers trembling:
I dreaded what damage I might find.

I was still fumbling under her chin when she opened her
eyes.

There was a flash of shock and disbelief; joy sparked in her
eyes but almost as it leapt it was gone and the shadows
shrouded their green depths.

There was an uncomfortable moment of constraint, of
waiting. Neither of us knew what to say to deflate the tension

with some trite or wryly humorous phrase. Her lids were heavy, perhaps with delayed shock from the crash.

Still silent, her eyes on mine, she brought the ring to the tip of her tongue and then touched the back of my hand with the tiny wet spot she'd made.

The sound of fire came from the wreck. I assumed she had heard it too and got to my feet with the intention of going back for the pilot. She however not having heard the crackling, misconstrued my move and looked aghast.

'The plane's on fire – I'll try and get him out,' I managed to say. 'It could go up at any minute.'

'Guy, wait . . . no, go.' Her voice was an uneven whisper. 'Save Peter . . . I heard the bullet go into him . . . but take care of yourself, for God's sake!'

The bullet had ripped into the airman's left shoulder and plugged the wound with a tear of his silk choker. I spotted its tiny entrance hole in the side of the cockpit. Spurred on by the brittle crackle of flames I hurried to get his safety strap loose. The blaze appeared to be gathering momentum and I was terrified at the thought of how soon it might reach the tanks. I struggled with the deadweight body, which seemed to hook on every projection, but eventually I got him to the ground. The flames a blow-torch on my back. I knelt to flip him on to my shoulders and somehow managed to pick him up and start off. We hadn't gone more than a few yards when the tanks exploded and threw us to the ground.

Little meteors of flaming fuel raced into the dry bush. One fell on to the pilot's jacket and I beat it out. With the tinder-dry bush for fuel, each incendiary spot became the start of a new fire. I humped the pilot up again and stumbled towards where I had left Nadine but saw her coming, white and shaky, towards me. I tried to wave her back but she joined me and tried to help me set the pilot down in her own patch of shade. I found my shirt and hands sticky with the blood from his wound. A tall plume of smoke rose above the burning machine and everywhere the bush was ablaze.

I welcomed the need for quick action about the wounded man. It begged off all the impossible questions in Nadine's eyes and quietened the devils inside me.

'Who is he?'

'Peter Talbot. My father's personal pilot. He . . . I . . .'

'The explanations can wait. He's in a bad way. The first thing to do is to get well clear of the fire.'

'Guy – you . . .'

She seemed to sway a little. I went to her. 'Here! You'll pass out from heat stroke in that jacket. Off with it.'

'It's not the heat . . . Guy!'

'We can't talk now.'

'Have you seen yourself? What have they been doing to you?'

She bit back the rest of her words.

I wondered if Rankin, too, had been shaken by my wild appearance. I suddenly became aware that my face was singed and stained from the Mannlicher misfire; one eye was blood-shot; my unshaven beard plastered with dust and sweat; my shirt ripped; an arm skinned and raw. I stank of petrol, sweat, cordite and fresh blood.

'There's a sort of cave over there.' I nodded towards my 'command-post', which merged remarkably well into its sur-roundings. 'We must move him out of the sun. It's a bit tricky crossing over . . .' I started to explain and then asked dubiously, 'Do you think you can make it?'

'I'm all right. I'm not really hurt. A bit dazed, that's all.'

However, the shock of the crash was catching up on her fast. Despite her brave show of words she looked on the point of collapse.

She indicated the pilot: 'When you think of all the flying risks he's come through, and then he crashes because of a bullet which wasn't his fault!'

There probably wasn't any imputation in her words but nevertheless I found myself replying defensively. 'I couldn't get there in time. I was just too late to prevent the shot.'

'We saw you waving to us. We both felt certain it was you.'

A billow of smoke, acrid with the smell of petrol fumes and *kanniedood* timber, swept over us.

'We must hustle,' I said. 'Soon this whole hillside will be ablaze. The "command-post" and its approaches are solid rock so we'll be safe there. I'll make the first trip with him. You wait where the wall ends and I'll come back for you. It's a nasty stretch and you're in no state to make it yourself.'

'What about . . . I mean, the man who fired the shot?'

I laughed grimly. 'You needn't worry. I took care of Rankin.'

Her constraint cracked. 'You must be joking – Rankin!'

I didn't feel up to meeting the emotional challenge which lay all the time just below the surface.

'I'll tell you later,' I replied, 'it's too involved. But Rankin's no threat to anyone at the moment. He's out – unconscious. Now help me get this man on to my back!'

I could sense the conscious effort she made to bring her nerves under control.

'Shouldn't we try to bandage the wound and stop the bleeding first?'

'I don't know enough to judge. Perhaps carrying him will make it worse. At a guess I'd say the slug is lodged inside him.'

She buried her head suddenly in her arm and cried out brokenly. 'It was all so good until . . . until . . .'

I couldn't find it in myself to comfort her. There were a score of questions I dared not face. I had not even started to come to terms with the situation which had exploded the moment I saw Rankin's sights tracking the aircraft; the range of events which had taken over extended much beyond Rankin now. At the press of a trigger he had brought unguessed-at forces into play and The Hill was somehow one of them. Without further ado I shouldered the pilot's limp body.

'Keep on the top side of the ruined wall and don't look down,' I told Nadine. 'Stay put at the gap until I come back for you.'

Heat bounced off the rocks and seemed to distort their shape. Its intensity made my head swim. There was nothing I could do to ease Talbot's passage and I suspected that we must have left a trail of blood behind us. Nadine kept close to me until we reached the unprotected section between wall and door. There I shifted my grip to steady myself: my arm muscles were kicking from the weight of my burden. I wanted to turn and reassure Nadine before starting off, but didn't know what to say. Looking up to take my line for the crossing, all I was aware of was The Hill: looming, blocking everything. *Our* Hill.

I cannot pretend to remember staggering to the other side,

blinded as I was by the insufferable light and my confused mental state, but the barred gate brought a return to reality. My earlier leap up the coping came back like a film flashback of which I was a spectator, not a participant. I put Talbot down and decided that once again I would have to attempt the stone face. This time, however, there was no revenge-induced thrust to transform my hands and feet into automatic instruments finding their own holds. The ascent was painful, slow and energy-sapping. Once over the breastwork, however, it was only a matter of minutes before I had lifted the door's rough-hewn log catch.

To my astonishment, Nadine was crouched beside the airman.

My general annoyance with her boiled over. 'My God! I don't want any extra casualties on my hands! I told you to wait for me!'

The sun was strong enough to burn all expression from her eyes except a bright carry-over of terror from her recent brush with death.

But her reply was a sensible one. 'You left a trail of blood all the way across. The sooner we do something for him the better.'

'Come on then.'

Together we hefted the inert body, Nadine carrying his feet and I his shoulders. We carried him into the 'command post'. But it was Rankin who held her attention. She became paler still at the sight of him, put down Talbot's feet, and went over to where he lay wheezing, standing back with a sort of shocked repugnance. She looked at me – reproachfully, I believed – and I stared back wordlessly.

'You did that to him, Guy? I wouldn't have believed it possible when I think of the gentleness I've known from you.'

I was in no mood for any criticism from her. 'Don't waste your sympathy on that hardline sonofabitch! He had two guns and a knife. There they are at your feet.'

She gathered up four shell cases – two stubby ones from the derringer and two lean ones from the Mauser – then with her earlier air of repugnance studied the fine 7 mm Mauser, with its ribbed barrel and glistening stock of African zebra wood, where Rankin had flung it before making at me. She picked up the derringer by its flick-blade between thumb and forefinger holding it and the spent cases out to me. I read this as a further accusation.

'Guy, I'm not reproaching you. I see the odds. I'm reproaching the whole situation we're in.'

'I'd cleaned it up – then you arrived.'

She turned away. The tension was punctuated by Rankin's gasps. I wondered if a rib had pierced one of his lungs.

I added a little more kindly, 'That's all over now. Our immediate problem is Talbot.'

She pitched the derringer and shell cases away and came back to help the pilot. The command-post was backed by a hollowed-out cliff of *holkrans sandsteen* similar to my safe spot on The Hill. To the front the post dominated an area so extensive that one machine-gunner could have held a whole regiment at bay. At the rear the original roofline had collapsed centuries before, converting what must merely have been an overhang into a cave. The entrance was to one side, the interior out of sight. The place offered reasonable living quarters under the most trying weather conditions.

Silently we carried Talbot into the shade.

We avoided each other's eyes.

'Let's see what's inside,' I suggested.

We edged past a rock pillar at the entrance and found ourselves in what was more a workshop than a home.

A curious wooden structure, something between a bench and a skeletonized cupboard minus panelling, dominated the centre of the shadowy interior. Two wheels were set into openwork beams at the top. From them a long cogwheel spindle ran almost to the floor, where it was connected to a treadle which appeared to have come from a sewing-machine. On the surface of the bench a heavy balanced arm rested on a revolving disc. It looked like an outsize gramophone turntable. Set about it were a series of screw-clamps and large butterfly nuts. On the floor was a cast-iron pot with burned-out coals. Among them was a metal crucible filled with solder; and a similar empty vessel lay on the bench.

Nadine shivered, maybe because of the contrast with the heat outside; the coldness I felt was my recollection of Rankin's hands in the moonlight. I puzzled over what strange craft those hands might ply on the bizarre machinery before us. Nothing could have been in greater contrast to his hovel on the diggings than this neat, clean, trim abode.

'What is all this apparatus for, Guy?'

'It stumps me. But the place looks as if it's been lived in for a long time.'

'It must have been he who booby-trapped our expedition.'

'That's for sure. Other things too.'

She waited for me to explain further but I couldn't bring myself to muck-rake details of the guard's murder and Rankin's attempt on my life.

'What is it, Guy? What are you hiding from me? What has got into you?' She was obviously making an effort to keep her voice even.

I tried to lower the pressure between us. 'Let's take a look round. There may be something we can use to help Talbot.'

'Here's a camp-bed, and a stretcher too.'

'Perhaps there's some water. We'll need it if we're to clean up his wound.'

We went deeper into the cave. There were two chambers, a smaller one leading off the first, larger one. The inner room was clearly Rankin's kitchen.

'There's our water,' I said. 'And I could use a drop of brandy in it too.'

I went towards three or four large, buff-coloured Aladdin-like storage jars. There were several dippers nearby, all decorated with a similar sort of triangular motif near the upper rim. There was also a spouted bowl with odd black markings.

'Guy! Please don't! Don't drink!'

Nadine was staring at the dippers as if they were instruments of torture.

'I doubt whether Rankin thought of poisoning me, among his other efforts,' I answered ironically. 'And by Heaven he owes me a drink! I intend to have it.'

'No, Guy!'

'Don't be ridiculous,' I said off-handedly. 'I haven't had any water since yesterday. Again because of Rankin all I've tasted is a lot of soapy pith.'

'Guy – what has been going on here at The Hill between you and Rankin? All I get from you are hints and a lot of evasions when I try to press my questions.'

'It can wait. If you won't let me use one of those things, I'll try my hands instead.'

'Let me get it for you. I . . . I can't explain.'

The constraint and touchiness was back in full force between us. I watched her with growing puzzlement as she avoided what were clearly containers for the water and filled instead a cup which she took from the table. I felt her concern for my thirst was more like the professional sympathy of a nurse for a patient than that of lover for lover. She had several small sips from my cup when I had finished.

The same sort of feeling was evident when we went back to the pilot, acting like compassionate strangers in seeing to his wound. I used the derringer flick-blade to cut away his flying-jacket. The wound had almost stopped bleeding and we bathed it clean. It looked harmless for so deadly a thing – a small bruised blue-black swelling on the collarbone with a puncture in the centre.

Nadine eyed me questionably when I proceeded to cut away the clothing behind his neck.

'Look,' I pointed out. 'There's no exit mark. That's bad. It means that the bullet went in from the front, smashed his collarbone and penetrated deeper still. If it's ended up lodged against his spine, he's had it. On the other hand, it may have shattered into fragments when it hit bone. Then he may still have a sporting chance. Rankin's rather fond of dum-dum bullets.'

She swung back on to her heels and the thing which separated us flared up.

'He's fond of dum-dum bullets –' she echoed. '*You know that!*'

'Yes – I know that.'

'Guy,' she burst out. 'You're not here with me . . . you haven't come back . . . from something I don't, can't understand . . . please . . . I can't reach you . . . please . . .'

I dropped my eyes and tugged the ripped sleeve clear of the wound. Then I looked up at her. There was something in her eyes I had never seen before. I should have taken her in my arms. But like a shell-shocked impotent I could not reach for the love *I* needed.

Instead I answered harshly: 'I found a man's head with the back of it blown away. Only a dum-dum bullet does that. Rankin fired the shot.'

She buried her head in her hands as if I had thrown the horrible thing on the ground in front of her.

'The head was off its body,' I went on. 'Rankin spent half last night trying to do the same to me.' I got up. 'Save yourself any feelings you may have about the way I roughed him up. I want him alive for one reason only.'

She looked up at me from where she knelt with a kind of uncomprehending despair. Suddenly, overwhelmingly, I wanted to be alone. I wanted to think, think, think. I even asked myself the savage question, looking down on her lovely face, whether a love born of so strange a thing as The Hill had the strength to neutralize the acid which was eating into me.

'See here, Nadine,' I said more gently. 'A great deal has happened since . . . since my . . .' I could not bring myself to use the word 'walkout' to her face. 'I'm sorry if I sound half out of my mind. Yesterday . . . last night . . .' The words would not come. I temporized and got a grip on my voice.

'Let's strap up Talbot as best we can. He could be dying. From the limp way he hung on my shoulder I'd say he's paralysed from the neck down. He needs a doctor and hospital care. So does Rankin. I want to check on him also.'

'Guy,' she replied raggedly, 'I want this thing your way. You've been through some awful hell you won't tell me about. Not long ago you would have. What is between us has slipped somehow. I don't know where anything begins or ends. But I'd like you to understand that for me it is simply enough that I've found you.'

My rawness erupted again. 'Sands?' I demanded.

'Don't say it like that! Yes, Dr Sands told me, but it was my idea! And I talked Peter into flying me to The Hill to look for you! He'd just bought the Tiger Moth for himself. He thought it was a bit of a lark. We told Father we were off together to a flying rally. He was all for it – daughter on the rebound with his personal pilot. He was only too glad to think I was getting you out of my system – a blasted jail-bird he called you – does all this really matter to you, Guy?'

'And you expected to find the flown bird?'

I regretted the crack the moment it slipped out.

She brought her voice under control and said softly, with only a shadow of rebuke. 'I expected to find you. The man I loved. I haven't. I have the person of Guy Bowker, it's true,

76

but not . . . not . . .'

Trying for a breathing-space to sort things out inside myself, I fenced: 'This man's going to die while we stand here talking. Somehow we've got to get him to hospital in Messina.'

My brusque voice annoyed but steadied her. 'We can put the mattress from Rankin's bed in your Land-Rover,' she said. 'I'll hold him firm over the rough bits of track.'

'There isn't a Land-Rover.'

'It's not possible!'

'Mine's a shoestring outfit. Everything I have can fit into a couple of gunny-bags. In fact, it's all lying right now at the foot of The Hill.'

'Did you *walk*? Through this sort of country?'

'No. I bought a boat in Messina. It's made out of an old flying-boat float with an outboard motor, but it goes. And it's shallow enough for the river.'

'But there's scarcely any water! Peter and I followed the river upstream from Messina.'

'It probably looks worse from the air than it really is. There are pools and shallow channels connecting them. You have to look for them, hard. Plenty of sand.'

'How did you manage to get over that?'

'Portage. The hard way. I dragged the *Empress of Baobab* as I call her across the sandy bits at the end of a rope. I guess I've got harness sores on my shoulders as a result. I'll never forget those sixty miles of pulley-hauley.'

'You really were keen to lose the world and me, Guy.'

'The boat's our only transport for Talbot.'

'From what you say it would be madness to attempt it.'

'In the first place I doubt whether we'd get him alive to the river. I've moored near a big pool at the confluence.'

'And . . . Rankin?'

'It's about time we took a look at him too.'

We went outside to where he lay. His face was puffy and mottled and he was deeply unconscious. His breathing frightened me. When I pulled open his shirt Nadine flinched. The red-and-purple welt across his chest looked far worse than Talbot's wound.

'You . . . you did that, Guy?'

It was one of those rhetorical questions which, under the circumstances, threw me on the defensive. 'You saw,' I rejoined. 'He had two guns and a knife. I was unarmed.'

She didn't reply immediately but gestured towards the looming, shimmering Hill.

'It was a place of love – that is what it meant to me. All the things that go with love. Now somehow it's changed, horribly, into something else. You're part of the change . . . oh, Guy, Guy, doesn't the queen's ring still mean what it did?'

I could not face her hurt, pleading look: there was too much to explain all at once.

'Nadine, neither of us is in any shape for the questions which are uppermost in our minds. We're pretty well at the limit. Let's leave it and get some rest. I'll clean up first. We'll talk later and also try to make a plan about these two. I can't see that we can do anything for them at present. We're as marooned here as if we were on a desert island. Now give me a hand with Rankin.'

She looked at me penetratingly for a moment; and when she spoke her voice sounded less overwrought. 'I'm almost afraid to touch him for fear of what it might do to him.'

We brought the stretcher over to him and, as gently as we could, lifted him on to it. We gave Talbot the truckle bed. When we had finished, the uncomfortable vacuum seemed once more to envelop us. This time it was Nadine who eased things.

'What we need is tea and something to eat. I'll fix it.'

The snack meal was a silent, strained little affair with only an occasional commonplace exchanged between us. Afterwards I sat on the rock floor by the cave entrance, meaning to keep watch over the terrain, on which the sun was beating remorselessly down. Nadine went inside. I loaded the magazine of Rankin's Mauser and put it by me – against what sort of contingency I wasn't quite sure. The unwinding process caught me unawares, and I fell asleep. It was dusk when I snapped into wakefulness. The Mauser had gone from my side and there was a soft leather cushion for my face to rest on.

Nadine sat ahead of me on a small stool, her chin, characteristically, cupped on her interlocked fingers. She was so still that for a moment I wondered if she too were asleep but she was in fact awake and staring fixedly at The Hill. It looked uglier and more menacing with, behind it, a setting sun as lurid as a film fake. A splendid tower of smoke hung over K2 and the remains of the plane. Its tip was chalk-rose in the sunset.

I remained motionless, not wishing to break the spell and wondering whether the things I had been through had really happened. There was only the faintest nimbus round her hair, which merged into the gathering darkness; her shirt was tinted yellow-gold at the shoulders. For a brief respite I felt good, good simply to be with her.

'Guy!'

The vignette of a few precious moments vanished: she swung round and got up. My sleep-soothed mind jerked into action at the imperative note in her voice.

I too now heard the distant sound and in a second was on my feet and with her at the parapet. It came intermittently, echoing among the fading hills.

'That's an airscrew.'

'Yes, Guy, it is! Listen! It's coming from somewhere over by the river!'

This could be salvation for Talbot and Rankin. We held our breaths. One moment the sound seemed close, the next far away. It was higher pitched than the Tiger Moth's engine.

'Someone must have spotted the smoke,' I said.

'It's much too soon for an air search; they won't know until tomorrow at the earliest that the Tiger Moth is missing. Peter and I flew from Pietersburg and that's hundreds of miles away to the south. We checked out a false destination on purpose to hide our trail. They won't dream of looking here.'

'I'd guess then that some other plane has come to investigate the smoke – we're right on the frontier.'

'The regular air route's far away near Messina . . . listen, Guy, it's stopped!'

The minutes ticked by. 'Nadine,' I said slowly. 'The most likely thing is that it's a relief plane come to pick up the guard . . .' I explained briefly about the murder at the hut.

'I begin to understand better now,' she replied sombrely. I wished I could see the expression on her face but it was really dark now.

'If it had been the guard plane, surely it would have made

some signal to the hut?' she argued. 'And anyway it doesn't seem a very likely time of day to come and fetch the guard.'

'There it is again!'

The noise came through clearly but we could not pinpoint it.

'It seems very light for an aeroplane engine,' she remarked. 'But that's the sound of a propeller all right.'

'It's stopped again.'

'If it's cutting on and off it means the machine's in trouble – perhaps it knows about the airstrip and is trying to locate it for an emergency landing.'

We waited for it to resume but after ten minutes there was still nothing.

'We would surely have heard it if it had crashed?' she asked.

'Yes. In this stillness you can hear a jackal bark miles away. Also, there's no sign of a fire. Think what a pyre the Tiger made – we're bound to see it.'

After keeping our eyes skinned for another ten minutes from our grandstand perch we gave up. The uncertainty disrupted our discussion of further plans for Rankin and Talbot. It would have been stepping from the frying-pan into the fire to leave The Hill when help might be at hand. Nadine held out her powerful torch, but I shook my head. Though as concerned as she for the plane's safety, I knew that any signal from where we stood would mislead the pilot into disaster. And any attempt to make our way to the airstrip miles away at night through the bush would be futile. We decided to stay where we were until morning.

The tip of the plane's smoke pyre vanished with the full onset of night. The stars grouped themselves in epaulettes on The Hill's shoulders. Its bulk was invisible but we still sensed its dominion. At moonrise it would re-emerge, like a centurion standing athwart Africa.

The disappearance of the need for further action or consultation over the injured pair inevitably brought about the confrontation between us. I dreaded it but there was no escape. The long silence before she began was an ominous curtain-raiser.

I half expected her to reproach me or plead but she did neither.

'Guy,' she said, 'What I am going to say now is something

I was reserving for the night we first make love. I've thought all along that would be the moment but I've changed my mind. I think you need to know it now that we're faced with a crisis in our love.'

Her quiet almost detached words about her own body being pledged to mine and the strong physical pull of her presence sent a powerful shock-wave of sexual charge through me. I yearned to see her face and eyes and slim figure but the hazed stars were too dim. The soundtrack of the African bush was silent.

'The queen and her ring are of course at the heart of it . . .' She smiled slightly, the first time since the crash . . . 'Oddly enough, those old dippers I stopped you drinking from are also involved. But I'm not doing this very well, kicking off at the end instead of the beginning.'

'The Hill's the start. I think we've all been so dazzled by its treasures – all that gold, the golden rhino and the crown and other stuff – that it's blinded us to another side which is equally important, if not more so.'

Her voice warmed and again I wished for some light, to see what I knew must be in her eyes.

'You remember how excited Dr Drummond became when I discovered the statuette?'

'I'll never forget that day, for more reasons than one.'

She inclined towards me on her stool; the thing sparked between us like two joined electric terminals.

'Well, it was proof of something he had suspected for years although he'd no direct evidence. You were out for the count in hospital when this was going on. All the treasure was proof enough of The Hill's temporal power, but the statuette revealed the other side of the coin.'

'What do you mean, Nadine?'

'The Hill was a symbol of spiritual power throughout the whole of Africa south of the Sahara.'

'One statuette couldn't have proved all that.'

'No. But it confirmed Dr Drummond's suspicions. You see, years before, he'd found an ancient inscription hinting at a powerful force marching down Africa towards where we are now. It was led by a general or a king – maybe both offices were combined – who claimed he 'knew God': and who demanded in the name of his God the allegiance of all the countries through which he travelled. And he got it. Backing this rallying-call was a quite remarkable political machine which enforced his rule. There's no doubt that he was some sort of oracular master-mind who gave supernatural revelations to the masses. Anyway, he surrounded himself with enough mystique and terror to ensure that long after he and his stronghold of The Hill had passed away he continued to hold superstitious sway over millions. Do you wonder The Hill is still regarded as taboo?'

'If all this is so, where is his grave? We both know that the one with the treasure was the queen's.'

'That's what is so curious – it never has been found.'

I wondered where all this was leading. I couldn't see that it had much bearing on Nadine and myself.

I think she detected some impatience in my tone and hurried on.

'Rankin's water dippers come into this – you wondered why I wouldn't let you use them?'

'I still do.'

'They're not for water at all. They're called funerary furniture. They come from a grave; not a human one.'

'I thought all graves were human.'

'The dippers were really sacred and symbolic things which were put in the grave of a bull which had been specially slaughtered and buried with elaborate ritual. The dippers are ritual urns and were cursed against being used by humans. It's known as a beast burial ceremony. The eggheads talk themselves into knots about them – all sorts of theories about their being relics of the bull cult of the Hamitic peoples of the Nile Valley, and so on endlessly. Yet here we have the same thing at The Hill, thousands of miles away, and not a trace of a link anywhere in Africa between. I think differently about them. You see, my . . . my heart tells me otherwise.'

I was still mystified, unable to equate anything she was saying with ourselves.

'I've put myself pretty ruthlessly in the mental dock since you left,' she went on. 'I couldn't just laugh you off, or the things which began our love. But I did ask myself whether I had allowed my emotions to run away with me.' She added, apparently at a tangent: 'But I know she did it for great love.'

We both understood whom she meant but I repeated the

word, to hear her explanation.

'She?'

'Our queen, Guy.' Now the answers tumbled out. 'When I saw it I realized that I had to have a ring like hers for our love too. I understood deep down that it was she who had offered the sacrifice . . .'

'Saw what, Nadine?'

'In all the other graves the bodies are buried in the traditional way: in a sitting position, arms flexed, chin on knees, facing north. Not she. She . . . she . . .'

'What are you trying to say?'

'She had them lay her body out – in the love-making position. She must have died after the king and she believed she was going to him again. They were both in their prime and it was their faith that they would meet again in the next world. And she expected him to make love to her. All the things the stuffy old professors call funerary urns aren't that at all. They're for her perfumes, her powders and her cosmetics. She wanted him to find her in death as he had done in life: beautiful, perfumed, lying waiting for his love. It was a *lover's* grave, Guy. Now do you understand about the ring? And the occasion when I had decided you should hear this from me?'

The picture of her standing in the trench flooded back to me. I was overwhelmed. I said the first thing that came to mind.

'What has all this to do with sacrifice?'

She started to reach out her hand to me but hesitated at the barrier still between us. Her words became a torrent.

'I should really thank you for what you did by walking out, Guy. You taught me to understand *her*. When a woman's heart cries out as mine did – and as hers must have done – it looks round for some physical thing to break in sympathy. It's just got to tell – the world, God, anyone – it's breaking. You've got to say it somehow or go mad. Her king went away in death and her heart burst. It's as if I had inherited her grief along with her ring. When a heart bleeds, there must be blood. I *know*. She found release in sacrifice. The difference between us is that I don't, like her, have to crash the barrier of death. That's why I'm here and I thank God I can still reach out and touch you.'

She choked and got up and went quickly to the stone parapet, staring in the direction of The Hill. I rose and went to her. Had I remained sitting, however, the invader could never have got past my gun and perhaps we might not have been drawn into the subsequent turmoil of events.

She said very slowly and deliberately. 'Since – you – went – away – '

The strange timbre of her voice was like the sound of bells muted by grief.

'. . . four short, simple, terrible words, my darling: "since you went away".'

I did not see, only sensed him. I wheeled round, every nerve taut. I saw the flicker of his shadow vanish into the cave. He had slipped past our backs.

I leapt for Rankin's Mauser and worked a bullet into the breech.

A voice commanded. 'Dika! Dika!'

Nadine and I swung towards the doorway.

'A charming fancy, don't you think?' said a mocking hidden voice. 'You have to dissect a hyena before you can tell its sex. My Dika could be male or female, I don't know. And Sappho's Dika – what was she? But I suspect that lesbianism is not unknown among hyenas either.'

He came forward so that I could make out the outline of his figure but not his face.

'I don't see any poetic wreaths or garlands for Dika but it's a pretty snug hideout you've got here. Without Dika I would never have found it.'

CHAPTER EIGHT

'Step forward!' I ordered, keeping the rifle trained on the newcomer. 'And stop talking crap. We're not a couple of gays.'

I was furious at the intrusion. That bare moment with Nadine might never come again.

'What the devil do you want? Who are you?'

Some quick calculation told me that, whoever he was, he couldn't have put down at the landing-strip some five miles away then made his way to the command-post in the time that had elapsed since we heard the aircraft engine. Moreover, if he had landed near The Hill in the sand and half-dark he had taken fantastic risks. Anyway, I did not believe it possible. His immediate discovery of the hidden command-post also added to my suspicions. All this, plus the off-beat introduction left me very uneasy. I was grateful for Rankin's Mauser.

Instead of obeying me he rapped out, 'Don't shoot! It's harmless if you leave it alone!'

One of the biggest hyenas I have ever seen slunk past me returning from the back of the cave to its master. I switched the gun from the man to the animal, following it all the way and ready to blast it. Except for lifting a lip in a silent snarl as it passed, it went to the stranger like a dog to heel.

Before I could reply the off-beat, bantering tone came out of the darkness again. It also had a strident quality which later was to become inseparable in my mind from the manner of the man.

'Whatever is the lowest of four-legged creatures, the hyena must run it pretty close, don't you think? Yet look how this one responds to a little kindness – just like a pet. One could almost say that the quality of mercy is not strained but distilled . . .'

'Cut out the bull,' I retorted. 'If you're anything to do with the guard, say so, because I've much to tell you.'

I waved him forward with the gun and he came leading the hyena, a twist of its mane in his fingers.

Nadine shone a torch on the pair. He had a thinnish, somewhat elongated face which was dark with beard stubble. His narrow eyes were close together, his hair long. His lips were thin and leathery-looking beneath a prominent nose and receding forehead, and the eyebrows continued unbroken across the bridge of his nose. He held his head to one side as if he had a crick in the neck. He appeared to be about my own age.

'I apologize for the intrusion but the blame is really Dika's – you must have something very attractive in here, a dead buck perhaps? Dika couldn't restrain herself, or should I say himself or itself, once we reached the area of the fire. She took off nose to ground . . .'

It was a barrage of words; with the hindsight of later events

I know it covered a tight nervousness on his part as he realized that he had reached the end of his road.

I wasn't in the mood for this sort of thing. 'Your pet smells human blood,' I snapped. 'There's an injured man back there. The sooner you move that brute out, the better.'

'Allow me to introduce myself.' His speech was too correct to be mother-tongue English, yet he was not South African. The slight pseudo-bow and stiffening, however, betrayed his German origin.

'Von Praeger. Doctor Manfred von Praeger.'

His tension further revealed itself in the manner in which he tugged at Dika's mane; I found myself revolted at the way the creature rubbed against him with a kind of brutish affection. The relationship put my teeth on edge.

He waited, as if he expected us to reciprocate with our names, at the same time shooting me a penetrating glance.

Before I could stop her Nadine asked, 'Are you a medical doctor?'

'I am.'

'Then you're a godsend at this moment. You see . . .'

'Wait a moment, Nadine.'

I had no intention of accepting von Praeger's help before I knew more about him. I was deeply suspicious of his stealthy approach. My experiences with Rankin had sensitized me.

Nadine, however, took him at face value, without reservation.

'We heard your plane, Doctor von Praeger, and we were worried because the engine cut. We thought you might have crashed.'

He seemed taken aback for a moment, then amused. 'Ah, yes, the plane! It is difficult flying country this, is it not?'

'You weren't in trouble then?'

There were odd nuances in his reply and I didn't care for his forced, toothy smile. 'No. I managed . . . ah . . . to come safely to rest.'

Nadine hurried on. 'Peter Talbot – my father's pilot – has been hurt. We think he's pretty bad.'

Again I had the feeling that events were running away from me, though I conceded that what we needed right then was principally skilled aid for the two men. I allowed necessity to lull my suspicions; if von Praeger could achieve something with Rankin I could still get my confession. Once that was done, we could sort the rest out later.

'Where is the man?'

(Praeger seemed too keen to investigate the command post.)

'Wait here – there's no light back there,' I said. 'And please do something about that hyena before I bring Talbot out.'

'I also have a torch. Two of them will give plenty of light for me to examine him by.'

I held back irresolutely, wondering if I were doing the right thing. My mental hackles bristled again at his remark. If he'd used his torch across the wadi and up the slope of K2 to the plane wreck we certainly would have spotted him.

'This is the way I want it,' I said shortly.

He gave his slightly stiffened inclination in reply. It didn't give anything away.

'Don't you carry a gun?' I asked. 'I don't want that brute to get out of hand once it comes close to blood.'

I handed the rifle to Nadine to have my hands free for Talbot but I was a fool to part with it. Immediately Praeger stepped forward and took the weapon from her. 'It is not necessary, I assure you. My words to Dika are stronger than bullets.'

The way he slipped the shell out of the breech showed he knew all about guns. He went on to take out the magazine and made play of returning the spare cartridge to the clip. The gun he laid aside. It was a smart piece of opportunism which increased my misgivings.

I still hesitated but there was nothing I could do about it. I turned, went inside, and dragged Talbot's bed out into the open. Von Praeger disregarded my instructions to stay out. He was close to the cave entrance with Nadine when I reappeared, staring about him inquisitively. I deliberately held the torch at his eyes to prevent his seeing the interior, and brought Talbot well away for the same reason.

'Here he is.'

In the flashlight's beam the pilot looked far worse than before. His face was deadly pale and blood had spread through his bandages. Praeger undid the dressings with short, competent fingers. I began to wonder how I would explain Rankin's injury when his turn came.

'Gunshot, yes?'

I didn't like the way Praeger regarded me.

'Yes, gunshot. That Mauser you unloaded just now.'

'He's lost a lot of blood. No wonder Dika picked up his trail so strongly. You must have brought him across the rocks here?'

Inwardly I cursed the hyena for revealing our hideaway.

'Yes. I carried him. His plane crashed on the hill slope where you saw the marks of fire.'

'Before or after the shot?'

'The result of.'

'I see.'

'I was with him,' added Nadine. 'It happened this way . . .'

'The story can wait,' I broke in. 'The first thing is to establish what must be done for him.'

Von Praeger left off for a moment and eyed us both. I could not help feeling there was some hidden triumph behind his scrutiny.

'A doctor is called upon to perform many strange tasks,' he said in a neutral, professional voice.

He sounded Talbot's heart perfunctorily by putting his ear against his chest. He turned him over, as I had done, to find where the bullet had emerged. Finally he rolled the pilot on to his back again.

'He is bad, very bad. Dying, in fact.'

Nadine caught her breath. 'Please – is there nothing you can do, Doctor? He did me a great service.'

'How did it happen?'

I resented his continued probing and said shortly, 'Is the history of how he was wounded of any importance in treating it, Doctor?'

'It might be,' he fenced. 'It's a very strange set-up here.'

'No stranger than a man having a hyena for a pet,' I retorted. 'No stranger than . . .' I bit back my annoyance. I wasn't going to play into his hands by giving away what I knew about the dead guard and the suspicion I nursed about the impossibility of his aircraft having landed near The Hill.

We glared at one another but now it wasn't the same as having a stranger at the wrong end of my gun. He was calling the shots; I was on the defensive.

Then a deep groan came from the interior of the cave.

Von Praeger swung round, startled. 'What's that – more casualties?'

'Yes,' I replied without elaborating. 'One more.'

He was about to make for the cave when I stopped him.

'Stay here. I'll bring him out to you. It's a different sort of injury, as you'll see. It was he who fired that bullet.' I indicated Talbot's wound.

I grew unhappier still about Praeger. It was nothing concrete but a matter of undercurrents, of straws in the wind. So far he'd been medically correct, if not enthusiastic, in his examination. If it had not been for the hyena sitting like an indictment at the command-post's entrance I would have had little firm ground for apprehension.

I brought out Rankin on the stretcher; he was beginning to stir.

Nadine held the light for von Praeger. He gave a low whistle.

'This is a hideous blow. He's lucky still to be alive.'

'He ran into something.'

'The chest cavity is smashed.' He explored cautiously round the wound. He pointed. 'A little pressure here and his heart would stop. One could do it easily with one's fingers.'

Nadine shivered. 'We wanted to move them both to Messina hospital but we haven't a vehicle.'

'No vehicle! It all grows curiouser and curiouser, as your English classic says,' he remarked sardonically, 'I am the doctor and am therefore automatically implicated. That doesn't mean to say I intend to be incriminated. Either of these men could die – soon.'

By inferring that it was a police matter he'd managed to put moral right on his side too. My objective narrowed down to one thing: to have Rankin talk, and as soon as possible. And for that I needed Praeger's help.

My gorge rose at the sight of his smug little smile.

'Do what you can for them, leave the explanations to me,' I said shortly.

'Very well. The flier first. His wound is very similar to that which killed your English hero Lord Nelson. The bullet is lodged against the spine. Already he is paralysed and if he lives he will never walk again. The bullet must be removed.

First, however, I must find out exactly how deep it is and whether there are any splinters. The proper instrument would be a surgical probe.'

'Would a knife do?'

'No. The blade is too broad. I need something long and thin and sharp. He won't feel a thing – he's too deeply unconscious.'

I felt in my pocket and held out the diamond pencil.

I looked back into the mouth of a pistol.

The barrel was unsteady and von Praeger looked as if he had seen a ghost. I should have jumped him before he brought up his other hand to steady his aim. I think, however, that what I had already been through with Rankin had punished my reflexes. Afterwards, too, I realized that the pistol must have been harmless because the quick draw from his pocket had probably snugged home to 'safe' the awkward catch of the heavy Russian war-time Tula Tokarev.

'Where,' he asked in a strained, high voice, '*Where is the hyena's blanket?*'

I simply couldn't credit what was happening. If it hadn't been for the reality of the blue-black mouth of the automatic I might have been tempted to flippancy at the way-out question.

I remained silent; Nadine was also stunned speechless.

Von Praeger got to his feet and moved behind Talbot's bed to use it as a barrier against attack. The pistol became rock-steady and he blinked his eyes rapidly; there was a glassiness about them and he stumbled over his order to Nadine.

'Put that torch on the bed. Facing your friend. Out of my eyes.'

Nadine remained rooted still, staring incredulously at the gun.

'Get on with it!' he snapped hoarsely. '*Schnell!*'

'Do as he says, Nadine,' I said quietly, 'and then come here.'

'No! Keep away from him!' He waved the gun at the diamond pencil which I still held extended in my hand.

'Don't come close with that thing, do you hear? Throw it at my feet. No tricks!'

There was no alternative so I lobbed it carefully on to the end of Talbot's bed. Von Praeger bent to pick it up and I missed another chance. He seemed spellbound by the ancient tool and for a second took his eyes from me, but before I

90

awoke to my opportunity he had straightened up and rammed it into his pocket.

His eyes had their same blank, frightened look when he repeated his earlier gibberish, *'Where is the hyena's blanket?'*

His own hyena gave a shrill little cry like a kitten in pain. It underwrote the dream-like quality of the scene, and it was the most frightening sound I have ever heard. Nadine ignored the pistol and ran to my side.

'Quick! Answer! Answer me!'

'Listen, von Praeger,' I said harshly. 'I don't like being pushed around, by anyone; especially at the point of a pistol. Nor do I like people raising their voices and shouting at me – I had enough of it in one of your precious POW camps. You've thrown enough bloody nonsense and crazy threats around. Now put that gun away and say quietly what you have to say, and say it plainly.'

Neither his smile nor its implication was pleasant.

'Ah, the tough approach! You were also too tough, or too guilty, earlier to do me the courtesy of telling me your name. Allow me to remedy your omission. It is William Guybon Atherstone Bowker – yes?'

'What has my name got to do with it?'

His eyes blazed. 'Yes or no?' he shouted. I thought he was about to fire.

'Yes.'

He cringed as if a bullet had seared him and gave two or three quick intakes of breath, more like gasps than sighs. Then the steam and tension seemed to go out of him all at once. His voice was strangely flat when he spoke again and he licked his leathery lips.

'Bowker. It had to be,' he muttered almost to himself. 'But I wasn't quite sure. Bowker . . . it's been a long, long chase.'

He held the pistol on me while he called the hyena to him. It shambled up and he said something in German and indicated us. The brute took up guard.

Nadine and I exchanged a swift glance. We were both convinced that Praeger was out of his mind. The gun and the hyena made the possibility of a successful attack on him very dodgy. I therefore left the next move to him. The only sound was of bats radar-pinging the cliffs in the darkness.

Finally he said. 'I will take this whole place apart with my bare hands to find it. But first I will take you apart if you don't tell me.'

'I've never heard such rubbish in my life – the hyena's blanket!'

'Perhaps if I refresh your memory on a few points it will all come back to you. We have plenty of time. You may remember that we Germans were adept at extracting information from reluctant witnesses.'

'You sound like the Gestapo.'

'Not quite one of them, but certainly on the fringes of their operations. Medically it is quite fascinating to dredge information from a mind whose owner is trying to hold back at all costs. Sometimes it is at all costs.'

'If you think you can . . .'

'Bluster is always the first reaction,' he retorted calmly. 'Later, under pressure, the patient usually becomes more amenable.' He held up his hand as I was about to explode. 'The methods are refined; no crudities like castration, which are self-defeating; for when a man finds he has nothing more to lose it increases rather than decreases his resistance. The target is the mind . . .'

'Von Praeger!' I broke in. 'The war's finished and done with. You're not operating now with your bloody Gestapo. This is a country with plenty of law and order, as you'll soon find out if you start anything. First of all, pointing a gun is an offence, in case you don't already know it.'

I think he must have been getting his mental breath back, so to speak, for he ignored my outburst and pulled the diamond pencil from his pocket.

'Where'd you get this from?'

'It was my grandfather's. It came to me in his estate. From Holland.'

He drew his face a little to the right, as if he could see us better that way.

'I wondered many times what had happened to it. You see, he had it in his hand the night he died. Then it disappeared. The fact that you have it is the last link in a search which I started that same night. Now the end is in sight and . . .' (a brief rictus showed his teeth and he gestured at us with the pistol) '. . . I have my fish in the net.'

'If you saw that in my grandfather's hand when he died

then you killed him,' I said slowly. 'Because he didn't die naturally. The Gestapo killed him. I know that much.'

'True,' he replied almost conversationally. 'The Gestapo *was* responsible. That is where the hyena's blanket comes in. Your grandfather was a spy . . .'

'A patriot.'

'What you call him depends purely upon whose side you are,' he replied levelly. 'I say he was a spy. The Gestapo intercepted a radio message from him to the Dutch government in exile. The code was amateurish as one would expect from an amateur. But the key to its meaning was a phrase which completely defeated them – "the hyena's blanket!".'

'They probably misread it.'

He shook his head. 'I think not. The only codebreaker in the war better than the Gestapo was the British Admiralty. It was hyena's blanket all right. The rest of the message was plain – all about providing finance for the Dutch to continue the fight in exile. Since Erasmus was a diamond dealer, it didn't require much imagination to know he was referring to diamonds. But,' and he squinted at us again, 'it would require one hell of a lot of diamonds to keep a whole government going in exile. And that's what Erasmus meant.'

'This has nothing to do with me or with Nadine.'

'No?' The pistol was rock-steady on us. 'It has everything, as you will realize soon. This diamond pencil proves it.'

'I tell you . . .!' I exclaimed angrily, while a knot of fear began to form in my stomach.

'Let me tell you,' he returned. 'The Gestapo rounded up Erasmus of course and interrogated him. Unfortunately they were too enthusiastic. The old man had a heart attack before they extracted much from him. I was called in as a doctor to try to keep him alive long enough for them to find out why he kept saying, over and over, "the hyena's blanket".'

'You bastard!' I burst out. 'You did a harmless old man to death!'

'Not so,' he replied. 'I used everything in my power to keep him alive. In fact, I thought at one stage I had succeeded. But he died, still moaning about the hyena's blanket.'

I felt a cloud of greyness rise up out of the past. I had been fond of my grandfather; automatically I blamed his tragic end on diamonds.

'I'm glad to learn the details of his death – even out of a pistol's mouth,' I said ironically. 'But I expect that when the diamonds were found the whole thing sorted itself out.'

'On the contrary, the diamonds were not found and nothing ever sorted itself out. Until tonight.'

I bit back a retort. Nadine stood close to me. 'Go on,' was all I said.

'The Gestapo shrugged it off after a while just as you have done. But I wasn't satisfied. First, that diamond pencil. Why did Erasmus cling so tenaciously to it? Where did it come in? Why something so intimately associated with the Cullinan, as I later discovered? Strange to say, it vanished while I was attending him. I suspected an old servant but the Gestapo didn't consider it worth pursuing. His house and shop were searched with a fine-tooth comb, of course, but what we found was no more than what would have been expected in the normal course of business. The thing became stranger as I probed deeper. Erasmus had assisted Asscher at the cutting of the Cullinan – that diamond pencil again! I became more interested still when I found that Erasmus's daughter – your mother – had married the man who had actually discovered the Cullinan. What if, I asked myself, that coded message about the hyena's blanket had in fact something to do with the Cullinan?'

'You could have checked on the Cullinan itself at any time, in the Tower of London,' I replied sarcastically.

He ignored my crack. 'I became more and more interested in the Bowker family. In war-time, of course, it is difficult to follow things up and I had no way of knowing whether the famous Bowker had a son. But imagine my pleasure when I located the mother – Erasmus's own daughter – hiding in Amsterdam.'

I felt a pinch at my heart. I guessed what might be coming.

'We picked her up. I tried everything to persuade her to talk. But I never got a word out of her about Bowker or the Cullinan or her son, whose whereabouts she professed not to know; William Guybon Atherstone Bowker. We had to shoot her in the end.'

'Guy! No, no!'

Nadine grabbed me as I was about to throw myself at Praeger. I would never have got across the dozen feet which

94

separated us. When my blind fury had subsided I started to shake with reaction. What he had related gave me the measure of his ruthlessness.

'Thank you,' he said with a brief cynical smile at Nadine. 'You saved me an unpleasant task. He's worth a lot more to me sound in mind and limb than wounded. I still hope he's going to be accommodating and tell me what the hyena's blanket means.'

'Damn you, I don't know, I tell you!'

'I see I'll let you have to help you to remember; time is, as I said before, on my side. Well, after the setback over your mother I went to work to check up exactly how Bowker and a fellow-digger discovered the Cullinan.'

'I'll let you have the press clippings,' I sneered. 'It's all been told and written about a thousand times. They thought it was a bit of broken bottle sticking out of the opencast face. Don't try to make a mystery of that.'

'I don't have to, Bowker. The mystery was already there, built in. The Cullinan in the rough had two natural faces and a cleavage face when it was found.'

'So what?'

'A cleavage face, don't you understand?'

'No.'

He tried unsuccessfully to control the rising note in his voice.

'If there was a cleavage face, it means that the Cullinan had been cut – before it was discovered.'

'Even my father never dreamed that one up.'

He edged round the bed nearer to me, the pistol held at my stomach.

'No, he didn't dream it. He did it.'

'You're crazy!'

He retreated to the hyena's side and fumbled with its mane, choosing his words deliberately and slowly.

'Your father was a master-crook, Bowker. He and Rankin planted the Cullinan in the Premier Mine – salted it, to use the jargon. The cleavage face proves that the Cullinan was only part of a larger, colossal diamond.' He shot out his free hand, clenching his fist. 'The Cullinan Diamond was the size of that! What then in the name of the Peacock Throne of the Great Moguls is the other half like?'

His fingers went on clenching and unclenching on the animal's mane in a kind of nervous spasm but his gun hand was steady enough.

'*Where* . . .' his words were slightly blurred like a drunk's '. . . *where is it?*'

I put an arm round Nadine's shoulders. She was trembling. but I sensed a quiver of relief at my gesture.

'Why,' I rejoined, picking my words as carefully as he, 'don't you ask the man who found it? There he lies on the stretcher next to you. Rankin.'

If I had thrown the Cullinan at his feet the reaction could not have been greater.

'*Rankin!* Is that – *Rankin?*'

If it had not been for the hyena I could have side-swiped him as he swivelled the torch on the digger's unconscious form. The pistol sagged and he was completely off guard. I slipped free of Nadine with the intention of going for him, but the animal leapt to its feet snarling. The sound seemed to bring Praeger back to earth.

'Bowker and Rankin! Bowker and Rankin!' he kept repeating, as if stunned. 'Now I have it all in my hands!'

The moon had risen and the enclosure was bright in its light. The little figure of the German in his too-neat safari suit, with his longish hair and thunderstruck face might have been the sort of image I would have conjured up had I been asked to embody the evil spirit of diamonds.

When he spoke the entire character of his voice had changed. It was flat and vicious, like a dud note struck in the middle of a concerto.

He addressed Nadine. 'And where do you fit into this?'

'I came to look for Guy. He . . . he . . .'

'Think quickly!' he rapped out. 'Think up some yarn, very quickly! Your companion's pretty smart at lying. What's your name?'

'Nadine Raikes.'

'Raikes. The millionaire?'

'Yes.'

He rounded on me. 'The jigsaw begins to fit together, doesn't it? Bowker and Rankin peddling the greater half of the Cullinan to Raikes the millionaire – deal and dealer!'

'Listen to my side of this,' I began in a sandpaper voice but he stopped me.

'Cover Rankin up with the blanket. I can't risk anything happening to him now! It's going to take everything I know to pull him through. Button up his shirt too, gently!'

I did as he bade me and straightened up to face the pistol again.

'I came to The Hill, alone,' I said, holding myself in. 'I had a score to settle with Rankin. He framed me and I got shopped. Nadine flew here with Talbot to find me. Rankin shot down their plane. That's my story in a nutshell. All this stuff about the bigger half of the Cullinan is so much bull as far as I am concerned.'

He laughed and I didn't like the sound of it. 'Very well improvised, at such short notice! But how about the truth? A shoot-out when thieves fall out after a double-cross in which the plane was deliberately set on fire to prevent the other party making off with the great diamond? Here's the evidence, and I believe what my eyes tell me.' He gestured at the two wounded men.

Nadine broke in desperately. 'Guy being here has nothing to do with diamonds. I give you my word. He . . . it's something personal between us. He was in prison. He left without telling me. I came to look for him in a plane, that's all.'

'All, eh, Miss Raikes?'

'No. Guy was here hunting fossilized hyena excreta . . .'

Praeger laughed derisively. 'Now I've heard everything! Well, at least fossilized hyena excreta is original! Somehow all roads lead to hyenas, don't they? Look at the debt I owe Dika here for tracking you down. She's justified the two years I spent training her.' He went on, with a grating note of self-apology, 'We Germans are a thorough and methodical people. I thought at the beginning that by training a hyena and studying its behaviour pattern something might emerge to give me a clue to what hyena's blanket meant. That's all unnecessary now. I've got you, Bowker, and Rankin as well. You'll tell me before long.'

'Why don't you stop kidding yourself, Praeger?' I asked. 'I've never heard such a lot of nonsense in my life. You're projecting God knows what sick fantasies into a code for something which is as dead as the man who sent it. Forget it.'

'I was beginning to think that way at one stage myself,' he answered. 'When all my leads ran dry in Europe I emigrated to South Africa. I scoured the country for traces of you without success. Then came one of those colossal breaks of good luck (like tonight) in my search. I'll come to that in a moment.'

While I listened I tried to hit upon some plan by which I could turn the tables on Praeger and grab his gun. That would also mean coping with the hyena at short range. The brute stood as watchful as a well-trained Wehrmacht non-com. I felt sure however that the heavy calibre of Praeger's pistol in my hands would be sufficient to stop the hyena. I left Nadine out of my calculations. I hoped I would be the focus of attack.

Von Praeger was saying, 'Good luck is followed by bad luck, as they say, and I certainly thought this was so a few days ago when I discovered that you and I had been under the same roof for the past eighteen months, Bowker.'

'It's a pity we didn't share the same cell,' I retorted. 'You wouldn't have had the advantage of that gun.'

'No chance of that: I'm the senior prison doctor. That's the job I took when I came to South Africa.'

It was my turn to be taken aback: the giveaway became obvious.

'Charlie Furstenberg,' I ground out.

'Quite. Charlie would rat on a rat. You were in the ranks of short-term prisoners, which are not my concern, so our paths didn't cross. I only heard your name after you had slipped away, and through my net at the same time. I came straight here, of course. And here you are, as Charlie said you would be.'

It was my turn to smile. 'Charlie held out on you, too. He didn't tell you about Rankin.'

'My time will come with Charlie.' The menace was very plain.

'If you're building castles in the air about a greater half of the Cullinan on the strength of the word of a small-time crook like Charlie, you're in for a disappointment.'

'I was sidetracked into telling you about Charlie. We are going too fast. As I said, I emigrated to South Africa and

98

became a prison doctor.'

'It seems a very appropriate post for a Gestapo handyman.'

'If you're trying to provoke me into attacking you, it won't work.' He nodded towards Rankin and asked in his unpleasant ripsaw voice. 'I suppose you did that?'

'Yes,' I replied with more bravado than I felt. 'And he had *two* guns.'

He shrugged but I noticed that he edged closer to his pet.

'A prison doctor occupies a unique and often all powerful position,' he went on. 'He's something between warder and confessor. There was a murderer called Kettler who was due to be hanged. He sent for me and tried to drive a bargain but it was already too late. Kettler had been the mine detective at the Premier Mine for a long time before his arrest. He never believed a word of the story of how your father and Rankin were supposed to have found the Cullinan. And do you know what he offered me to help him escape? – the other half of the Cullinan Diamond.'

'If you fell for that one, you're an even bigger sucker than I thought.'

Von Praeger remained unruffled. 'He had only a few hours to live. Who knows, if he could have brought himself to the point earlier? Then, when the rope was already round his neck, he asked for me again in place of the usual priest. What he told me put the clincher on what Erasmus had said when he died. Kettler whispered to me – he couldn't bear to part with the whole secret even then – as the gallows lever went over, "the hyena's blanket".'

Rankin's wheezing and the bats' thin metallic cries punctuated the still night.

Von Praeger said after a tight pause, 'Bowker; Rankin; the Cullinan; The Hill; all those links in the chain are now complete. All that remains is that key phrase, the hyena's blanket. I intend to find out what it means. Somehow the Cullinan has something to do with hyenas. You can make it easy for the girl and yourself by telling me.' When I did not answer he glanced at Rankin. 'Perhaps he'll be less intractable, but there's a lot of work ahead before he'll be conscious.'

I reasoned that the longer I kept Praeger talking the greater would be my opportunity of jumping him. Moreover, I wanted to keep him out of the cave where the confined space would make action more difficult.

'You're on very thin ice basing such a preposterous idea on a criminal's word,' I said. 'Everyone knows there are always so-called eleventh-hour confessions by murderers. Can you think of one that turned out to be true?'

He responded brusquely. 'Kettler spent his whole life on the trail. I consider that I'm much more qualified to judge on the question of condemned men's confessions than you. I know that Kettler was right.'

He jerked his head towards the cave. 'What's in there?'

'Rankin's hide-out – a lot of junk. There's no light, either.'

'March!' He waved us ahead of him. 'Dika!'

We had no chance but to obey. Praeger's flashlight threw long shadows before us and when the shaft of light traced the outline of the weird structure of beams, spindles and gears and rested finally on the turntable with its peculiar treadle, von Praeger rapped out. 'Halt! Turn and face me!'

I saw that he was excited; there was a feeling of danger in the air.

'I quite understand why you were reluctant for me to see this, Bowker! A lot of junk, eh?'

'You tell us what it is. I haven't a clue – a workshop of some sort, I suppose?'

'They learn to lie like that in jail,' he scoffed at Nadine. 'No one ever knows anything about anything. I suppose that goes for you too?'

She shook her head wordlessly.

'Let me tell you, then. It is a diamond polishing mill.'

CHAPTER NINE

The word kept coming back with the recurring persistence of a nagging musical phrase which despite all deliberate effort to exclude it intrudes and thrums through one's mind – *camisado* night attack!

I was teased into wakefulness through the long night which followed and into the small hours of the morning as I lay imprisoned in Rankin's inner cave by the tantalizing question

100

of what manner of night attack I should resort to in my predicament; as the hours passed without a solution there came a growing sense of impotence on my part. Over and over I formulated fresh plans for a break-out. Each one, when I came to evaluate it, would abort on some initially unsuspected snag. Then I would abandon it and start the process again, working round in seemingly endless, unproductive circles.

My eyes became completely accustomed to the inky blackness and I could make out various objects in the kitchen cave: the Aladdin-jar water vessels; Nadine's ritual pots next to them; a table and a diamond boiling set, which consisted of a small lipped mug resembling a sauce boat, over a spirit burner standing on a screened asbestos pad. My eyes moved from one object to another; there was simply nothing else to look at. I came to the conclusion that Rankin must use his diamond mill equipment for the secondary purpose of kitchen utensils.

I consulted my illuminated watch dial for the hundredth time as my hundredth plan collapsed – 2.15 a.m. In three hours it would be dawn and still I had concocted no plan of night attack. I became jumpier and more frustrated, both of which hindered clear thinking.

I compelled my mind to go back right to the beginning when Praeger had forced us into the cave, in the hope that by going over every detail some ray of light might emerge. There were two interconnecting caves and I was in the deeper one, the shorter leg of the L-shaped hide-out. The diamond polishing mill occupied the longer section. This in its turn opened via a crooked entrance to the outside enclosure with its commanding view. Nadine was held in the mill section while Talbot and Rankin were in the open, out of sight beyond an invisible line drawn by the glint of moonlight on the pug barrel of a machine-pistol held by our guard. The cave ran dead against solid rock where I was lying and as far as I could discover there were no cracks through which I might possibly have wormed my way to freedom.

I attempted to recall everything I had seen in the mill section when von Praeger had shone his torch on the curious complex. I might have recognized it for what it was if it had looked like the equipment I had seen often enough at my grandfather's, but it didn't. Praeger himself was amused at

101

it and remarked that it was the sort of thing shown in pictures of diamond cutters' workshops a century ago. The light had come to rest like an accusing finger on a collection of unfamiliar objects grouped round the turntable. One of these resembled a miniature metal crane's beak set into a heavy iron base. It was, in fact, a pair of tweezers mounted in a double ball joint so that it could be swivelled in any direction – a kind of 'third hand' to hold a diamond while a craftsman worked on it. All round were other tools and equipment which blew the gaff on Rankin's secret operations. Praeger had detailed them for our benefit; any of half a dozen of these would have been a useful weapon for me, but he had been wise enough to clear them out of the way before leaving us for the remainder of the night.

Up to the moment when his torchlight fell on the mill I had still cherished hope of overpowering Praeger and his hyena; but his next words hit me like a bucket if icy water.

'Koen will certainly be interested to see this.'

'Koen?'

My dismay made him laugh.

'You didn't think I was fool enough to come to The Hill alone to tackle you, did you? Koen's my partner. He's also got a vested interest in the Cullinan. The name's enough to tell you why – Koen Kettler.'

'You said they hanged Kettler.'

'This is the son, and every bit as tough as the father. Now he's also on the trail.'

I bit back what I was about to retort about never-never pursuits, in the hope that he might relax and enable me to get closer to some of the potential weapons. Meanwhile Nadine had started towards the bench with the purely innocent intention, I felt sure, of examining some of the strange things more closely.

Praeger, however, was on the alert against any tricks we might attempt. 'Back! Stand back!'

Nadine halted in bewilderment.

'Men – and women – do remarkable things under the lure of diamonds. You're probably no exception: even the gentlest become savages. In fact, that was the cause of Kettler senior's downfall. He had the answer to Rankin in his hand but he couldn't restrain himself.'

102

'Murder,' I snapped.

'I like to think of it rather as over-enthusiasm.'

This remark gave me a further insight into what I was up against.

'Let me tell you briefly about it and you'll see what I mean. Your father and Rankin pulled the big job to end all big jobs over the Cullinan. But even so, Rankin couldn't leave diamonds alone afterwards. In fact, he tried the same thing again.'

'Never! There's only been one Cullinan, ever.'

He moved round so that he stood between us and the bench while the hyena cut off our escape to the rear. He put down the torch with its beam still directed at us.

'Remember Jagersfontein?'

'Remember it! God's truth! I was dragged there by my father on one of his sentimental tours of diamond mines! A dreary, clapped-out village not so very far from Kimberley, living in the shadow of its past under a derelict mine head-gear!'

Von Praeger eyed me curiously. 'This diamond thing burns you up, doesn't it, Bowker?' Then unexpectedly his tone changed and the harsh note softened to an overtone which came close to reverence. 'Well, don't be too hard on Jagersfontein. It *had* a past. The world's biggest diamond came from there – before the Cullinan was discovered, that is.'

'The Excelsior; you don't have to tell me!' I jerked out. 'I know every bloody detail by heart. Nine hundred and ninety-five carats. Purest blue-white. Anything else you want to know?'

'And Asscher cut that one too!'

I made an impatient gesture which von Praeger miscon-strued and he raised the pistol, level with my face. When he realized that I was not about to attack him he went on.

'Jagersfontein was just the sort of place which Rankin was on the look-out for: a worked-out, has-been mine where a few old-timers scratched and pecked amongst the tailings for a diamond crumb or two which might have slipped past the sieves. Then suddenly Jagersfontein came into the headlines again. It yielded a perfect 120-carat blue-white of purest water.

'But Kettler wasn't fooled. He read the Indian signs. To a man who had studied every minute aspect of the Cullinan's discovery it was like a detective seeing the hallmark of one particular professional burglar on a safebreak. The master-hand was Rankin's, of course. Kettler rushed post-haste to Jagersfontein. But the fox, Rankin under an alias, had already gone to ground, but not his partner in the venture. He was still there; a young chap called Fouché. Kettler worked on him but handled him too roughly. They hanged Kettler for killing him. But not before Kettler had told me – enough. I'm sure Koen won't repeat with you his father's mistake of being too impetuous.'

He gave us time for this to sink in, then the stretching of the thin lips which was his travesty of a smile took in Nadine also. 'You'll soon realize that Koen's ideas about women are somewhat primitive. He won't hesitate to smash up your face if necessary. After that, no amount of diamonds in the Raikes millionaire bracket would hide your disfigurement. So be careful, Miss Raikes.'

Words gargled in my throat. 'Listen, you scum . . .'

Nadine put her hand restrainingly on my arm. 'Please Guy! Give Doctor von Praeger a chance to check on our story and he'll find out that we have nothing to hide. Peter, for a start, will bear it out.'

'I've made my own checks, all right,' retorted Praeger. 'But if you're relying on your pilot to carry on your bluff, you can forget it. He won't see morning.'

Before we had time to digest his callousness he startled us by moving to the entrance and firing three shots into the air. The flat claps, obviously a signal from the spacing, struck back like a Spanish dancer's heels from the silent audience of hills.

'We've plenty of ammunition to spare,' he remarked, anticipating my calculation that there would be five rounds left in the automatic. 'You'll see for yourself when Koen arrives: he'll be along in a hurry now.'

Praeger and the hyena escorted us to the entrance to await Koen's arrival. He left me no opportunity to turn the tables on him: he even handled a lantern himself, hanging it over the door to guide his companion.

And it was ammunition indeed and a wicked-looking Czech M-25 machine-pistol which was my first impression of Koen. Von Praeger highlighted the weapon with the torch, keeping the beam low for Koen to see his way across the stepping-stones; with the result that his face and upper body were in shadow. The light showed a skeleton butt at the end of a long kinked metal stalk and an ungainly magazine of 9mm shells projecting underneath a pug barrel.

Koen reached us gasping and sweating from the dangerous crossing. He was much shorter and stockier than either Praeger or myself. He wore tight whipcord pants tucked into half-calf boots; his clothes generally had an air of cheap flashiness which belied the rugged toughness of his square chin. His thick pelt of black hair was glossy with pomade; a wisp fell over his forehead, giving him an old-young look. His fingernails were foul.

Von Praeger indicated me. 'I got him, Koen! It's Bowker. Watch your step though; you should see what he's done to Rankin.'

The newcomer unshipped the machine-pistol and covered me.

'*Allemagtig,* Doc! Both of 'em, eh?'

The crude vowels and gutter accent came from the Lichtenburg diamond fields. The association made me crawl inside.

'Come on in and see.'

I reached out unobtrusively for the lamp. Thrown, it would become a flaming Molotov cocktail.

'Keep away!' snarled Praeger. 'Back! Watch him, Koen! All the time. And don't let him get close to you. He's got all the tricks and some besides!'

The two of them, weapons at the ready, led us through to Rankin's bedside where Praeger showed him the wound. Koen's response was to hold the M-25 on me and give me a long, silent, threatening stare. It was my main impression of him and I saw little else of him that night for shortly afterwards he and Praeger busied themselves clearing out all the equipment from the cave while the hyena kept us securely pinned in the outer enclosure. At the beginning of this operation Praeger spent some time treating Rankin and from time to time checked on him.

Finally I was ordered into the inner cave and Nadine confined to the mill section. Koen took up sentry on a stool out front. For the first couple of hours he used the torch to make frequent checks on us. It grew weaker, however, and after midnight there was no further check. From time to time I caught the murmur of the two men's voices, but as it grew late they became silent. Koen remained very much on the alert, however, blocking our escape route, as I discovered by creeping to the boundary of the kitchen cave.

The words *night-attack* continued to gnaw away at my brain and, try as I would, I could not dispel them. Sleep was out of the question; I felt no tiredness but only an increasing sense of bafflement and frustration. I mentally reviewed every geographical feature of the area, reconnoitring them in thought, weighing the merits of possible hidden strongpoints at The Hill, of the semi-desert places round about, and of course the Limpopo and Shashi waterways. Every workable plan I framed was scuppered by some major flaw.

I was pulling off my boots in order to give myself a quick bout of warming exercise – a chill had risen up out of the rock – when out of the blue came one of those strange flashes of thought which seem to be born fully grown when one has been devoting all one's time to another stream of pre-occupation.

The crucial remark had been crowded out of my mind by the non-stop action since my encounter with Rankin; now it blazed before me like a comet in the sky.

Rankin had said as I hit him, *they were cut diamonds.*

I could have laughed out loud: it is not a crime to possess a cut diamond. IDB means trading in uncut stones. That admission in itself, whether he lived or died now, was a starting-point towards clearing me. I realized at once, however, that it would involve big technical questions. The detective who had arrested me had said that Rankin's diamonds were foreign to the Lichtenburg fields: he could only have cut them here at The Hill but at the same time it must have been a crude job. No one, not even my lawyer, had thought of requesting expert, microscopic examination of the diamonds. Rankin all at once became vital to any escape plan, for I had to get him to blow up that tenuous admission into a full-scale confession, with all the accompanying involvements of his own underground 'salting' activities.

Paralleling this dramatic revelation, the hang-ups and self-agonizing which had dogged me since I became involved with Charlie Furstenberg fell away as unexpectedly and I free-wheeled to a similar moment of truth regarding Nadine. I found myself confronted with a need greater than that of escaping: to restore the love which – for my part at least – had been progressively eroded for over a year. With an intuitive flash I knew in my heart that she was more important than anything else and that the time was overdue for clearing the junk out of my emotional attic and taking up our love again where it had begun: here, at The Hill.

Not half a dozen machine-pistols in Koen's hands would have kept me from her in that moment of insight.

Still without my boots, I squirmed silently towards where she lay faintly visible near the bench under a cheap grey cotton blanket that Praeger had given her.

I crouched immobile for a long moment when I reached her, looking down on her loveliness. There was only a memory of light in the face; the rest of her, including the dark hair, was indistinguishable from the night.

I kissed the parted lips.

Her eyes opened, staring up at me in disbelief, and her lips took on the frame of my name without saying it.

I looked into her eyes, not speaking either.

And I wondered, in that mute and magic moment, if the tide of her spirit would do the same at other deep occasions between us. Her features remained composed, as if still sleep-bound, but the pupils of her eyes grew wide and then contracted. Then she raised her lips to mine and the pupils widened again. A lifetime ran by.

At length, at a silent signal from me, she slipped from under the blanket and made her way with me to the inner cave. There was the danger that Koen would check and find her gone: to fox him, I used a variation of the schoolboy dormitory trick – wrapping the blanket round her water jug in imitation of her head on the pillow.

We crept to the farthest wall of my cave so that Koen would not hear our suppressed whispers. There remained Dika, however. The brute's ears were twice as keen as a human's. We lay in each other's arms saying the things lovers say, cajoling and teasing a little, our words gaining an extra dimension from our danger.

'It can't be true, can it, Guy?'

'It is, my darling.'

Her laugh was low and soft, full of a new joy.

'Not this, not us – the Cullinan, I mean. Rather, that fantastic yarn of von Praeger's about another half to the Cullinan. Is it remotely possible it could be hidden away here at The Hill?'

'Rankin is a crook,' I replied. 'This place is both his base and his funkhole. It's easy now to understand why he didn't want the scientific party ferreting around. But to Praeger it's the clincher on the most way-out bit of nonsense it's ever been my misfortune to hear. "Hyena's blanket", my foot!'

She snuggled close and kissed me deeply, fervently. 'It's our Hill, not theirs. You're mine, not theirs,' she said, between kisses. The tip of her tongue was a soft electric caress against my palate. I crushed her to me; for a brief desperate moment all we knew was the thing our bodies cried out for, then she took my face in her hands and made us separate again, running her fingers over my features in the darkness as if to use them as eyes to remember.

'The Hill to me is a place of love, my darling. Remember that when we've sorted out this other side. And my love is for your taking then.'

She put her palms against my lips and her fingers to frame my face. I do not know how long she held me like that: her trembling told me how the current sparked between us, until finally it ebbed a little.

'Escape,' she said huskily. 'We must talk about escape, my love; not about us.'

'Escape!' I echoed. 'I've lain awake all night thinking only of that!'

'Somehow there must be a way.'

'We'll have to take Rankin with us . . ' I explained to her quickly his remark about cut diamonds. 'We need him. What he has already admitted is enough to have the case against me re-opened. But I must have a full confession. I want the world to know it was a plant, a frame-up. I'll make Rankin swear an affidavit in front of the first policeman or magistrate I can get him to – alive.'

'How do you intend to do that, Guy?'

'I've got half a dozen half-baked plans. None of them works. But I know this, I'm not including any heroics in them – no getting even with Praeger or Koen. Just plain flight.'

'If only we had a vehicle!'

'I can't think even in terms of annexing Praeger's because he hasn't one, as far as we know. Yet this business of putting down a plane near The Hill has me licked. I simply don't know how he managed it.'

'A plane's no use: neither of us can fly. If only Peter . . .' she broke off, choking slightly. 'Guy, I think he must be dead.'

'Why?'

'I caught something von Praeger and Koen said when they were talking between themselves outside. Koen said something like, "well, that's one less to worry about".'

I refused to let my anger rise but I answered grimly.

'I believe Praeger could have saved him if he'd wanted to. He's concentrating everything on Rankin.'

'In a way, the more he helps Rankin the more he helps us.'

'True, though it doesn't excuse Praeger's gas oven mentality. We've got to play this thing coolly and not let our anger run away with us or we're sunk. It boils down to our having two alternatives for escape – first, to try and make a break on foot; or second, to use my boat. For both of them there's one hell of a prerequisite and that is to give Praeger and Koen the slip. Let's by-pass that one for the moment and assume we get clear of them. What do we do? Without transport we'd be lucky if we got ten miles before the sun killed us. If we try and work downriver on foot our problems are almost worse. The water is poison to drink and the sun reflects at double strength off the white sand. It would burn us up quicker than if we used a bush route. There's no real choice between upstream and downstream; either the Limpopo or the Shashi. We haven't any food here either, remember. It would be straight suicide. Think of Rankin. He can't walk even one mile in his present state.'

'It all seems to point to transport of some sort.'

'I hid the boat pretty carefully under a palm clump and we'd be unlucky if Praeger sighted it. It depends, of course, where he landed but the sand and mud seem to rule out that particular area.'

'He appeared very taken aback, didn't he, when I blurted out that bit about our having no Land-Rover? Perhaps he'll simply assume that the plane which crashed was how we got here and never even think of a boat. It seems unlikely when you consider the state of the river.'

109

'If that's so, it gives us the edge on him at the outset. The first four miles downriver from here isn't too bad but farther on the rough stuff really begins. I wish to Heaven I had one of those shallow-draft water-jet affairs which are specially designed for these conditions! We could then work our way without portaging through all the shallow channels and stagnant pools. Make no mistake, Nadine, if we do manage to escape it's going to be a hell ride. Our biggest advantage will be if we can win the headstart of those first four miles of clear water. That'll give us room to play with.'

'They'd pick us up from their plane within an hour,' she objected. 'You can't hide in this bare countryside.'

'What good's a plane? They can't land it in the bush. They could try shooting us up but they wouldn't manage more than a few pot-shots. Firing from a fast-moving plane is a dead loss anyway: the odds against one are enormous. We'd hear the machine coming into the bargain and have plenty of time to take cover . . .'

'Guy, Guy, it's all ifs and buts, all hit-and-miss, this sort of plan! If this, then that!'

'I know, I know! I've been worrying at it all night. If we plump for the boat to escape by, we still haven't touched on the initial hurdle – just how are we to overpower Praeger and Koen before we even begin?'

'They've got a sub-machine-gun now as well as everything else.' There was a tremor in her voice.

'Machine-pistol,' I corrected her gently, kissing her hair.

She pressed her cheek hard against mine and spoke close into my ear. 'Promise me, my darling, promise me above anything else that you . . .'

'I won't,' I smiled in the darkness. 'Not now.'

'Not ever,' she whispered passionately. 'Not ever. I couldn't bear being left alone like the queen. I . . . I . . .'

I calmed her and she lay warm against me.

'Koen's gun in my hands would be the answer,' I resumed thoughtfully. 'He's very cagey, though. It's a dicey chance that he'd drop his guard long enough for me to jump him.'

'Rankin isn't going to rush at our invitation to come along either.'

'He's a very slippery customer and a dangerous one, even

hurt as he is. The last thing he wants is to be brought to book. He'll vanish like a puff of smoke if he's given the slightest chance.'

'It's not only him I'm thinking about. What if we do escape? What happens to von Praeger and Koen? Do you think they'll simply wait around for you to return with the police?'

'We could burn their plane.'

'Guy, do you really believe the police will swallow your story about a secret diamond works hidden in a cave? You'll be suspect in their eyes right from the start, having just come out of jail. How will you explain away a couple of bodies? If you view it impersonally it sounds like an elaborate attempt at a cover-up for yourself. That's the way they'll look at it, I'm certain.'

I felt an apprehensive knot in my stomach. I said with more assurance than I felt, 'Praeger and Koen can't destroy all traces of this machinery . . .'

'What if the whole plan misfires?' she persisted. 'What happens to you? And to me? Von Praeger and Koen aren't the sort to stand by with their arms crossed. They're capable of anything! And you've still to tell me how you intend overpowering two heavily-armed, desperate men. How *are* you, with the added handicaps of an injured man and a woman round your neck? It won't work, Guy! Its success hangs on a series of chances which we may never get!'

I knew in my heart that she was right; I answered defensively, 'What do you propose in its place then? Simply string along with them in the hope that the mad Gestapo doctor comes to his senses and realizes we don't know anything about his super-gem? We'd both be dead from torture before that happened! Under no circumstances can he afford to let us go. We know too much about him.'

I felt her body stir against me. 'I've got it!' she continued to keep her voice low but there was a ripple of excitement in it.

'The Hill!'

It came with a rush: 'There's the perfect place we've been looking for on the tabletop! It's near the queen's grave! There's a kind of deep underground chamber hewn from the rock and behind its innermost wall is another small room almost completely hidden.'

'Steady!' In the darkness I smiled at her spate of words. 'Step by step, please!'

Her animation continued to bubble. 'It's perfect, perfect, Guy! The more I think about it the better I like it! One would never suspect there was anything there if you didn't know: the chamber has hardly been excavated or explored properly. I think it must have been what Dr Drummond was anxious about when he and Jock Stewart climbed to the summit after the damage to the Land-Rovers. He called it an armoury – they'd found some intriguing ivory arrow-heads and there's a beautiful inlaid mosaic floor.'

'Have you actually seen this hidden room?'

'Yes. It's not big enough to be called a room really: more a minute hollow cut in the solid rock, about the size of a wardrobe and half blocked with rubble. It's a very tight squeeze. We could hide there and be absolutely safe from von Praeger, I'm sure.'

'It sounds good.'

'The spring's close so we wouldn't be short of water. I know my way up the secret stairway and the layout of the summit.'

'Food – I have it! We could pick up what's left at my camp.'

She kissed me cheerfully. 'Everything for surviving a siege!'

Although I too was sold on the idea I said cautiously, 'It doesn't solve our problem of how to break free of Praeger and Koen or how to take Rankin along.'

'Perhaps we could use the place as a sort of staging post on the way to your boat if Rankin isn't fit enough to make it at one go,' she replied. 'Whatever we decide eventually, it gives us a firm objective to start with.'

'Transport!' I exclaimed. 'That's what sinks us at every turn. I can't carry Rankin to The Hill.'

'Rankin doubles the odds against us.'

'He's a built-in hazard and we've simply got to face that fact. He's got to come along; we must work on it.'

A fragment of dawn seemed to be penetrating the darkness. I held her close, reluctant to let her go, but we both knew that she could not stay.

'The Hill,' she whispered as she left me to crawl back to her blankets. 'Everything always comes back to The Hill, doesn't it, Guy?'

I grinned back, not explaining. 'Thanks for the *camisade*.'

CHAPTER TEN

'Out, Bowker!' Koen jerked the machine-pistol towards the cave entrance. 'Quick as kiss-my-arse. Out!'

Day seemed to have followed unbelievably fast after Nadine had left my side to return to her part of the cave; a few minutes before Koen had appeared to escort me I had heard him shepherding her out into the command-post's enclosure where I had first spotted Rankin.

I decided to play things in a low key and did not react to Koen's tone. Daylight revealed him as an even tougher proposition than I'd thought. He had a weather-beaten face and powerful shoulders and chest. His arms were sunburnt the colour of seasoned stinkwood. He brought with him a stench of sweat, leather and gun-oil. His breath in the confined space was metallic with stale brandy and he was red-eyed from the night's vigil.

'All right. As you say.'

'I warn you, don't try to be smart with me, Bowker. It's the Doc's idea that you and the doll should have some coffee. If it was me, I'd let you sweat it out, march or no march.'

'March?'

'You'll see. Now – out!'

We passed through Nadine's mill section and the first warmth in the open was welcome after the ground-chill of the cave. There was the faintest surprise touch of moisture in the early air which made the nostrils tingle. I greeted Nadine with studied casualness. However, a remarkable sight greeted us: Rankin sitting up on Talbot's bed, drinking coffee. There was no sign of Talbot. It amazed me to think that a man of his age could have put up such a fight but he was as hard as nails from a lifetime spent in the open amongst the tough breed of diamond diggers; and he looked at least twenty years younger than his age. Although he was balding, his sparse brown hair was only slightly flecked with grey and merged into his deep mahogany tan. His hatchet face was sullen now and his eyes below a high forehead had the kind of angry glassiness of a bird of prey – winged, wounded, watchful, dangerous. His chest was bandaged and I guessed that Praeger must have spent a good deal of the night working on him. I got nothing from him except a hard stare from his pale eyes.

The woodsmoke and coffee smelt good. Two mugs had been placed on the breastwork.

'Get it yourselves,' snapped Praeger without preliminaries. 'It's all you'll get, so make the most of it. You're going for a walk with Koen.'

I took one mug for myself and the other for Nadine, moving unobtrusively in von Praeger's direction. His pistol was in his belt.

I hadn't reckoned with Koen, though. 'Keep away from the Doc with that mug, Bowker! Back!'

I halted. 'What are you up to now, Praeger?' I demanded. I felt self-confident in spite of the odds. Having come from my long self-induced emotional vacuum I felt keyed up, ready for anything.

I rounded on Rankin. 'It's about time you started talking, Rankin! You've got a hell of a lot to answer for to me and still more to explain to this idiot here. He says there's a bigger half of the Cullinan and that you and I have it.'

'The Great Star of Africa,' Praeger prompted.

I noticed then that there were bubbles of dried saliva at the corners of the leathery lips and that his grim pet was sniffing at tiny flecks of blood on his clothes: I wondered if I were seeing evidences of a sadism which had put an end to Talbot during the night.

Rankin showed no sign that he had heard; an eyelid may have flickered, but it could have been from the drifting smoke.

I indicated Nadine. 'They've dragged her into this as well, Rankin. It needs only half a dozen words from you to put her in the clear.'

He looked at her, not at me, across the top of his mug and said in a hoarse, inflexionless voice. 'The Hill is mine.'

'Is that all you have to say?' I burst out angrily. 'You

double-crossing . . . !'

'Keep away from him, Bowker,' warned von Praeger. 'I'm relieved to hear he can utter, though. They're the first words I've had from him and I trust there'll be plenty more – all about the Cullinan.'

'Damn the Cullinan! All I want is for this crook to confess that he framed me!'

'It seems that at least we have one thing in common: wanting Rankin to talk,' retorted Praeger. 'You've made a great show, Bowker, of trying to buck off the responsibility on to Rankin. But it doesn't fool me. You're both in this and you are both going to tell me – separately – all about it.'

A tiny muscle pulled in his face as he looked down at his hands, like a surgeon before an operation. I didn't care for the gesture.

Rankin remained silent. I wondered how long he would hold out under Praeger's methods.

Then I turned to Koen: 'You must know from what your father told you that I have nothing to do with all this.'

'I visited him once, in the death-cell. He never uttered a single word about the Cullinan. Why should he, anyway? I meant nothing to him as a son: I was just a hand to work the trommel on the diggings. Afterwards he cleared out and got a good job and didn't want to know me. Fair enough. But he told the Doc and I believe that.'

'It's so much utter rubbish, Koen . . .'

He grinned unpleasantly. 'I may be sucking on the hind tit, Bowker, but thirty million dollars is one hell of a tit! I'll keep it that way!'

I regarded the three men, feeling cornered. Nevertheless, I kept working away at Koen.

'Take a cool look at this Cullinan thing, Koen. Okay, say Rankin here and my father salted the Premier? Those were the old days when only a couple of mines outside Kimberley were known. We've all heard romantic old-timers' stories about men crawling round with tobacco tins strung round their necks, picking up diamonds. Everything has come a long way since then. Every inch of South Africa has been prospected. There isn't a diamond area that isn't well known and hasn't been exploited. Answer me two things if you believe von Praeger: just where did the Cullinan come *from?* And do you think that under any circumstances the other half would have been left stashed away all these years? Thirty millions' worth?'

Koen appeared a shade nonplussed. 'My old man knew. He told the Doc.'

I forestalled Praeger. 'No, he didn't, Koen. What he did say was, "the hyena's blanket". He never mentioned the Cullinan. Your Gestapo helper here killed my grandfather and kidded himself he first heard that same absurd phrase from him.' I rounded on Rankin. 'What, if anything, does it mean, Rankin?'

The injured man's granite mask did not alter.

'I hope he'll be more communicative when we're alone,' said Praeger. 'It's taken everything I know to have him sitting up there drinking coffee this morning.'

I could believe it. Praeger's eyes were more bloodshot than Koen's and he looked as if he were living on his nerves.

I said harshly, 'I did you a favour, Rankin. Now's your chance to make amends for eighteen months of hell I spent in jail because of you.'

Nadine added softly. 'That includes me, too.'

Koen took a half-jack of brandy from his hip pocket and deftly laced his coffee, without relaxing his grip on the machine-pistol. He eyed us consideringly.

Suddenly Praeger's strained voice broke in: 'Talk, talk, talk! Round and round in circles! That's all I hear!'

He strode across to me and thrust his face close to mine.

'A cleavage face, do you hear! The Cullinan had been cut . . . !'

It was the moment I had been waiting for. I jostled him and whipped the automatic from his belt with my left hand, keeping him between me and Koen.

Koen faced me but the M-25 was aimed at Nadine's waist. She stared at us in horror. I had von Praeger fast in a kind of half-nelson with the pistol aimed beneath his left arm.

Koen said, 'I'll cut her in half, Bowker – drop that gun!'

I lowered the weapon, seeking desperately for some last-minute way of getting a shot in. I still had the pistol.

'In five seconds her guts'll be all over the floor – drop it!'

I let go and the pistol clattered on the rock. Praeger jerked loose, snatched it up and swung blindly at me.

There was an ugly clunk from the M-25.

'Stop! Keep still!'

Even Praeger came to his senses at the note in Koen's voice and he drew back from me.

Koen rapped out. 'For Chrissake, Doc, is there shit in your eyes? Do you want to get yourself killed?'

A child could have taken the pistol from him; he was shaking and biting his lips.

'For that, Bowker, I . . . I . . .'

'Let's get cracking,' snapped Koen. 'I'll see he doesn't cause any more trouble, Doc. You get on with Rankin. Let me know when you want me back. Same signal – three shots.' He leered at me. 'That'll be the time for you to start saying your prayers! Come on, both of you!'

Nadine moved but I hung back. I felt Rankin, the key to everything, was slipping through my fingers while I remained powerless to do anything about it.

'March!' ordered Koen. 'March, you bladdy *gomgat*!'

We had already started for the entrance when a thought struck me. It was so monstrous and yet so likely that I stopped short and Koen jammed the muzzle of the M-25 savagely into my back.

I ignored him and swung round to Rankin. 'Rankin,' I said, 'Did you kill my father too?'

We made a tight, nerve-shot little group, all eyes focused on the hard-faced man on the stretcher. I think he was about to reply, for my words brought a spark of animation to his face, but Praeger spoiled it.

'I'll ask you that on his behalf, Rankin!' He laughed a grating high laugh which set my teeth on edge. 'Think it over!'

'Get on!' repeated Koen. 'It's a long way to the river.'

I read dismay in Nadine's eyes and I tried to keep my face expressionless. Discovery of the boat would rob us of our last chance of escape and this was inevitable once we got anywhere near the pool at the confluence.

'If you don't want us to hear Rankin's screams when you start torturing him, The Hill's far enough,' I threw at Praeger. 'The heat will be pretty tough later on for such a long slog to the river.'

'We want you to see our aeroplane.' replied von Praeger and they both began to laugh. The implication was lost on us.

We reached the entrance. They had made the dangerous crossing safe by rigging a handline from door to wall: the risk was cut to nothing. The thought of my action in negotiating it carrying Talbot appalled me in retrospect.

'The girl first,' said Praeger.

Nadine pulled the cowl of her flying-jacket over her head as protection against the sun, whose heat was becoming evident. Koen stood at the rear, the M-25 trained on our backs. I rejected a plan to try and unsnick the rope once I had crossed, so as to maroon him temporarily while taking cover behind the wall, because the range was so short that he could spray the place with bullets and finish us off before we could hope to reach safety.

'Bowker! You next!'

With a growing feeling of helplessness I sensed that the crunch was at hand and I had nothing left to fight with but words.

'Von Praeger,' I said levelly. 'There are already two dead men at The Hill. I'm going to see that you and Rankin hang, if it's the last thing . . .'

'You'd be a fine poker player, Bowker,' he laughed in my face. 'Your hand is empty yet you go on calling as if you had a full house.'

'I warn you, Praeger . . .'

'Let *me* warn you, Bowker. Do a lot of thinking on this little walk of yours with Koen. If you don't, it may be the last walk you take.'

'Shut up and get across,' snapped Koen.

There was nothing for it but to obey. While Koen made the crossing Praeger held his pistol on us and kept the hyena at the ready. Once clear of the wall, we three followed a well-defined path, which was clearly Rankin's own, down the side of K2 towards the Wadi. It wound steeply but entailed no risks. Although it was still early, the heat was already becoming trying. There was a mirror-like dazzle off some very high thin cloud which magnified our discomfort. The suggestion of moisture earlier had vanished and the unmoving air seemed to throttle the countryside. The short hike underwrote the futility of any plan of ours to escape on foot. I marvelled at Koen being able to take the heat without a hat.

As we neared the foot of K2 I said to Koen, 'Where's your

plane? It might be easier for us to make a circuit rather than go directly via The Hill. The entrances to it are blocked with barbed wire and gates . . .'

'I know. I'll shoot 'em open.'

I simply couldn't think of any other argument to forestall Koen's taking the direction which must ultimately reveal my boat.

Shortly afterwards Koen called a halt in the shadow of a big rock before starting on the shadeless, sandy crossing of the wadi. Ahead lay The Hill, sticking up like a long grey stone cruiser; the warship image was carried further by the projecting section below the tabletop resembling a naval cutwater. Koen drank some water from a canteen and followed it with another slug from his half-jack – a home-distilled fire water made from peaches. I eyed the bottle, thinking it could become a deadly weapon if broken and jammed into Koen's throat. He passed the canteen on to Nadine and me.

'Apart from the gates, we'd make it much easier for ourselves if we kept to the hard ground along these hills,' I persisted. 'Also, the wadi's at its narrowest farther along opposite the tabletop and there's less sand . . .'

Koen considered me curiously. 'You're very keen to stop me getting near The Hill, aren't you? What have you got there?'

'Gold,' said Nadine.

I'm not sure whether Koen or I was the more thunderstruck.

She pulled off her cowl: the inclination of her head as she pretended to shake her long hair free told me everything: I read the double meaning in her lips and played up to it.

'We're in the hot seat through absolutely no fault of our own,' she told Koen. 'But I don't intend to be made mince-meat of by your crazy doctor friend. I can't confess to something I don't know. And I don't know about the Cullinan. Nor does Guy.'

He appeared to eye her with a new respect but his reply was unconvinced. 'Go on.'

She said vehemently, play-acting splendidly: 'I'm tired of being pushed around by a couple of bullies and I'm prepared to pay to get shot of you. You know who my father is.'

'Don't give me that line! Harold Raikes couldn't pay thirty

million dollars ransom for his daughter!'

She went on angrily. 'You talk as if you *had* thirty million! Where is it? Just tell me that and I'll go along with your story!' She waved at the blanched countryside. 'Fine – where? Just *where*, Koen?'

'The Doc says . . . Bowker and Rankin . . .'

'It's a dream; you're chasing shadows!'

I threw my weight in with Nadine's. 'I'll give you a playback of everything connected with the Cullinan, Koen. Just you tell me when you've heard it if your yarn makes sense.'

'I know the story,' he answered sullenly. 'The Doc told me everything.'

'Including the hyena's blanket?' I jeered. 'Just what the hell does that mean, Koen? It's the ravings of a sick man.'

'Listen to me, Koen,' added Nadine. 'Von Praeger was a Gestapo doctor. We don't know how many people he killed then. A man has got to find a reason for murdering if he's to stay sane. So what happens? Praeger carries on by justifying his conscience in the name of a bigger diamond than the biggest in the world. It's so far removed from reality that he had to invent a way-out code for it. I don't have to tell you what that is.'

Koen was clearly rocked, but still sceptical. 'The Doc heard those words *the hyena's blanket* from Bowker's grandfather and my old man. He didn't make them up himself.'

'Who says so?' I retorted. 'You can't check that one either: they're both dead. It's part of Praeger's cunning. He fixed his story so that there couldn't possibly be witnesses.'

Nadine followed up crisply. 'Believe it if you want to, Koen. Neither Guy nor I are stopping you. Go chasing your thirty million dream if you wish. What I'm offering you is a lot less, but it's right here and I can take you to it in the next couple of hours.'

His glittering brown eyes went from Nadine to myself. I began to feel we had him on the ropes.

'Have you ever heard of the Ancient Ruins Exploration Company?'

He shook his head.

'It doesn't matter,' replied Nadine. 'It's a company my father set up to exploit gold from old ruins.'

'You can't do that legally,' objected Koen. 'I'm not that dumb.'

Nadine sighed with mock patience. 'Gold is where you find it, Koen. Why do you think Guy and I came here with the scientific expedition in the first place? It was legal, perfect cover. We reconnoitred the place. Then, when everyone left we came back. We were using a plane because the treasure's in bits and pieces: it's light and easy to fly out. Then along came Rankin and spoilt everything by shooting the pilot.'

Koen remained mulish. 'Rankin was here. You came to fix things about diamonds with him. The Doc says so.'

'For God's sake stop saying the Doc says this and the Doc says that!' I burst out. 'Talk about sucking on the hind tit! Let me tell it you, Koen, the way it was. I didn't know Rankin was at The Hill. Rankin shopped me. IDB . . .' I gave him a brief summary of the case. 'What Rankin is up to is nothing to do with us. Ours is a separate outfit – gold, as Nadine says. You and Praeger have got your lines hopelessly crossed. When I ran into Rankin here – after what he'd done to me before, well, he got hurt, that's all.'

Koen unscrewed the stopper and took another drag at the brandy. He half closed his eyes against the harsh sunlight.

'Where's this treasure then?'

Nadine indicated the tabletop. 'There. Hidden. I know where. Half a million in solid gold. And *there,* Koen, not a dream. We'll cut you in on the deal if you let us go free.'

The frustrated greed of a thousand aborted diamond washes was in his face. 'Well I'll be damned for a fiddler's bitch! Right there, you say?'

'You won't find it without me,' said Nadine. 'Take your choice, Koen. It's not thirty million but it's real. There aren't any risks. You'll get your whack in hard cash.'

'*Allemagtig!*'

I laughed in what I hoped was the right conspiratorial manner.

'Listen to what she's got to say, Koen.'

Suddenly his face was transformed by suspicion. 'The Doc said you were a smart talker, Bowker. What if I say I don't believe a word of it?'

Nadine came to my rescue. 'I'll make you a gesture of goodwill. I'll take you there and show you.'

I was out of my depth but I strung along with her.

'I don't leave Bowker behind. Not on your nellie!'

'Of course Guy will come,' she added calmly. 'We have to go up the secret stairway. We must also be very careful at about three-quarters of the way up. Let me explain: the stairway is actually a narrow cleft which is open to the sky. However, at this particular spot a big boulder has fallen down and nearly, but not quite, blocked it. As a result it's very narrow and you have to crawl through slowly. It's almost like a sloping chimney, in fact, for a while and I warn you it's tricky.' She took in the machine-pistol and Koen's broad shoulders. 'Do you think you'll be able to make it?'

He laughed grimly. 'You two will lead; I'll be behind with this in case of tricks.'

She shot me an almost imperceptible glance, then resumed: 'Right. Then I'll go first and Guy will follow. You will have to wait in the open while we negotiate the covered section one at a time. While Guy's there I'll slip up to the summit and make quite sure there's nothing loose which could fall down . . .'

I got her message; my part in the plan was clear. I was to obstruct Koen by taking my time over the slow section where the rock cover protected me while Koen was exposed out in the open. She would then race on to the summit and pitch a rock down on his head. I remembered that during the expedition there had been talk of a stack of fashioned stones at the head of the stairway which the ancients had used for exactly that purpose against their enemies.

It brought me satisfaction that I was to be the Judas-goat who would lead Koen to the slaughter. However, the operation would require co-ordination, split-second timing and strong nerve. If Nadine's first brickbat missed him there wouldn't be a second chance. He would be behind me at point-blank range and Nadine would be equally vulnerable on the skyline above him.

'Okay, no harm in talking, is there? If this gold of yours is really there, maybe we can get down to business. But I want to see it first. You're still my prisoners, so watch your step! Let's go!'

The growing tension was almost as energy-sapping as the

stiff hike across the sand-filled wadi. Nadine kept up gamely. Koen gave us no opportunity to exchange even a whisper. I wondered what he meant to do about the rolls of barbed wire which blocked the gully we were heading for. I couldn't imagine he'd be fool enough to involve himself in a crawl through it and lay himself wide open to attack. I accordingly kept my mouth shut when we got near; the last thing I wanted now was for him to change his plans and head for the river.

Koen surveyed the wire-blocked entrance, backed by a high fence.

'On!' he said briefly. 'We'll try the next one.'

We trudged farther, our discomfort growing steadily in the sun. After a while the remains of a wall appeared on the terrace above our heads and where it became less ruined the wire barrier had been discontinued. Soon we were confronted with a broad eroded gap in the terrace itself, new since the time of the expedition, which was stoutly fenced with a big double gate and lock. Because of its width, the customary rolls of barbed wire were absent.

'Stand clear!'

Koen fired a short burst from the M-25. The echo magnified it to sound like a heavy machine-gun. Nadine was shaken. I think it brought her an added sense of dismay at what Koen would do if her stone missile missed him in the stairway.

Koen gestured at the remains of the lock fastenings which still held.

'Bowker! Get this damn thing open!'

A couple of kicks from me and we were through. I wanted if possible to keep him away from my camping-place but our footpath to the secret stairway led directly past it. I was worried that there might be spent cartridges lying around near the fire which could blow the cover on my story about meeting Rankin quite by chance. The Mannlicher, too, gave me qualms. We were almost past when Koen caught sight of my orange-yellow gunny sack.

Looking suspicious, he led us into my camp, examining everything. The fire was a mess and ash was littered about. It was obvious that it had not died down of its own accord; in fact, it looked as if two wild animals had fought in its remains.

'What's all this?'

'Only my camping-place.' I tried to keep my voice neutral.

He spotted a spent shell from my clip and picked it up. My heart missed a beat.

'You're lying, Bowker. Look at the fire. Look at this.'

The spent case was dulled from being in the embers. I took it from him, commenting casually with a confidence I did not feel, 'That's an old type of cartridge, if you look closely. It's probably been lying around for years.' I had a sudden brainwave about the fire: 'Baboons,' I said. 'They'll tear up anything – and they're starving. I'm surprised they've left anything in one piece.'

A scatter of tins bore out my story. Koen, however, appeared to want to investigate further.

'I'm famished,' I added. 'I'm going to collect this stuff and put it in the shade so that it won't spoil.'

Unexpectedly, Koen sat himself down in the shadow of a rock with the machine-pistol across his knees.

'We'll all eat. I'm hungry too. I've been up since sparrow-fart.'

'There was some brandy somewhere, provided the baboons haven't raided that as well.'

He cast about and found the bottle on its side and uncorked, but there was a little brandy left, which he added to his half-jack.

'Gesondheid!'

We toasted him back in water from the jerrican I had filled at the hut tank. Then we all had some food, though I, for one, was too tense to do more than nibble at it.

After what seemed hours we made our way under Nadine's guidance to the entrance of the secret stairway in my fig tree's root cage. I prayed that the Mannlicher might not show up and break Koen's somewhat relaxed mood. Fortunately there was no sign of it.

Nadine took the lead, I followed, and Koen brought up the rear. From the cage itself the start of the climb was easy but higher up we had to resort to wedging ourselves by our backs and legs across the rocky funnel for purchase, and worked our way upwards in that way. It was slow and tedious and we made frequent stops to rest. About 150 feet from the ground Nadine called out from above.

'Here we are! Come up, Guy, and I'll show you.'

I relayed her message to Koen. He made himself secure across the passageway by the same method of legs and back: his arms were free for the gun. The M-25 pointed up at us. He couldn't miss at that range.

The way ahead ran underneath the big boulder Nadine had described – a kind of upward sloping corkscrew – which would take us temporarily out of Koen's sight. The place seemed impossibly narrow and somewhat dark, too, away from the hard sunlight.

I edged close to Nadine. She reached down a hand and clasped mine. It could have meant goodbye, or encouragement. High above her head on the summit I detected the top of the stack of missiles.

'This is it.'

Then she was gone, her slim body squirming easily through the narrow aperture.

In a few minutes I guessed she must be through but made no move myself. The longer I held back, the better became our chances.

I felt the tension in my bowels and for the first time in my life a slight vertigo. I therefore didn't look down when I spoke to Koen.

'I'll start off in a moment. She's not through yet.'

'What the hell's holding her up?'

'It's very narrow.'

'Get on!' snapped Koen. His voice changed and hardened. 'I tell you . . .'

'Up! Get up!'

I had no way of knowing whether I had given her time enough for her plan. I still delayed as much as I dared: moreover, while I was exposed she could do nothing with the missile. I was scared Koen would sight her near the stack.

I jack-knifed upward suddenly, to be out of her line of fire, then flung myself full length to wriggle into the narrow space.

I lay where I was, deliberately scuffling and pretending to make heavy weather of negotiating the passage. I could hear Koen breathing hard less than ten feet below me. Every second seemed an hour.

'What's up?' he demanded.

'I'm stuck.'

'I'll give you a shove.'

125

It was the last thing I wanted. *Where was Nadine?*

'Okay, Okay, I'm free now . . .'

His smothered oath and the loading clunk of the M-25 sounded as one. My fingers clamped involuntarily on their holds and a spasm of terror shot through me as I expected a burst to rip into me from below. Simultaneously there was a heavy crash of stone on metal, the scream and slam of one isolated shot, followed by a long volley whose racket in the confined space stunned me. Sick with anxiety for Nadine and marvelling that I was unwounded, I clawed my way upwards into the open.

I dreaded what I might see on the summit, but to my relief Nadine, her eyes wide with horror at what she had done, looked down into mine.

Her primitive missile had smashed the stubby barrel and long magazine into Koen's head and chest, breaking its force, which otherwise might have brained him. It was probably some animalistic survival instinct which had caused him to glance up, throw up the weapon and try to fire at the last moment before the thing crashed on him but he had been too late. A whole long burst had discharged as he fell; and his broad shoulders had eventually saved him, lodging across a narrow section of stairway and suspending him senseless a hundred feet above the ground.

I was numb with reaction and couldn't make the rest of the climb. Nadine came down to me. Her tears fell into my face.

When we had recovered we worked our way carefully down to Koen. Between us we managed to lever him safely to the bottom. Exhausted, we hid ourselves and him behind the curtain of fig roots, out of sight of Praeger.

CHAPTER ELEVEN

Inside the cage formed by the overhanging roots the air was blessedly cool, with the same hint of concealed moisture as in my baobab hideout. Welcome, too, was the roots' filtering effect on the sun's scorching light – it was now a little after midday. Nadine and I hardly spoke: we were in the process of unwinding, reliving each risk and finding it magnified in retrospect. We tacitly avoided discussing Koen, whom I had dragged into a far corner.

It was I, however, who unintentionally set off Nadine's latent nervous explosion.

I indicated an ooze of sticky white sap which streaked a big main root. It resembled rubber latex.

'Look at this, Nadine. That happened a moment after my clip exploded in the fire in front of Rankin. It was meant for me. It's where one of his bullets went in.'

She stared at it for a long moment and then threw herself into my arms, shaking and sobbing. She kissed my lips, my eyes, my face, and her tears became part of the wild wetness of it all.

'I'm changed the way The Hill's changed – oh God, how I hate myself for it!'

'Nothing's changed, my darling. Our love's more wonderful than it ever was.'

'I looked down at him with that rock in my hands and something took hold of me. I wanted to kill him!'

'You haven't killed him – he's not even badly hurt.'

'I *wanted* to, Guy! He stood between me and you.'

'It was a wonderful plan. It worked.'

'It was *my* plan! I didn't want this!'

'It's the way of it, Nadine. It had to be done.'

'No, no, Guy!'

'Of course it had to. It was very clever. I was at my wits' end to think of anything.'

'I was in the grip of something, up there. My brain was burning – *I'll kill him, I'll kill him*! I couldn't think of anything else.'

'You were very brave and clever.'

'Brave, clever – but it wasn't love; that's what I'm saying. It was hate – hate, Guy. At The Hill itself, which means love to me. I feel unclean.'

I reached out a foot and pulled the M-25 to me. I held the barrel against her bare arm and the still-warm metal seemed to stem her rush of anguish.

'There were maybe twenty rounds in there. Koen meant them for us. See it that way.'

She gained control of herself and said in a small, flat voice.

'Are there any left?'

'I don't think so but I'll check. Even a couple of live rounds would put a different complexion on our entire strategy.'

My words rekindled her nightmare. 'Strategy! Why has it got to be strategy, tactics, plans, plots, bullets? Why must they come between us and our love?'

'I was the first to sell us down the river, remember. That day with Charlie Furstenberg. For a long time I've wanted to confess to that.'

She closed my mouth with her lips. 'No, no, I won't have you say it!' Her body tight against mine wrote off the past and promised the future. Gradually, as I held her, her sobs subsided and when the storm was past she held up her face with the ghost of a smile.

'I'm sorry. We'll see this thing through first and then things will be all right again in every way.' She went on, making a deliberate effort, 'We could say now that stage one of our master-plan is behind us?'

'We could,' I smiled back. 'Thanks to you. We have the initiative now. We're past one of our biggest hurdles: breaking free from them. We'll make the rest of the plan work out too, I promise you.'

She brought my lips to hers with her ring finger in a strange, lingering caress.

'We'll make it work,' I repeated. 'We've got to play this thing strong.' I gestured towards K2. 'First, I'd like to know what that devil Praeger is up to.'

'What about Koen?'

She couldn't bring herself to look at him. I bent down and listened to his breathing and checked his pulse.

'He's probably been worse off than this a dozen times in pub fights,' I comforted her. 'Concussed, I'd say. He'll be out for a couple of hours. He'll have a headache when he wakes – and a big grudge too.'

'Shouldn't we . . . tie him or something?'

'We'll get round to that later. I'm worried now about that burst of fire from Koen's gun. Von Praeger must have heard it.'

'I doubt it. It was magnified for you, right beside Koen as you were. I believe the stairway would have absorbed the sound. Just think, von Praeger didn't appear when he shot the gate to pieces.'

'Von Praeger may have been very occupied.'

'When you say things like that I don't feel safe unless I'm close to you. Do you think . . . ?'

'I stop myself thinking. We must never again allow Praeger the chance to get his hands on us.'

'I don't know which of those two is the worse.'

'Koen's a big mouth and a bully! Praeger's a different kettle of fish; far more dangerous. I wish I knew for sure about those shots. The echo, too, would boost the sound.'

'It wouldn't resemble the three spaced shots signal they arranged.'

'Praeger said he would signal Koen, not the other way round. He was also reckoning on Koen hearing it as far away as the river. We're only halfway there. I think we must assume that Praeger heard Koen's volley.'

'Why assume?' She parted the screen cautiously. 'There are your binoculars in the camp. Why not see what he's up to in the command-post?'

'You're the real brains of this outfit,' I tried to jolly her out of her dark mood. 'Wait here and I'll collect them.'

'No,' she replied. 'I'm not staying alone with Koen.'

I checked him once more by lifting an eyelid.

'He's still out cold.'

'He looks even worse unconscious.'

'I must admit that personally I prefer Koen in the horizontal position rather than the vertical.'

I slipped off his belt and secured his hands behind his back with it. Then I removed his boots.

'That'll make him slightly less mobile.'

'I'll hide them later, high up in the stairway,' said Nadine.

'Good. Here goes.'

I crawled across to the camping-place and retrieved the glasses. I felt naked out in the open despite the fact that I knew that Praeger had no binoculars of his own. I hurried back to Nadine.

Together we scanned the slopes of K2. The command-post harmonized so well with the surrounding rock that it was difficult to pick out. There was no sign of Praeger.

'Heaven help Rankin,' I remarked.

'Guy, where do we go from here?'

I looked into her troubled eyes and for a moment I was tempted to flee downriver and damn the consequences.

That conditioned my reply. 'Our escape route's wide open. We don't have to stay and face that madman. There's nothing to stop us beating it for my boat.'

'Except Rankin. Except for a future which won't be a future for us. You'll never be your own man. At every turn we'll be waiting for von Praeger to show up and plunge us back into this nightmare. He'll be behind every bush. The farther we run, the farther he'll follow.'

'Unless Rankin comes clean.'

'About what? About something that doesn't exist except in von Praeger's own fevered imagination?'

'We've added more fuel to the general fire by having to tell Koen about non-existent treasure. He won't forget that in a hurry.'

I examined K2 again. I knew she was right. She was expressing my own deep-down conviction when she said very quietly and decisively:

'We must stay and stick it out, Guy.'

'That's the way I see it, too.'

'Rankin has got to come with us.'

'If we can get our hands on him long enough to obtain a signed confession from him, we needn't take him along.'

'It wouldn't be the answer, Guy. He could always deny it afterwards and say it was an admission extracted under duress. You're also assuming that he'll be willing to confess. I doubt it. Look at how he kept his mouth shut in front of von Praeger.'

'Right. Let's say finally then that Rankin comes with us.'

'That means seizing him out of von Praeger's grasp. It'll be very tough, Guy. Rankin's worth just as much to him as he is to us.'

'Transport!' I exclaimed. 'If there were only some way of transporting Rankin to the river!'

I had a sudden idea. 'What about those two old Land-Rovers which were wrecked during the expedition? Where are they? They must be around somewhere.'

'Over against the cliff beyond my trench,' she replied. 'But you ought to see them, Guy. The rock that fell on them was the size of a room.'

'Surely there's something left in the way of wheels we could use for Rankin.'

She was dubious. 'A couple of years' lying out in the open won't have improved them either. But let's go and look. It's not far.'

We made our way as unobtrusively as we could to the wrecks. I had previously missed them in the dark because they were partly hidden under an enormous boulder. Wheels and chassis, which had buckled from the initial blow, had rusted and collapsed. The vehicles were simply useless junk.

The sight jerked me into a sense of cold reality.

'Nadine,' I said. 'We won't succeed with a series of woolly improvisations: we must have a clear-cut plan. Yours worked because it was simple and straightforward. That's the sort of thinking we need now.'

She was charming as she defended me to myself. 'It was worth coming, Guy. You might have spotted something of use.'

'Forget it. I was carried away by the thought of wheels. We need wheels for Rankin if he's to be moved. And there simply aren't any wheels anywhere.'

'Let's by-pass that problem for the moment and hope that something will occur to us when we've mulled over everything. We didn't know how we were to get away from Koen and von Praeger at the start, but we finally did. Let's tackle the Rankin dilemma in the same way.'

'Right. First task is to get hold of Rankin. Consider what we're up against. He's held in a place from which anyone approaching can be seen for miles. It's guarded by a barred door and inside is a maniac: with a gun and a savage animal. Our prospective snatch victim can't be moved by ordinary means. I can't simply sling him over my shoulder: the pressure on his heart which Praeger mentioned would kill him before he'd covered fifty yards.'

'You're over-simplifying,' she chided me gently. 'You're forgetting the ace in our hand. We have Koen.'

'We can't hold him to ransom and say to Praeger that if he doesn't surrender Rankin we'll bash Koen on the head with a rock.'

'I haven't thought how we can play our trump, but a trump nevertheless he is. Guy, we can't sit here at The Hill shadow-boxing with the problem at long distance. We must get close to the command-post and be ready to snatch Rankin when the opportunity offers.'

'In that case Praeger's bound to see us crossing the wadi.'

'In about six hours it'll be dark. We'll cross then. We'll use your hollow baobab to keep watch on von Praeger.'

I had a brainwave and the whole operation fell into place. 'Nadine! Wheels! What a clot I've been!'

'Where, Guy?'

'The plane wreck! The undercarriage was torn off when it first hit the trees! It's lying there for the taking – two wheels and an axle!'

'The tyres wouldn't have survived the fire.'

'It doesn't matter about the tyres. The wheels alone are enough for our purpose. We'll fix them to his stretcher and we'll have a mobile litter. We'll make him fast to it with some of the plane's strut wires which are also lying around. It'll be a piece of cake hauling him across the wadi and on to the boat.'

'It's perfect, Guy!' She kissed me lightly. 'Absolutely perfect!'

However, a sense of caution curbed my enthusiasm. 'Don't let's get carried away too soon. Praeger still holds Rankin. We haven't beaten that part of the problem yet. We've got to get our hands on him, which means that somehow or other we must overpower Praeger – and his hyena.'

'If only we could lure Praeger out of the command-post for long enough, we could manage Rankin.'

'It bristles with difficulties. We'll have to be on the alert, to act fast. We'll also have to construct the litter in the dark almost under Praeger's own nose.'

I kicked at the Land-Rover wreck. 'What we need is weapons. We're pitting our bare hands against guns.'

'Plus our wits.'

'Do you remember if the tools were removed from these wrecks?'

'No. Only the petrol.'

I reached into one of the mid-section tool compartments as far as I could and after a while I managed to extract a rusty tyre lever. I had no luck with some other things I could only touch. However, with the lever I prised loose a heavy mesh grille protecting a radiator.

'If we wedge that across the narrow section of the stairway it'll make an effective seal,' I told Nadine. 'It's not part of the Rankin kidnap plan – at this stage. It's merely an insurance in case things go wrong and we have to use your hide-out on the summit.'

'As I understand it, we cross the wadi tonight, somehow or other overpower von Praeger, grab Rankin, put him on the litter and make all speed for the boat?'

'Correct.'

I was peering under the crumpled bonnet at the engine compartment when, at the sight of the plastic brake fluid reservoir, a thought struck me like a sledgehammer.

'Fire!' I exclaimed. 'I've got the answer to what we can use for weapons! I'll make a petrol bomb out of my empty brandy bottle. If Praeger and his pet start getting tough, I'll toss it into the enclosure like a grenade. That'll bring 'em up short! They'll have to get out, with flaming fuel all over the place!'

'Where's the petrol coming from? There's none in these tanks.'

'From the boat,' I answered. 'We can come and go to it as we wish.'

My mind was on the technicalities of fixing a wick through the brandy bottle cork when an odd thought made me burst out laughing.

'I've just thought of something else for our arsenal: a mini-bomb using Koen's brandy! That stuff of his is practically pure alcohol. Like my petrol bomb, it'll kick up hell's delight. I'll reserve it specially for Dika!'

Nadine did not share my enthusiasm: 'It all sounds very ingenious and terror-like, but where does it get us? A petrol bomb in the command-post won't entice von Praeger out long enough for us to do anything about Rankin. We want him out of the way – well out of the way – for a long time. Instead, why not burn his plane tonight and create a major diversion that way?'

'Sounds good, but the time factor's against it. We'd never make it from the burning plane near the river to the command post and back again to the boat with Rankin. And we'd lay ourselves wide open to bumping into von Praeger somewhere along the line. Also he'd be sure to discover our boat if he passed near the river on the way to his plane. In which case our whole plan is shot.'

'We seem to be going round in circles.'

'No. The main plan's straightforward, but if things start getting snarled up we'll have to improvise, and improvise quickly.'

'What's the alternative if we have to?'

'It's all yours. Your cubby-hole on the summit of The Hill.'

'I don't like it, Guy, because it presupposes that we must abandon Rankin.'

'Not necessarily. Assume we transport him safely as far as The Hill en route for the boat, then have to take emergency action and hole up on the summit for some reason we can't foresee at this stage. We hide Rankin in the root cage as a temporary measure while we shoot up to your hideout. We'll block the secret stairway with this radiator grill. We'll take the litter with us. Praeger is bound to find Rankin but his problem then will be exactly what ours was without the plane's wheels: he can't move Rankin without killing him.'

'Checkmate.'

'Just the contrary. We can stand a siege on the summit by taking up food from my camp. The spring will give us water. We'll hamstring von Praeger and Koen as far as food goes by dumping the contents of Rankin's kitchen over the cliff. They haven't any other provisions that we know of.'

'Then let's hump some of your supplies up to the summit right away,' she answered. 'I think it would also be a good thing if you made yourself familiar with the layout there.' She tried to smile but it didn't come off. 'As a matter of tactics, not of the heart.'

CHAPTER TWELVE

After our return to the root screen I checked the command-post again with the glasses before beginning the food-lift operation. I was uneasy about von Praeger, of whom there was no sign. The place was too far away for him to be able to distinguish individuals but it would be possible for him to see figures moving about, and the nature of our various movements might have aroused his suspicion. I did not want anything to foil our main plan now that we had firmly decided upon it. After a couple of minutes the bright, hard light hurt my eyes too much for me to go on looking; moreover the heat waves reduced the outlines of the rock to vagueness. Nadine also took a long look but could see nothing.

Somewhat reassured, we crossed to the camping-spot and quickly loaded the gunny sack which was our sole container with a manageable weight of supplies for the stiff climb. We reckoned they would last us about five days if rationed carefully. I was of two minds about Koen's machine-pistol. It was too heavy and cumbersome to take along and yet it was a big risk leaving it. I didn't want to smash it in case I should find a spare magazine when we broke into the command-post; something which would completely alter the balance of power in our favour. I compromised by removing the empty clip and part of the firing mechanism, which I pocketed.

Koen, lying at the foot of the stairway, still showed no signs of consciousness. We left him there and started off, Nadine leading and carrying his boots to stash away in some rocky niche high up out of sight and reach. She outdistanced me but waited at the tricky section which had been Koen's downfall. We worked through this bit together; then she went on ahead to the top.

This was new territory to me and I became strongly aware of that sense of being watched which had struck me previously, as if the long-dead sentries' eyes had burned something of the intensity of their vigil into the rocks themselves. This impres-

135

sion was heightened by the sight of the empty ladder-sockets cut into the rock on either side of the passageway; the rungs had apparently been removable when danger threatened in order to isolate the summit to withstand siege. My idea of the radiator grille was a variation on this same theme. There was also another sensation – less tangible and a little chilling – especially where the ascent straightened out for the final few yards. I imagined that a pilgrim seeking oracular guidance from the great king would have felt it strongly: something vaguely ominous and awe-inspiring about the threatening dark jaws of the cliffs on either hand. I also thought grimly of the other side of the coin – if one had come in the role of an attacker – above me were several piles of stone missiles stacked ready and a natural slot between giant boulders guarding the head of the stairway where bowmen could have fired into the faces of any enemy who got that far. On the very edge of the cliff top there was also a man-made fortification, terminating in a tall stone pillar.

Nadine did not hear me reach the summit; she was standing staring abstractedly at what appeared to be an irregular pyramid-shaped heap of bright, small stones of the kind I had seen below the river terrace. Some of them reflected colour from blue and green inset crystals. It was a puzzling little edifice whose purpose I couldn't guess.

The tabletop ran away at a slight incline, bare and smooth, to the north-western cliffs; and here and there it was intersected by untidy trenches dug by the archaeologists to probe its mysteries. The end near the queen's grave looked like a miniature version of the Lichtenburg diggings but near where I emerged there was only one excavation, running steeply through the cap of soil to the solid rock beneath. A red and white excavator's staff, marked in feet, projected from the bottom like a wrecked ship's mast.

Nadine started from her reverie as I approached and I noticed that she flushed slightly.

She indicated the staff. 'Our hideout's down there. There are a couple of chambers, all at a lower level. They have a natural rock ceiling, so where we go in is actually the top part of an old door. As you can see, there's been very little work done.'

'Are you sure it's safe? It looks a bit spooky to me. No wild animals holed up? What about baboons?'

'Let's investigate: there weren't any last time.'

'Before we do that I'm going to check on von Praeger.'

The declining afternoon light tended to iron out all the shadows against the distant slopes of K2, making it harder than ever to pick out the command-post. I had a grandstand view as I faced southwards across the wadi and overlooked the complex of hills beyond. I thought I spotted something moving when eventually I located the post but I couldn't be sure.

'Nothing,' I told Nadine when I rejoined her. 'It somehow seems too good to be true.'

Nadine, however, was in high spirits and didn't share my uneasiness.

'Feel better?' I asked.

Our eyes met. There was almost no need for words.

'I'm at home here. I feel . . . good, that's all.'

She took me impulsively by the hand. 'There's no time to show you all the wonderful things but there's one of our essentials – the spring, at the back of the rooms.'

'And the baboons?'

'Their rest colony is farther along beyond the spring itself. They don't seem to want to shelter here, for some reason. Come!'

She insisted on leading the way into the dimness below. I didn't share her confidence about the place not being used as a lair. She used the top of the lintel as a handhold and swung down. I followed. The interior was twilight-dim, although a shaft of long light made it possible to see without artificial means. It was chilly by comparison with outside and there was a faint odour of midden gas. Floor and walls were of living rock and there was room to stand comfortably. In a far corner was what appeared to be a patch of moisture, probably seepage from the spring.

Nadine was delighted that I could not locate her hide-away.

'It really takes a lot of looking for,' she said. 'It's right there below the drip. It mightn't be man-made but simply a water fissure which has widened out with time.'

I went to examine it more closely, my mind occupied with its possibilities, so was not aware of the mosaic pavement until I trod on it.

137

But to me it wasn't a mosaic pavement at all – it was an *isifuba* board.

Isifuba is a game as old as Africa. It can be played anywhere, any time, simply by crudely sketching a squared board as for draughts. Pebbles are used as pieces. *Isifuba,* it is said, was the game the Roman soldiers played at the foot of the Cross. If there are no wayside shrines in Africa, at least the traveller's road is cheered by innumerable *isifuba* boards scratched in the rocks and distinguishable immediately by slightly hollowed places for the pieces.

However, I could not imagine the purpose of such an ornate and sophisticated *isifuba* board hidden out of sight in an underground chamber. It was about three feet square; which to begin with is about twice the size of a regular board. It had three squares each way and every hollow seemed inlaid with a different coloured stone, and one was missing entirely. They could have been semi-precious but I wasn't sure: the dim light and a layer of dust didn't help.

'What do you make of it, Guy?'

'I'm foxed. It isn't a mosaic in the usual sense.'

'I suspect this is what brought Dr Drummond rushing up here after the Land-Rover business.'

'Didn't he give you any clue as to what these stones really were?'

'No. He was puzzled, but from the way he spoke I'd say it was a lead to something else.'

'A lead to what?'

'He didn't say. As I told you, this chamber hasn't been examined properly: there wasn't time. All I know is that Dr Drummond found a lot of rather peculiar-looking arrow shafts in here made of ivory, which he took away with him. They were very short and had odd markings. That's why he called this place the armoury, for want of a better name.'

'Let's take a close look at your hideout and get this stuff stowed. I have a feeling that Praeger is breathing down our necks all the time.'

'He's miles away, Guy. Try this gap for size.'

The way into the cubby-hole was a very tight squeeze past a jag of sandstone. Because of the loose debris it was virtually undetectable.

Standing jammed across the entrance, I pitched a tin from

the gunny sack into the inkiness. As I did so there was a sharp prick in my shoulder and what seemed to be a clatter at my feet; simultaneously I heard what I thought was a distant shot. From the darkness I caught a gleam of mother-of-pearl.

'Nadine! Stand back! It's a puff-adder! It got me in the shoulder!'

For a split second we stood rooted, but her eyes were better than mine in the poor light.

Her voice shadowed the curiosity inside her. 'Puff-adders aren't made of ivory!'

She picked up the thing and we hurried to the light. It was a curious gauntlet-like object cut off above the knuckles and thumb-hole and with a wicked, backswept hook at the wrist. Its sharp point had jabbed me. The lethal glove had been carved from solid elephant tusk.

Nadine was delighted. 'Guy, what a find! It must be an archer's arm-guard to prevent backlash from the bow-string!'

I slipped it on. 'No,' I replied. 'It's much more dangerous. Look!' I made a dummy sweep with my arm. 'It's meant for in-fighting.'

The echo of a far away shot slapped through the hills. This time I knew I was not mistaken and Nadine heard it too.

'That's von Praeger's signal – he wants Koen back.'

'It's our turn to be grilled, Guy.'

'We haven't any means of bluffing him by giving an answering signal. When Koen doesn't reply he'll know there's something wrong. Let's leave this for the moment and take a look outside.'

'I'll hide the arm-guard right here by the door.'

I hurried ahead of Nadine and once outside I heard a repetition of the three signal shots from the direction of K2. They sounded like the Mauser.

'Keep down and well out of sight. Even if Praeger's a very long way away,' I warned Nadine, 'he'll be looking for any sign of movement.'

We crept to the cliff under cover of the wall and I used the glasses. K2 looked the same as before. When my eyes became fogged Nadine took over.

We waited.

'He's coming!'

'Where, for God's sake!'

'He's just leaving the post – starting to move across the bad bit above the precipice . . .'

She pushed the binoculars into my hands. Praeger was crossing very slowly on the handlines, guiding his pet by its mane. Rankin's Mauser was slung over his shoulder and I reckoned he'd be armed with his pistol too.

'If that damn brute would only slip and break its neck a lot of our problems would be over,' I remarked.

Nadine took a look. 'He's being very careful, Guy. That animal gives me the horrors.'

'It's a nasty piece of work, but don't overrate it. Hyenas are natural cowards and no amount of training will beat that.'

'He'll use it to track us down.'

'It's not a dog, Nadine: it only found us last time by following a trail of blood. And it can't climb – that's another point in our favour. Above all, like all wild animals, it's afraid of fire. A chunk of burning wood should be enough to scare it off. My Molotov cocktail would probably send it skidding over the nearest horizon.'

'He's across now, Guy! He's heading our way!'

I checked the height of the sun and the time and calculated how long von Praeger would take to cross the wadi.

'Good! This is a break we didn't expect. Now we don't have to winkle him out of the command-post.'

Nadine was very taut. 'Are you just going to stay here and wait?'

'Not on your nellie, as Koen would say. We're getting across there and bringing Rankin out. This is our golden opportunity.'

'He'll see us! He can't help it. It's still hours before dark!'

'Right. He'll reach The Hill before nightfall. But we're moving out – now. He can't possibly see us descending the stairway. Once we're down we'll work our way westwards, as I did when I escaped from Rankin. Look down there at the long shadows. We'll use 'em. We'll have to choose our moment very carefully, though, so as to stay out of sight while negotiating the terrace wall.'

'If he spots us from a distance he'll send Dika to cut us off.'

'Dika will never manage the drop off the terrace. I half wish it would try. I'd like to get close to that brute with a fire-bomb.'

Nadine continued to be apprehensive. 'Are you sure it will work, Guy? What if he sights us when we cross the wadi?'

'We wait for darkness before we do cross. Until then we hide amongst the rocks.'

'What's the time?'

'Nearly four.'

'Three hours until dark! He'll be here at The Hill long before that!'

'We'll buy extra time by making him search for Koen,' I replied. 'I'll gag Koen and hide him in my *holkrans sandsteen* shelter. Praeger must find him eventually, of course, but it will take time.'

'I've got butterflies in my stomach already.'

'Let's go,' I said. 'Once we have Rankin, we're on our way.'

'Where to, Guy? In the river, or back here? What about food?'

'There's a little left which we can stretch for the river trip. We'll pick that up now. As I see it, The Hill falls out of our plan. We strike for the river during the night as fast as we can manage with Rankin to carry. There's nothing to bring us back here.'

She didn't respond and I looked at her sharply.

'I'm just being silly I suppose, darling, but I feel rather let down that The Hill isn't part of it.'

'It's the cut of the cards, I'm afraid. Now fetch the gunny-sack and we'll be on our way.'

While she went for it I kept tab on Praeger moving with ant-like deliberation down the K2 path. He was taking his time and I noticed that he carried the Mauser at the ready. I checked again on the sun. The light wasn't sharp but sickly and hazed and it appeared as if the high cloud cover had thickened during the day. The heat remained overpowering in spite of it, but there was also a new, added feeling of oppressiveness. It was as if everything was cringing away, waiting for something to happen.

During the descent we both had to hold ourselves back from rushing it and courting unnecessary risks. Praeger seemed to our over-anxious eyes to be making fast progress, whereas, in fact, he was not. He too wasted time by checking frequently

141

in the bush about him. I was careful to keep my lenses out of the sun for fear of a giveaway flash.

By the time we reached the root cage we were completely exhausted. Koen was still unconscious, though he groaned when I moved him to tie his hands more securely. Then I bundled him unceremoniously into the *holkrans sandsteen* shelter, removed his shirt and tore off a wide strip to gag him with. As a further precaution I used some of the material as a running noose round his neck and secured it to a stone. The idea was that if he moved his head or upper body the noose would choke him; if he kept still he would come to no harm. While I was busy with Koen Nadine crawled on hands and knees to the camping-spot and collected the remaining provisions.

We met again in the root cage, both tense.

'How's von Praeger progressing?' she asked.

'Slower than expected. He's not reached the edge of the wadi yet. He's like a cat on hot bricks about being ambushed.'

'He couldn't have watched us crossing in the first place or he'd have known that Koen was all right up to the point where he himself is now.'

We exchanged a glance of unspoken fear for Rankin.

Nadine said with a shudder, 'I think he tortures for kicks, Guy.'

'More than ever I wish I had some ammunition for this gun of Koen's. But since I haven't, I'm in two minds about taking it. An empty gun may bluff a human but it won't frighten Dika. It's fire we need for her.'

As I reluctantly shouldered the M-25 and the tyre lever, I saw a possible answer in the form of a dried branch of the fig tree. This soft wood would flare up if we needed it in a hurry. We'd each carry a piece of it and if Dika attacked we'd light it and keep her at bay. I hacked off two lengths but retained the machine-pistol.

Then we set off, moving cautiously from rock to rock. Von Praeger began the wadi crossing, obviously following our tracks in the sand, for he headed towards the first blocked-off gully which we had been unable to get through. I was pleased at the thought that this would mean a further delay for him. We moved as quickly as we dared, certain that we had not been spotted. When we arrived at The Hill's westernmost limit

142

we had the benefit of the deep shadow cast by the tabletop while Praeger was open to view in full sun plodding across the wadi, Dika at his side.

By the time we reached a point where we considered it safe to descend from the terrace, von Praeger was lost to view. We didn't attempt to force one of the wire-blocked gullies but plumped for an unguarded spot which offered likely-looking rock holds for the 30-foot drop. We pitched our gear and the M-25 on to the sand below and were about to start our climb down when von Praeger's signal shots echoed again through the hills.

'He's very worried about Koen,' I remarked. 'I'll see what he's up to now.'

I crawled back a short distance with my binoculars until I could see him. He had stopped, and was staring at The Hill. His pockets bulged.

'I might as well ditch the machine-pistol,' I told Nadine when I returned to her side. 'Praeger seems to have all the spare ammunition.'

'They seem to have all the cards, Guy. I daren't even think what might happen if von Praeger catches us.'

'He won't. In a couple of hours it'll be completely dark. We'll hole up until then.'

She glanced up at the soaring tabletop.

'I felt safe up there. It's like abandoning a friend.'

I looked into her eyes. 'We'll come back when this is over, I promise you.'

She did not reply, so I said gently, 'This is the only way, you know.'

It was a difficult rather than a dangerous descent, the main hazard being the crumbly sandstone which several times nearly let us down but eventually we reached the bottom safely. A temporary hiding place was provided by a huge rock close to the edge of the wadi. We lay face down in the sand behind it until the sun went down. Although we had lost sight of Praeger, we knew that by now he must hold the advantage of height on the terrace: his present position and ours were reversed.

I finally got rid of the M-25 by burying it deep in the sand. We had a drink of water and set off across the wadi, heading for the same group of hills which had sheltered me from

143

Rankin and following approximately the same course.

After a time Nadine asked, 'What when the moon comes up? Surely the light will give us away?'

'We must reach the post before then. We're making good time.'

I aimed to pick up hard ground on the K2 side of the wadi and then make our way quickly parallel to The Hill until we struck Rankin's path to the command-post which both we and Praeger had used. As we progressed farther into the thick sand our fig-tree branches became a nuisance, and I was considering abandoning them also like the machine-pistol, when the chilling laugh of a hyena echoed through the still night. It appeared to come from The Hill.

Nadine stopped in her tracks. 'Dika! It's Dika, Guy!'

'There are scores of other hyenas about,' I comforted her. 'It's not necessarily Praeger's.'

The sobbing scream echoed and re-echoed again.

'They sound worse than they really are,' I went on. 'They're not near enough for us to worry about.'

We trudged on but Nadine remained apprehensive as a general chorus got under way. It was impossible to pinpoint where any one scream originated because of the cross-echoes.

After what seemed an interminable time the going under-foot started to harden and we knew we were across. Then some dead trees loomed and we changed direction, using them as cover to work our way eastwards towards where we knew Rankin's path must intersect our course. The Hill blanked out a slice of star-horizon; we could not distinguish it clearly beyond a dark looming mass.

'Guy,' observed Nadine. 'There's no light in the command-post.'

I didn't want to let my fears regarding Rankin run away with me. 'Perhaps Rankin's in his cave. A light wouldn't show. The whole place is too high to see from our present angle anyway.'

'I don't like it,' she said, with a shiver.

'We'll know pretty soon what's happening. We should hit the path any moment now. Praeger and Koen seem to be keeping mighty low, too.'

'Do you think Koen's come round by now?'

'Sure to have. He'll be after our blood for sure.'

'What if the two of them are also heading for Rankin's cave?'

'We've got a good start. By the time we reach the cave the moon will be up. We're bound to sight them crossing the wadi – if they are.'

Despite our long trudge, Nadine managed to put on speed. We kept on for a while but then I began to worry that we might overshoot the path. The sky was somewhat lighter in anticipation of the approaching moonrise, but we dared not risk showing a light. However, our anxiety vanished when we found the big rock where we had sold Koen the phoney treasure story. We gave ourselves a short rest and then set off on the steep climb. It took longer than we had expected and by the time we reached the top the moon was above the horizon. By its light we found the plane's wheels for our litter, and some strut wire. As we suspected, the tyres had been destroyed but the wheels themselves were undamaged.

The command-post lay in a shadow unbroken by any gleam of light.

'It's too easy!' Nadine said in a low voice. 'I don't like it, Guy. Something's wrong.'

'Let's get up higher where we can see down into the post.'

'Look, the door's open!'

The handlines, we saw, were still in position and our uneasiness grew. We made a circuit to reach higher ground. The Hill became visible as the moon grew stronger but of Praeger and Koen there was no sign. We were feeling our way over the rough going when I stumbled over a mound of earth. There was no mistaking its grave-shape.

'Oh God!' cried Nadine.

I took her by the arm and led her away.

'Peter – or Rankin?' she whispered.

'We'll soon find out.'

The better vantage position did not in fact provide the answer: the enclosure was deserted and the cave mouth was a black shadow. Yet the weak light and deep shadows made it impossible to pick out any details.

'I'm going in, Nadine.'

'No, Guy, it might be a trap.'

'I must risk it. Rankin's the key to everything.'

'Is – or was?'

145

'If that's Rankin – ' I jerked my head in the direction of the mound – 'it changes everything. If it isn't, our original plan stands and we've got to get him out.'

I checked the wick of my improvised bomb and tested my cigarette lighter behind my hand to see if it was sparking properly.

'Do you see anything at The Hill, Nadine? Your eyes are better than mine.'

'No . . .' she replied, a little uncertainly. 'No, Guy, nothing. Von Praeger couldn't have doubled back and arrived here before us, could he?'

'He could, but it's unlikely.'

'Don't go, Guy.'

'I must, my darling.'

'I'm coming too.'

'I'd rather you stayed.'

'The whole plan's ours, not yours or mine '

'Is this still the way you want it?'

'Yes. We could have run after we fixed Koen. We didn't.'

I gave her the tyre lever. 'We won't want the truncheons: Dika's not here.'

She shivered and kept silent. We made our way quickly and quietly to the old wall and the rock crossing. The half-open door was unnerving; it beckoned yet repelled. We used the handlines and trod silently. When we reached the door I eased it wide and paused but there was neither sound nor movement. We gave it a few minutes and then, with the bomb at the ready, I led the way inside. The place was deserted; utterly silent.

We had begun to make our way towards the cave entrance when a subdued moan came from the interior. We froze, but when it was repeated we felt our way inside the kinked entrance until I was sure that a light could not be detected from the outside.

I flicked on my lighter: the tiny flame, by emphasizing the shadows, made Rankin's face look worse than it probably was. It was hideously pulped and his lips were swollen; he had dragged himself along the floor and had stripped off his bandages in doing so, leaving a blood-stained trail. He was spread-eagled on his chest with his right hand extended, the fist clenched, and the left doubled under him.

146

I knelt down and held the light close to his eyes.

'Rankin! It's Bowker – Guy Bowker!'

He moaned again and his face tied in a spasm.

'Water – quick!' I said to Nadine, who stood stunned at the sight. 'No, wait, he's trying to speak.'

Something incomprehensible bubbled from his lips but neither Nadine nor I could make it out.

His head did not seem able to support its own weight and fell sideways in my hand. I thought he was dead but he managed to speak, and this time we understood.

'They were cut diamonds, Guy – from The Hill.' Both of us craned towards him and we heard his next words distinctly.

'The hyena's blanket.'

'What does it mean, Rankin? *What does it mean?*'

He tried to articulate again but it was lost.

'Water! Get some water, Nadine!'

She rose and he threw out his arm in a sort of jerky, un-controlled movement as if to stop her and something fell out of his fist and rolled out of range of the tiny light.

I had an inspiration. I passed Nadine the lighter and got the top off Koen's half-jack. We tipped back Rankin's head and poured some of the strong liquor into his mouth.

He didn't open his eyes but said in a weak, faltering voice. 'It's the way in . . . the King's Messenger takes you there . . .'

We couldn't get him to speak again, and ten minutes later he died. We found a lantern and watched him die without being able to do anything for him. After the final death-rattle we searched the floor for the thing which had fallen from his hand and found it easily because it shone faintly with a curious glow.

It was a large dark blue hexagonal bead.

CHAPTER THIRTEEN

The yellow flame of the lantern was an oasis of normality in the cave's grim interior and we clung to its slight cheer under the shock impact of Rankin's death. We knew we ran a risk in burning a light but this was masked by its position in the longer leg of the L-section. At the moment we simply couldn't bear the dark. We stood close together near the lantern for comfort, our backs turned on Rankin's body sprawled upon the floor.

'I've never seen anything like this.' Nadine's voice was wobbly. 'What did he mean, *King's Messenger*?'

'I haven't a clue. It's as mysterious as *hyena's blanket*.'

It cost me an effort not to turn towards the body, as though I was still hoping to extract the mystery from Rankin.

Nadine said in a small voice, 'I wish we hadn't been here for . . . for his end. What he said means that *hyena's blanket* isn't just a phrase von Praeger cooked up. It's real, something terrible. I would rather not have heard.'

'Rankin knew he was finished by the time we found him. I believe he was trying to make amends for what he'd done to me. If only he'd gone a stage farther! What he did manage only serves to compound the mystery.'

'*King's Messenger* – my mind's a blank.'

The great bead was about two inches long and three-quarters of an inch across, with a large hole through the centre. The hexagonal facets were beautifully worked. Even the poor light seemed to penetrate to its heart, which glowed with a kind of lustrous, regal hue somewhere between dark blue and indigo. We turned it this way and that.

'I simply can't think straight with Rankin lying there,' she said.

'I'm not too bright myself. Let's go into the kitchen cave.'

'I'd rather be outside.'

'The moonlight makes it too dangerous. It's anyway not strong enough if we want to examine this thing more closely.'

Rankin's last words churned in my brain and a score of might-have-beens crowded in at the sight of the twisted face as we stepped past the body on our way farther in. From the trail of bandages and bloodstains it was possible to reconstruct his last movements: they led from the stretcher into the inner cave and back.

I pointed this out to Nadine. 'It looks as though Praeger didn't get anything out of him. When he'd finished his hellishness he left, and Rankin somehow or other managed to make his way into the inner cave. I'd guess that he then collected the "King's Messenger" from some hiding place and was struggling out again when we arrived.'

It was a relief to reach the kitchen and be away from the body but I was still very uneasy.

'This place is a trap now, Nadine. If Praeger and Koen walk in we're sunk.'

'But you barred the door, Guy.'

'If I could climb over the gateway, so can Koen. We mustn't stay long. We'll throw everything away if we do.'

Nadine said quietly. 'There's only one place where we can go now, isn't there, after what Rankin said?'

'The Hill.'

'It holds the key to your innocence, somehow. Rankin made that plain.'

I echoed his words. 'They were cut diamonds – from The Hill.'

'Hyena's blanket – King's Messenger!'

'There can't be any diamonds at The Hill, Nadine! Dammit, it's sandstone: crumbly rotten sandstone, not diamond-bearing gravel!'

'If you're sure of that, then that leaves only the possibility of a cache there. That would tie in with Rankin's remark about the "King's Messenger" being the way in. But "hyena's blanket" . . . !'

'Let's keep our cool,' I interrupted. 'Let's also play this step by step and keep realities firmly in mind. That applies especially to the geography of The Hill. We must rule out linking the hyena's blanket with the sort of wild improbabilities von Praeger fell for – the Dika business, for example.'

'Let's accept it as a fact that your grandfather used the words as a code. He didn't know anything about hyenas or The Hill, as far as we know. He'd never been here: had your father?'

I gestured in the direction of Rankin's body. 'We'll never know, now.'

She tossed the 'King's Messenger' up and down and the blue fire burned in its heart.

'Why call a bead *the King's Messenger*? At least we can thank our stars that he came clean and revealed that it was linked with the way in.'

'To what? We know no more about that than about anything else in this infuriating business.'

149

'Cast your mind over The Hill's layout and it's pretty apparent that the way in to whatever Rankin intended must lie on the summit.'

My mind jumped ahead of our reasoning and I saw the answer in a flash.

'*Isifuba!* The *isifuba* board! One of the pieces was missing!'

I took the bead from her with excited fingers.

'It could be, Nadine! This could be it!'

'They were mosaic stones, Guy, not beads. They were decorative pieces in a pavement.'

'How do we know? We didn't explore. All we saw was a strange collection of coloured stones. We don't know what they really are.'

'Then the sooner we get back there and find out, the better!'

'Rankin wouldn't have cached anything where he couldn't get at it fairly easily.'

However, as I speculated further the balloon burst.

'No, Nadine, it can't be! It all presupposes that there was an excavation trench there previously, leading to the underground chamber. That only came to light with the archaeological expedition. It must be somewhere else on the tabletop.'

'No, I think you're wrong! Dr Drummond got on to the underground chamber in the first place because he spotted what he called a sinkhole. The present trench is only a development of it. The hole where we entered has been there all along, long before the expedition arrived on the scene.'

'We were there!' I exclaimed bitterly. 'My God, we were right there: we had the solution in our hands!'

'But we didn't have this.' She indicated the bead. 'We're guessing still, but our line of thinking sounds good to me.'

'And if we're correct, Koen and Praeger are now in possession. Maybe they're working on the *isifuba* board at this very moment. Perhaps that's why we haven't seen anything of them,' I added.

'That's assuming Rankin blew the gaff. There's an additional reason against that. Didn't you see the mess as we came in? Von Praeger had ransacked every single item from the workshop.'

'I'd overlooked that. It looked like a hurricane's trail.'

I drew her close and drew her face up to mine.

'You see where all this is leading, Nadine? We've plumped

for Praeger's own line of thinking.'

'The other half of the Cullinan.'

'It could be – and yet it needn't be. We know from Praeger himself how he arrived at his deduction about another huge diamond. The actual secret may in fact be something entirely different.'

'But it has to do with diamonds, Guy. Rankin said so.'

'My innocence has to do with diamonds,' I replied grimly. 'We're at the cross-roads again, Nadine. All we have is a lot of damnably tantalizing loose ends.'

'Could you walk away from it now, Guy? – I couldn't.'

'Then that's settled. The Hill it is.'

She ran the smooth surface of the 'King's Messenger' over my face, as if she were sketching me with an artist's chalk.

'I don't fear The Hill, my darling. It has given me everything I want.'

I continued to be restless and edgy at the thought of our being trapped in the cave.

'Don't let's rush our fences after we leave here,' I said. 'Breaking through Praeger's lines at The Hill will be tough, make no mistake. Nor must we let any emotional spin-off from Rankin's death interfere with clear thinking.'

'We've decided; and I'm happy.'

It was clear that our resolve had given her an immense shot in the arm.

'After Praeger's outfit, the moonlight is enemy number two,' I went on. 'The shadows will be risky as we move along the edge of the hills but frankly it's the open crossing of the wadi that scares me.'

'Must we retrace the route we took coming here?'

'There's no alternative but I don't like it.'

'We've beaten them all along the line so far, Guy, and we can do it again. We've simply got to get back to the *isifuba* board.'

'And darkness is the only time for doing it. Let's face it, we can't hike for miles, break through Praeger's defences, climb the secret stairway and set about solving the problem on the summit all in a few hours tonight. We're going to be pretty short of sleep, even by the time we've reached The Hill.'

'I'm fine, Guy – ready for anything.'

'We must also make up our minds that once we do reach

the tabletop we'll have to sit out a siege there. Five days is about our maximum with limited food. After that what happens is anyone's guess.'

'We do have the edge on them as far as food goes.' She indicated Rankin's shelves. 'Let's dump all this over the precipice. Then even if they come back here they won't last out as long as we do.'

I smiled at her enthusiasm. 'We'll eat some of it first – now – and take away what little we can carry. I'll start the dumping right away and make a recce at the same time.'

First, I covered Rankin's body with a blanket, gathered up an armful of supplies and crept out on hands and knees to peer cautiously over the breastwork. I needn't have been so concerned: the light was hazy and diffused, and the country-side far from being illuminated. The high thin cloud which had masked the sky during the day had thickened and, to the north-east – the weather quarter – a long black line showed.

'Nadine! Come and look at this!'

I must have sounded more excited than I knew, for she came running and I had to warn her to keep down.

The cloud bank – it looked almost like a front at sea – appeared about a hand's-breadth above the horizon. But the moon which had travelled about a quarter of its way across the sky was consequently ahead of the oncoming bank.

'It all depends on how fast that cloud is coming up,' I said. 'It could overtake the moon within an hour. If it does, we'll be home and dry. It'll be a dark, dark night.'

'Can we risk waiting here so long? – Guy! I just saw something!'

'Where? Where, Nadine?'

'Near your camp, slightly to the right – no, I can't be sure now. I thought I saw it.'

We craned our necks, trying to pierce the uncertain light but couldn't make out anything.

'It moved,' she breathed. 'It seemed to flit from one rock to another.'

'The bastards!' I exclaimed. 'It looks as if they're on the alert. And there's Dika too.'

'We'll make it, Guy.'

I pitched the supplies carefully over the parapet to avoid clatter and when I had done that, I tried to measure the respective rates of climb of the cloud bank and the moon in relation to the stars. Eventually I gave it up, concluding, however, that by and large the bank appeared to be gaining. After we had eaten I checked again and returned to Nadine, feeling much happier.

'Now I'm sure. This is a break we couldn't have foreseen. We'll hang around here until it's dim enough for a safe crossing via the handlines. Then we'll put as much distance behind us as we can while the going's good.'

The ensuing minutes dragged like hours and we became more and more impatient to leave; the moon and the rising cloud bank were like two tortoises competing for the world's slowest race in the sky.

Eventually, however, the distance between them did narrow to the point of safety and the haziness increased to a general blurred dimness in which The Hill was swallowed up.

Then we left. As a precaution I ripped the handlines loose after we had crossed but I had to leave the door ajar, as I dared not risk being seen climbing over if I should decide to barricade it from the inside.

We made our way from patch of shadow to patch of shadow down the steep path off K2, keeping a watchful eye on the wadi; but before we were halfway down the moon lost its race with the cloud bank and the night became pitch black. We moved as quickly as we dared, speaking in whispers only. Nadine took the lead, finding her way with surprising certainty, apparently untiring and buoyed up by the thought of returning to the The Hill.

It was after midnight when we arrived at the western limit of our route and made a right-angled turn to cross the wadi. The whole sky was now blacked out: it had taken place without so much as a whisper of wind at ground level. To my tight-strung senses this silent blackness seemed to add a touch of the sinister.

'If the drought should end at this moment we could find ourselves in trouble,' I told Nadine. 'The wadi could become a quagmire. If it does rain we'll be trapped on this side. Daybreak is our deadline, remember.'

'It's very hot and oppressive. It does feel as though it could be working up for something.'

'If we lose the boat in a flash flood we're done for.'

153

'I know, I know. Nevertheless I'm quite drunk with excitement!'

I kissed her. 'The Hill alone is enough to send you on a trip, any time.'

'Any time – but not without you, my darling.'

We rested briefly before crossing the wadi. By the time we were over we were both stumping along mechanically, exhausted.

It was with relief that we found our course had brought us directly to the boulder which had previously sheltered us.

'We're in no shape to climb the stairway,' I said. 'What we need is a good couple of hours' sleep.'

'Isn't that rather tempting the gods, seeing we've got this far safely.'

'The most dangerous part is ahead. We'll need everything we've got for it. I'll wake, all right. I've got a sort of built-in alarm in my brain.'

She nestled down against me and it seemed like only minutes, not hours later, that I jerked awake.

'What is it, Guy?'

'Wind. Listen!'

We heard its rustling approach among the kiln-dry grains of sand and shortly afterwards we were smothered in dust from a passing squall.

'The weather's really lining up on our side,' I said. 'If the wind goes on like this it'll deafen Praeger and Koen to any sound we make.

'Do we have to go near them?'

'Right past, if they're at the camp. There's no other way to the secret stairway.'

'What's the order of battle from now on, then?' There was the slightest tremor in her voice.

'First we have to shin up the terrace: it'll have to be done carefully, feeling our way for holds. I don't much fancy that in the dark. Then we'll backtrack on yesterday's route until we're in the vicinity of the camp. After that it's hands and knees and by guess and by God until we get to the root cage. You hang on to me – I'll lead now. Later on in the stairway you'll be the boss. Let's go!'

'I love you. I'm going to say that over and over to myself

all the way and I'm going to say it again to you when we're safe.'

'I love you, Nadine. If I don't get another chance . . .'

Her mouth came hard against mine and we tasted the blown sand on each other's lips.

'I won't have you say that, ever! We'll make it. We must, we will.'

We set off into the gusting wind, which made an unpleasant but effective cover. It was so dark we had to link hands. We reckoned we must be near the camp when we picked up a foot-path, and we dropped flat to a crawl. When the ground began to rise we knew we must be slap against the camp's protecting boulders but it was too dark to make them out. One behind the other we went on to higher ground, moving only when we had the wind's sound to mask our own; lying, scarcely breathing, during the intervals. Once on the slope proper we cast about for a time in the inky blackness until we found the root screen. It was with a sense of immense relief that we found it was deserted. We made rapid progress up the secret stairway and by the time we reached the tricky section we began to feel a growing confidence that we had achieved our objective.

'There's only one real danger point left,' I said in a low voice. 'Those last few final steps of the climb. If they're not waiting to ambush us there, we can be pretty certain that we've broken through.'

'Let's wait until day,' she whispered back.

'No, it's better to attempt it now. It's just on dawn anyway – the cloud cover's delaying the light. They've had nothing to alert them that we're here.'

'I'll lead then, Guy.'

'No. This is my party.'

I worked my way up and my heart pounded when my head rose to a level where I would be an easy target. I couldn't see a hand's-breadth ahead and I took it slowly, hoping that a possible ambusher would not hear my exertions. Finally I hauled myself on to the summit and when Nadine appeared we crept silently away to the underground chamber. On the summit the light was slightly better and the first signs of day were apparent in the east through the cloud, making the out-

155

lines of objects vaguely discernible. The wind was stronger and less gusty than at ground level, with a tendency to hold steady from one direction.

We went straight to the *isifuba* board, of course. Immediately I switched on the flashlight I realized that we would have to work fast if we were to discover anything before it failed altogether. Nevertheless, when Nadine produced the 'King's Messenger', the bead had the power to pick up the faint light.

'Why didn't Dr Drummond clean up the board?' I asked. 'There's a lot of sand and grit here that we'll have to get rid of before we can begin to examine it properly.'

'There wasn't time and the layer wasn't thick enough to impede our first tentative look at it . . . Guy! Why, it can't be!'

'What, Nadine?'

'There must have been hundreds of wind storms over the years – why then isn't the dust inches deep in here? There's nothing to stop its entering. These mosaics should have been completely obliterated. And yet, look! There's some dust, but it's certainly not the coating of centuries.'

'What are you trying to say?'

'Rankin. He kept it clean.'

'By God you're right!'

'Yes. And another piece of the jigsaw falls into place. Rankin kept it free of dust because . . . because he was using the *isifuba* board!'

She snatched up the torch to shine it more closely while I started to puff away the fine covering layer. As I did so my eyes came close to the glowing 'King's Messenger' which Nadine had put down.

'Look at this, Nadine! Here, the torch!'

I directed the beam into its heart.

'There's a chevron pattern cut inside!'

Nadine craned forward to see and her hands rested on the mosaics.

'Guy! Here's one that's loose!'

'Damn this light! It's dying on us!'

What had appeared to be an inlaid coloured circle revealed itself under Nadine's excited fingers as another bead. It was smaller than the 'King's Messenger', round and not hexagonal, and deep green in colour.

'Look, look, it's also got a pattern cut inside!'

The fast failing light showed us a different design from the 'King's Messenger': this one was a triangle etched above two lateral bars.

Then I explored with my finger-tips in the hole it had come from, and at the base I detected a stubby little shaft, smooth as ivory, with some notches in it.

'Nadine – give me the "King's Messenger"!'

I tried fitting it to the notches but all it did was to revolve loosely.

'I believe we're on to something!'

'What do you make of it, Guy?'

'I'm guessing, but the beads and notches could be some form of locking tumblers – like a primitive lock.'

'Let's try the others . . .'

I sat bolt upright in astonishment.

Nadine looked at me. 'What is it?'

'The lay-out of the board itself. Look. There are three squares each way. It reminds me of a so-called magical square whose numbers always add up to 15 whichever way you total it . . .'

'What? . . . I don't follow!'

'The ancients used to set out figures on a square in an order which was supposed to endow it with magical properties: a top line of three squares containing the numbers 4, 9 and 2; a second having 3, 5 and 7; and a third with 8, 1 and 6. Add it across, down or diagonally and the answer is always 15.'

'Where does that get us?'

'My guess is that those numbers will tally with the number and design of the slots inside the beads. If we fit them correctly into their corresponding positions on the board I believe we'll be able to move this whole slab of rock – like opening the door of a combination safe . . . blast!'

The flashlight had flickered and finally died.

Nadine found my hands in the dimness. 'I'm frightened of what we might uncover, Guy.'

I tried to revive the torch and juggled with it but with no result.

'Most of all we need light – daylight.'

'I'll slip outside and see how the sky looks,' she said.

'Right. Meanwhile I'll have another bash at this damn torch.'

The entrance was a greyish rectangle and I gave Nadine a leg up through it and continued battling with the flashlight. After a couple of minutes I was rewarded with a faint gleam and immediately went back to the mosaics, praying the light would last. It was only the last kick of the batteries, however, and I achieved nothing before it eventually fizzled out. I stood for a while longer, engrossed in the puzzle.

All at once I realized that Nadine had not returned.

I went to the entrance and was about to call her when I saw two figures struggling on the skyline at the top of the excavation shaft.

Koen held Nadine fast with one hand clamped round her mouth and was dragging her towards the secret stairway.

I stood transfixed while a wave of cold fear and hot rage swept over me and then I reached for the only weapon I could think of: the torch, which I had dropped. As I felt for it my fingers encountered the ivory arm guard. In place of my surge of confused emotions came an icy clarity of purpose. I slipped it on and threw myself through the opening.

I leapt up the shaft and ducked behind the fortification wall running to the edge of the cliff. I saw Nadine break half free from Koen's grip: he whipped out the derringer with its flick-blade and struck at her. I saw her sleeve rip and she went limp. It took all my self-control to stop myself flying at his throat. It was only when he spoke that I realized Nadine was still alive.

'You bloody little bitch! Treasure, eh? I'll teach you!'

I could not make out her choked reply but he laughed unpleasantly and dragged her farther towards the edge.

'It's you we want alive – he'll come after you, all right . . .'

I sprinted, crouching behind the wall, until I was between him and the head of the stairway, right at the stone post overlooking the drop.

I steeled myself as I heard him say, 'Wait till the Doc starts to give your boy-friend a work-out like Rankin! If he doesn't come clean, you will. You'll wish you'd torn your own tits off before the Doc's finished with you!'

I couldn't see him because of the post but I heard his shuffle on the other side. With it still between us, I threw my karate-arm encased in the arm guard round his neck and trapped his head against the post and with my right I jerked his gun hand full stretch to send any shot into the ground. I felt – I could not see – Nadine fall clear.

Koen lashed out instantly at my shins but he had overlooked the post and gave a strangled grunt of pain. Then he dug his bull neck hard down and tried to rip my arm with his teeth but the ivory guard saved me.

He was tremendously strong and I soon realized that he would either break free or tear his derringer hand loose, then shoot or stab me at a range of less than a foot. I threw all my strength into trying to throttle him, at the same time attempting to kick the derringer away; but he hung on. He was a clever fighter and, once he realized I couldn't choke him, weighed up the odds with lightning speed. He managed to loosen my hold on his throat a little and swallowed a lungful of air. It seemed to give him added energy and he tore the gun half out of my grasp. Sweat poured off me as I tightened my stranglehold, jamming my face hard against the post as I sought purchase.

With the sudden flash of thought that is born of deadly danger, my mind took in what the stone post was really for. It was notched at the height of man's throat: the hook on the arm guard was the complementary half of a deadly garrotting set-up. One had only to trap one's victim's head against the post in order to break his neck with the hook. But Koen was facing the wrong way for it to operate for me.

So I feinted and shifted all my force to his gun arm and at the same time deliberately eased off his throat. He fell for it and swung to face the post, exposing his neck to the hook – and the kill.

It was all over in seconds and needed surprisingly little effort. I hung on when he went limp and the derringer discharged harmlessly into the ground. I think it must have been a dying nerve reflex which tightened his finger on the trigger. When his body started to sag I braced my knee against the post and jerked him backwards over the edge of the cliff.

I climbed slowly over the wall and walked towards Nadine, who was still crouched where Koen had thrown her, her glorious hair dusty and dishevelled and a smear of dirt from Koen's hand across her mouth.

When I came up to her, we simply stared at one another as if in a trance and then I leaned forward and kissed the tiny trickle of blood coming through her torn sleeve. It was salty and warm and near to her breast.

The gesture brought her with a blind rush into my arms, her mouth crushed against mine, her words hardly distinguishable through her sobs. She tried to kiss and smile and cry all at the same time, caressing my face and murmuring endearments as if her heart would break. 'Oh my love, my darling, my beloved . . . there aren't words for this sort of thing . . . I want to say prayers and incantations and your name all mixed up together but they won't come . . . Guy, Guy, Guy!'

She shook all over and held me: she loosened my arm and slipped off the ivory guard; she drew me back farther from the drop.

Suddenly there was the whang and whine of a ricochet off the stone post and almost simultaneously the blast of a shot from below.

'Praeger!' I said, moving still farther away. 'But I'm sure he can't see us: that's simply blind anger on account of Koen. The hell with him! Before anything else I'm going to attend to that wound of yours.'

'It isn't a wound, it's just a scratch. It was only meant to scare me.'

Nevertheless, I bound up the cut with my handkerchief, thinking that Koen must have been an expert with a knife to have been so precise. As I did so Nadine winced as another harmless bullet bounced off the cliff and screamed into space.

'We're under siege, Guy.'

'In more ways than one,' I replied. 'Just look at that sky. I've seldom seen anything more threatening.'

It was a wild-looking morning. In the early light the clouds were black and ominous and they seemed to block every point of the compass as far as the eye could reach. They were low, too, and the horizon was in-drawn, which added to the feeling of being hemmed-in.

'This poor light puts paid to our doing anything more about the *isifuba* board for the moment,' I said.

The terror of her experience was ebbing fast but it had left behind a lovely light in her eyes.

'Let's get our breath back before we start anything else

exciting. To begin with, let's learn to live with a siege.'

I caught her light-hearted mood. 'Right! Then the first thing on my list is to clean myself up at the spring.'

'Philistine!' she mocked. 'No soul! Mysteries and magic pavements go overboard in favour of a bath!'

'They'll keep. My dusty body won't.'

At the spring, which had fashioned a crude basin out of the rock by virtue of centuries of dripping, I stripped and rejoiced in the cool water.

I rejoined Nadine at the small pyramid of coloured pebbles. The colour had come back into her face and she was smiling and serene.

'You're not going to have the edge on me – I'm next!'

'It's glorious; absolute heaven.'

She kissed me before going and her eyes were very bright. I said, 'I'll keep a watch on Praeger.'

'I'll be back.'

There was a shade of meaning about the way she said it which I didn't catch. I watched her trim figure disappear, then I moved carefully under cover to the strongpoint at the head of the stairway. There was no need for my glasses because I could see Koen lying near my camp with his head slewed unnaturally to one side. Von Praeger, with Dika, was near, his rifle barrel resting on a boulder and aimed at the summit. For a moment I toyed with the idea of taking a pot-shot at him with the derringer but its short range would have been just the waste of a bullet. I wanted him to know that we were in good heart, so I collected one of the shaped stone missiles and pitched it to fall as close to him as I could judge.

The result was spectacular. Von Praeger blazed off a whole volley of shots indiscriminately at the spot where the rock had fallen, the stairway and the rocks all round my hiding place. When the racket had died down I risked a glance below but he was nowhere to be seen.

Then, without apparent reason, but by a compulsion I could not explain, I felt my attention drawn to the tabletop itself.

Nadine was standing by the little pyramid, her hair as black as the lowering storm. She was looking across at me, her lips parted, her eyes like stars. Her breasts, dappled with an aureole of drops from the spring, shone luminously white against the backdrop of the storm.

She was completely naked.

The blood throbbed in my ears; then I was taking her to me. A dozen strides covered the space which separated us. The tiny living muscles at the corners of her deep eyes spoke a world of obvious and emphatic messages as well as nuances of doubt about her nakedness, a host of nerve-tingling ambiguities, expressing all things since woman was woman.

'It had to be here!' she whispered. 'Love me – love me right here!'

And the pulse which before had been only in her eyes spread into the thighs and breasts thrust hard against me.

But the blaze of emotion which overwhelmed us was matched by the storm, of which we became oblivious. All I know is that a moment before the thunderbolt struck the pyramid and exploded I caught a glimpse of it flaming towards us like a meteor and I threw our locked bodies to the ground out of its path. Then our spellbound world erupted in a burst of flame and dust and at the same time the solid rock under us seemed to split and heave like an earthquake. A fissure opened next to us and raced across the summit like a seam unthreading and there was a heavy rumbling from the heart of The Hill as it started to break in two: while on the river side the tabletop seemed to be toppling over the edge in an avalanche.

Fear emptied veins which a moment before had been pulsing with love.

We clung in terror now to one another while rumble succeeded rumble. Until eventually everything grew quiet, except for the sound of the sluicing rain beginning.

CHAPTER FOURTEEN

The individual drops were huge, falling cold and raw on to our naked bodies and making muddy little explosions all round us. The horizon was down and the east was a dirty grey; the rest of the sky was low and black and hostile. There was a hot, wet smell from the demolished cairn, like steam round an old-fashioned locomotive. Our cold bodies clung together and I noticed the tiny rivulets of rain that chased down her breasts and puckered nipples. So we lay in an ebb tide of reaction until pools from the downpour began to form round us. Then there was another small rockfall. We couldn't stay where we were.

We sat up. Her face was white and strained and her eyes great dark pools. She drew my own face against hers and made a tent over our heads with her long hair. It was half-dry inside and warm compared with the cold rain, and the smell of her hair and skin was sweet in my nostrils. She touched my cheeks and eyes and lips with her finger-tips, then kissed me with cold lips.

'It's the big thing. We'll never know about it unless we have it here.'

'Darling,' I said. 'Darling, darling.'

The rain broke through her hair and drew an icy line between us where our bodies met.

'We'll come back. It's not for now. The moment's past.'

'What made the bolt strike the cairn?'

'Some special attraction in those stones, perhaps. The Hill people didn't see it as a heap of stones but as a person, a sort of deity who kept a watchful eye on lovers in order to bind them in their vows.'

I laughed shakily. 'It certainly put on a king-size show for us.'

'Queen-size.' She tried to smile, too. 'Which reminds me. All I've got on is the queen's ring, It's a good thing I didn't leave my clothes in a heap at the spring instead of here.'

We found our soaking garments and dressed while the rain drove down and it became darker. It must have been about breakfast-time. Nadine had her flying-jacket and tucked her hair under the hood. It seemed to emphasize the shadows under her eyes. I hunched up my shoulders and tried to protect myself against the rain but it was useless.

Suddenly I exclaimed. 'We've lost the "King's Messenger"!'

'No, Guy, here it is. I still had sense enough when I left the spring to put it in my pocket.'

I surveyed the tabletop with dismay. 'No "King's Messenger" or anything else is going to be much use to us now, Nadine.'

'What a shambles!'

Between us and the way into the underground chamber a crevasse about ten feet wide had opened. It narrowed in the direction of the secret stairway and widened on the opposite side facing the river. Thousands of tons of soil and rock had collapsed into it, forming a rubble-littered sloping ramp from the summit to the terrace.

The implication struck us both.

'It's the end of The Hill, Guy! Look, anyone can simply walk to the top now. It's not even a climb.'

'The rock supporting the tabletop must have been eroded and rotten and ready to split and the thunderbolt did the rest. We must get off here – quick. Look there!'

We were only about a dozen feet away from the crevasse, and soil and rocks were tumbling into it as the rain undermined them.

Nadine looked with anguish towards the underground chamber.

'The *isifuba* board, Guy! We just can't abandon it!'

'The whole place has probably caved in. We can't risk our necks trying to find out. Anyway, the crevasse is too wide to get across.'

'Where can we go, Guy?'

'My boat – down that ramp. It's the only route left open.'

Another tremor shook The Hill.

'It's breaking up under us, Nadine! Hurry!'

The tattoo of rain sent muddy runnels pouring over the lip of the crevasse but we picked a spot which didn't look too dangerous. I went first. It was only an eight-foot drop to the ramp but it felt like eight hundred. I was muddied to the knees when I landed and so was Nadine in spite of my help. Soaked, cold and dejected, we struggled and sloshed down the slope with our arms linked. The farther we plodded, the trickier the going became, as we stubbed our feet and shins against obstacles we couldn't see. The rain, too, became heavier.

'It's developing into a cloudburst!' I called out. 'If this goes on the river will come down!'

There was a heavy rumble and we froze in our tracks, wondering whether a new avalanche was on its way which might overwhelm us, but it was thunder we heard. Flickering tongues of lightning leapt from cloud to cloud, illuminating the terrace below us like a gigantic flash-bulb. It was the onset of a new spectacular display which blinded, deafened and frightened us. At the same time the wind steadied into the north-east and, since we were heading north, it whipped the sheets of rain into our faces, which had the effect of making the downpour seem to increase in intensity. Everything was now a water-swept haze; the sun, too, had given up and all there was left in the way of light was an opaque dimness, like twilight.

We still had about halfway to go down the moraine-like incline and plugged ahead doggedly, heads down, slipping and stumbling, sometimes falling waist-deep into softer patches until we looked like scarecrows. Finally, at the level of the terrace, the crevasse broadened out to about three times its upper width. On the open terrace we felt more exposed to the vivid flashes of lightning and one of these underwrote our danger when it struck the wire fence and blazed along it like a magnesium flare. We made our way as quickly as we could through ankle-deep water and where the terrace ended, fronting the river, we found torrents of dirty water pouring over like a small flood. We negotiated the wire where I had originally cut it and it was like crawling under a small water-fall. The thought of another lightning strike to the wire lent wings to our crossing feet and we breathed easier when we were safely through and across the ladder with which I had bridged the rolls of wire. Then we reached the outer limits of the river bed proper and squelched our way slowly and tediously through a semi-liquid mess of mud until we located the boat by the palm clump, and crawled thankfully aboard out of the storm's uproar.

It was dry and snug in the tiny, low cabin and stuffy, too, because the air in it had heated during the blazing days and had had no opportunity to disperse. The main cabin was for'ard and there was another smaller one aft: they were linked by an open, self-draining cockpit. I had named her the *Empress of Baobab* because she had bulges where no craft should have had bulges. As a boat she was a herring-gutted bitch; as a sanctuary from the storm she was heaven.

It was difficult to hear one another speak above the drum-beat of the rain on the cabin's thin aluminium roof.

'Get dry and help yourself to some of my clothes from the

165

locker,' I told Nadine. 'I'm going over the side with a rope to make her fast. I'm scared of a sudden flood. If the river does come down we could be wrecked.'

'Isn't there an engine?'

'Of sorts. It's seen better days. It wouldn't hold her head into a flood.'

The wind caused me more concern than the rain which it brought slanting and cutting into my face when I opened the door. At sea it would have been considered a moderate gale. It blustered in from one direction only, the north-east, and this is what puzzled and worried me. A normal thunderstorm is usually accompanied by strong erratic gusts, but judging by the lightning flashes, the force of this one was already falling off in intensity. Yet the powerful wind continued.

I took a rope and dropped into the mud, which gave off a kind of stale flatus. The palm seemed firmly enough anchored though its trunk was whipping and the tattered fronds streamed like a battle ensign. I was making the rope fast when a brilliant flash spotlit the streaming river front. By its light I saw a propeller turning in the wind some distance up the main river channel and I realized immediately that it was von Praeger's plane. I finished double-lashing the moorings and then hurried back to Nadine.

'Now we know where von Praeger landed,' I explained. 'I wouldn't have thought it possible unless I'd seen for myself.'

Nadine had changed into a shirt, sweater and pants of mine. She'd rolled up the bottoms and tied back her wet hair. There was an air about her almost as withdrawn as on that day I had seen her in the trench during the expedition, and her eyes were equally inscrutable.

She replied almost detachedly, 'A plane can't offer him any shelter.'

'No. But I know that if I had been in his place I would have beaten it to Rankin's cave post-haste once The Hill started falling down.'

Her eyelids flickered when I said 'The Hill' as though I'd been discussing a person.

'Yes.' Her tone remained non-committal.

'I've got a solid-meths stove in the for'ard cabin and some coffee – I think we could both use some. While I'm still soaked I'll run and fetch it.'

I wondered what was eating her and I found out when I had changed and we'd had our coffee almost in silence.

'Guy – are we going to run away? Is this the end of The Hill for us?'

'I hadn't thought that far, Nadine. We needed shelter and safety and the boat was our obvious bet.'

'Do you *want* to go back, Guy?'

'My innocence is locked up there and so is whatever Praeger is after.'

'The other half of the Cullinan.'

'If we accept that, it makes a mockery of Rankin's admission. He said cut diamonds, not one diamond but many, and certainly never mentioned one great diamond.'

'It would have been much simpler if he hadn't dragged in that business of the hyena's blanket.'

'That takes us right back to square one, Nadine.'

She came swiftly and knelt in front of the low locker I sat on and rested her arms on my knees.

'We must go back, Guy! We must!'

'If there's anything left to go back to.'

'We must be sure! We know we were on to something with the *isifuba* board. We can't throw it away.'

'The decision may be taken out of our hands,' I said. 'Listen to that!'

The boat rocked under a more powerful gust from the north-east. The rain went on hammering on the deck but the electric storm had clearly lost steam.

'It's ominous,' I went on. 'It's not an ordinary storm. My guess is that it was a thunderstorm at the start but that wasn't the major thing in itself: it was the small stuff on the fringe of a major blow-up. You don't get rain and wind like this from anything as local as a thunderstorm. It's coming in from the sea. And if I read the signs right, it's a cyclone which has run amok inland from the Indian Ocean, which isn't more than a few hundred miles from here as the crow flies. It's pouring in on that north-easter and it scares the pants off me, especially in this cockleshell.'

'Let's get back ashore, then.'

'That's impossible: we're too late. Feel that. She's just starting to ride the water. I went up to my waist in muck over the side just now. There's already enough water in the river to drown us before we could reach firm ground.'

'Are we simply going to wait for the river to sweep us away?'

The boat lurched farther upright and began to snatch at its mooring.

'Now's our moment of decision, Nadine. We're so to say afloat. If we're to keep the idea of somehow getting back to The Hill as soon as possible we'll have to fight the river. Otherwise we can simply hang around until we judge there's enough water under the boat and hightail it downstream.'

While I was speaking the boat swung cleanly on to an even keel and brought up with a jerk at the end of her rope.

'Do you still want The Hill, Guy?'

I took her hands and kissed the palms. 'More than anything in the world.'

She buried her head against me, still kneeling, and the warm drops fell on my hands.

When finally she drew back her eyes were very bright.

'I'm under captain's orders.' She threw me a mock salute.

'The captain and crew had better go and take a look at the situation on deck.'

I gave her my oilskins and wrapped myself in a kind of improvised poncho made of tarpaulin.

To my mind the wind seemed to be gaining momentum, and it sent sheets of rain slanting at us so that it was almost impossible to face the weather for more than a few minutes at a time. We turned our backs on the north-east and, hunched and streaming, tried to assess our chances.

The river front was a breath-taking sight. The formidable sky was a little less black in the east where the sun should have been, and gave off a smudgy grey, watershot light which made all outlines indeterminate. There was no horizon to be seen – just the slanting curtains of rain. The Hill appeared once or twice through the murk like a ship pitching in a sea-way and throwing water all over itself. Nearer at hand, the edge of the terrace looked equally strange. Torrents of froth-ing, chocolate-coloured water pouring over it were caught by the whipping north-easter so that it had the appearance of a great roller breaking on shore. What had a short while before been a stagnant pool at the confluence of the two rivers was now a flowing river beginning to flex its muscles. It was difficult to estimate its strength because the gale was churning it up against the run of the stream into masses of small waves. From every quarter came the roar of pouring water and the moan of the wind through the bare trees. Some of those near the terrace were already half submerged.

I pointed this out: 'No good there – the water's banking up,' I shouted.

'The edge of the terrace looks like Niagara!'

'The opposite side in the Shashi channel is our best bet,' I told her. 'Look at its big trees. They'll give safe moorings. This palm isn't going to hold much longer. Once the storm's blown itself out, we'll recross to The Hill.'

'How wide can the river become in flood?'

'A mile – two miles – who knows?'

The *Empress of Baobab* was now straining and tugging at its mooring like a dog on a leash. Her shallow draught and high freeboard made her very cranky in the gale.

'It's no use trying to plug into the teeth of this wind; the engine simply won't make it,' I said. 'We'd do better to strike diagonally across the confluence and then allow the current to carry us down to the tree we choose.'

'Isn't that pretty dangerous?'

'Anything's dangerous in this. You steer and I'll nurse the outboard.'

I pointed out as our target a large tree on a high bank opposite, slightly above the confluence.

'Steer for that and don't let her head fall off, if you value our lives, or we'll be swamped.'

'Isn't it simply Hobson's choice which bank we go for? Why not strike to this side where The Hill is?'

'If I'm right about a runaway cyclone, we can expect still more wind. Those high Shashi banks will shelter us. We'll make fast right under their lee.'

'What about your flash flood?'

'The Shashi's gradient isn't steep like the Limpopo's and therefore the run-off won't be as fast. Let's go!'

I stripped off the waterproof engine cover and prayed the electrics would work. It took half a dozen pulls on the starting cord before it kicked but it sounded healthy enough. Of course, her head fell off as soon as I cast off but I managed to bring her back on course by gunning the motor to its maximum.

The crossing was as slow and tedious in its way as our plod on foot through the wadi's sand. The engine's power against the combined forces of the river and the gale was weaker than I had expected and we chugged across the choppy water (with the bows trying to break away all the time) with a kind of hellish single-mindedness. Nadine was kept busy compensating but our course was as zig-zag as a war-time convoy under attack. We finally made it across and then nearly came to grief when the current bore us down on the tree I had selected. The boat's unexpected speed caught us by surprise and she was snared by a sunken branch which luckily snapped before ripping the hull.

I secured the boat fore and aft to the big tree and, with the lesson of the underwater branch in mind, lashed several small trunks to the boat's above-water bulges to serve as buffers. It was mid-morning before we crept below out of the wind and driving rain.

It stormed all day.

By late afternoon the river was in full flood and presented an awe-inspiring sight. Muddy water roared by, making a kind of deep-throated complement to the sound of the gale, which had increased in violence to a long dismal howl. It simply threw the rain at us, and it became impossible to stand and face the wind quarter, which remained north-east. Its con-tinuous pressure was broken at intervals only by fiercer squalls. The air was full of flying debris; these squalls seemed to pick up objects which the otherwise steady thrust of the wind passed over. The way the weather was developing made me more certain that a cyclone from the sea had indeed broken loose overland instead of veering characteristically back into mid-ocean. I explained to Nadine that I had heard of this happening on occasions in the past and that on these rare occasions thousands of square miles of countryside had been swamped. The pool at the rivers' junction had now vanished and in its place was a swirl of chocolate water by virtue of the down-current becoming stronger and running head-on into gale-lashed water. We checked at intervals and saw the waves grow in size until they were about three feet high. Two great natural forces were testing their strength against each other.

By midday we were certain that our decision to move to the Shashi bank was a wise one. The main torrent was in the Limpopo channel beside The Hill and the water there was banked right up to the terrace. The trees near the palm to which I'd originally tied up were under water, or had been washed away. The choppy water was full of floating timber and we saw some dead animals too.

As the storm grew in intensity I double-lashed the boat to our big tree. At first I secured her both bow and stern to its trunk and later to the overhanging branches as well. It was risky working on the exposed deck which the rain had made as slippery as glass and the wind plucked at one's clothing making it dangerous to stand. From time to time we had to bail out the cockpit when the waves came aboard and added their quota. As the afternoon wore on I became anxious about our tree's holding power in the wet bank. I checked and felt reassured: it still stood firm; and I thought that by fending off the drifting debris and preventing a dam forming round the boat we would safely ride out the gale. The boat had also the advantage of the lee under the bank but this decreased as the water rose and increased her exposure to the gale. And as the day progressed the weather grew colder.

We spent some time examining and discussing the 'King's Messenger'. The fresh, strong torch we'd found in the boat showed clearly the chevron pattern in the centre of the stone and we made a cast of it by softening a candle and pushing it through the hole. Afterwards we felt surer that my hunch about its being part of an ingenious 'combination lock' was correct. However, trying to talk above the racket of the storm was tiring and as it grew worse we conversed less and even dozed at intervals.

About five o'clock in the afternoon I left Nadine and went on deck. The air was full of storm sounds. There was a weak smudge of light in the west where the sun was sinking but I reckoned that it would be dark soon. I couldn't see anything in the direction of The Hill and the river seemed to be boiling and churning worse than before. I checked the boat's moorings because there appeared to be a new degree of play in the way she bucked and swung on the ropes. I wondered if the tree was working loose from the wet bank and decided to get a light and inspect it after I had cleared away the build-up of loose stuff round the hull.

I was busy on this with a pole and had my head down, so still don't know from which direction came the wall of water which hit us. One moment I was shoving the debris clear; the next the boat had flipped on to her side, throwing me to the cockpit's bottom-board. The tree came loose and fell with a crash on top of us. Its weight must have plunged us completely under water because everything became a choking mess of muddy water. Mechanically, I grabbed hold of something and held on and then the boat and the tree, tangled together by ropes and branches, broke surface and shot away on the current. I had no idea which way we were going. The cockpit was full of water and the boat was still pinned on her side by the tree, which now began to bump and crash and threatened to hole her at every lift and fall.

I tried to get across to the cabin door to find an axe to cut away the tree but the angle of list made my first attempt impossible. For a moment I was held by evidence of how powerful had been the force of water which had hit us. A big tiger fish lay on the gratings: it had been sliced lengthwise on some metal projection and its guts lay pulsating while its razor-toothed jaws snapped feebly.

I managed to reach the door at my second attempt, and found Nadine safe but bewildered and up to her waist in water.

'Bail, Nadine! For God's sake, bail! I'm going to try and cut her loose!'

I thrust a bailer – a saucepan I found floating about – into her hands and seized my axe. I thought when I began to work on deck, however, that she would never rise again: the tree and boat swinging together in circles made my task doubly difficult. I went for the ropes first, then switched my attack to the entangling branches. Some of these were dead and hard and too much for the small chopper, so I concentrated on the smaller ones and cleared them sufficiently to enable the boat to float more upright. Nevertheless she was still trapped by some big limbs which banged down on the deck and punched some holes through it. I selected one which I thought was the main danger and after a tough struggle succeeded in hacking

172

it off. This gave me room for manoeuvre: I got the engine going and awaited my moment for trying to break free. The dizzy slewing went on and on and the way the boat rode heavy and dead brought fear into the pit of my stomach. I could see no sign of the banks: nothing but dirty brown water everywhere. I watched my opportunity and it occurred during one of the merry-go-rounds. The stern pointed clear and I snapped the engine into reverse and gave it the gun. She barely pulled clear of the tree because of the weight of water inside her; then, despite full power on the screw, she too began the same sort of swirling movement. I moved the rudder in every direction but it didn't help. So I cut the engine and went below to help Nadine bail out.

'Are we sinking, Guy?'

'Not yet. She's not badly holed, as far as I know. If we can lighten her and get control before she crashes into something we'll be okay.'

She touched her pocket. 'I've got the "King's Messenger" safe.'

'We'll need all the luck it can bring us.'

We bailed and bailed and brought down the water level inside the cabin but the worst part was the way the boat was listing first to one side then the other, as she went round and round with a slow spinning movement wherever the current chose to take her. As soon as the water in the cabin was below the immediate danger level I decided I must again try, using the engine, to bring things under control.

'I don't know if it's got enough guts to make any difference but I'll try,' I told Nadine. 'I must bring her head steady.'

'Where's the shore, Guy?' Her voice was very small and flat and her face looked peaked in the light of the swinging lantern.

'God knows. We may hit it at any moment. I daren't even think about floating obstacles.'

The roundabout movement seemed worse up on deck, though I had no fixed point to assess it by. The light was too bad to see more than a few yards ahead and all that was visible was the bucking water with its white caps of dirty foam looking like capuchino coffee. I couldn't spot the banks but from the force of the current judged we must be in midstream. I wanted something to steer for, something to end

173

that sickening motion. I tried to get the boat's head steady by using impetus of an outward wing plus full throttle but it didn't work. I tried a similar tactic when it seemed that the stern offered a hope, and revved the motor in reverse under full power until it felt it would jump clean out of the transom; but that didn't help either. I abandoned my efforts for a moment when I spotted a big tree trunk with broken-off branches whirling close in the same orbit as the boat and managed to pole it clear. There were suddenly more logs and trunks all round us now. I went into the bows with the pole to see whether there was perhaps a whirlpool or some obstruction which was causing the debris to bank up.

Through the murk and rain I saw what it was – a moment before the boat struck – a low brush island with debris of all kinds heaping up against it. The boat was still running and yawing like a hunted animal and there was no time to make even a gesture with the engine to avoid it. We tripped over a seething white reef fronting the island and bumped across it with a sickening crash-grind, crash-grind.

I was caught on the open deck with only the pole in my hands and nothing to hang on to. The jar on the keel shot me headlong into the water and I was carried away downstream on the current and into the night.

CHAPTER FIFTEEN

The water was very cold and I thought I would never come up. My boots and the tarpaulin poncho were a deadweight pulling down as the flood turned my body over and over. When I did surface I grabbed a lungful of air and tried to see the island where the boat had grounded but didn't know which way to look. It was dark and the waves splashed into my eyes and the swirling water completely disorientated me. The weight of my clothes and boots took me down again and I knew that I would drown if I didn't get rid of them or find something to hang on to. I was being whirled about, fairly deep under the water again, in a kind of blind-man's buff; then rose to the surface a second time, almost bumping into a piece of floating timber spinning about as I had just been doing underwater. I was too keen and snatched at it too quickly; it span and slipped away out of my grip. I tried to follow it but my boots and clothing stopped me. I attempted to thrash with arms and feet but the waves kept slapping me down and filling my eyes and mouth with ice-cold water, full of sand and grit.

I tried not to panic and told myself that the river was full of things to hang on to and that I had seen big trees about just before the boat struck. I'm only a fair swimmer and couldn't float because of my boots. Then I saw a trunk near by and it swung round as if it were meant for me. I held on to it and seemed to be moving very fast but there was nothing static against which I could judge my speed. Now that I could move my head freely, I looked for the island and the boat, and thought I saw them sliding away out of sight behind me. I couldn't be sure, however, what with the dirty water slapping into my face, but I hoped to guide the log towards where I thought the boat might be by thrashing with my feet and paddling with my free arm. But I couldn't work against the current and after a few minutes my throat tasted sour from the effort and my stomach muscles were strained; I wanted to retch but couldn't.

The rain on my face had a different quality about it from the water blown into it off the river. The latter was thick and muddy, and a silly phrase kept beating about in my brain about its being 'too thin to plough and too thick to drink'. I steadied the log and tried to face the wind, which I knew would be north-east, but every time I achieved this by paddling, a new eddy would swing us round and I would lose direction again.

It wasn't until I knew I wouldn't drown that I started to panic about Nadine. Until then I had taken it for granted she would be safe below in the cabin because the boat had grounded on an outlying spur of the island. But now the thought tore at me that she might have struck an isolated rock and not an island at all tearing the bottom out of the boat, with Nadine trapped in the cabin before she could escape. I lifted myself on the trunk as high as I could to see if I could spot the boat but it was dark and streaming and even the coffee-coloured wave-tops were invisible beyond a few yards.

It was colder out of the water than in and the wind seemed to cut into my chest through my soaking clothes. I fell back to my previous position, numbed by an inner chill and sick with despair.

I do not know how long I was in the river. There was nothing by which to judge distances or speed and my watch had been smashed. I was held in a tiny world of darkness, slapping water and cavorting tree trunk. I wondered if I would fall off if I got cramps or if I could do anything about a crocodile if it came my way. It was so dark, I told myself, that I wouldn't see it coming anyhow and the end would be quick. I also wondered whether any of the dead things in the river were hyenas and I cursed Dika and everything to do with von Praeger. I tried not to think of Nadine and clung to the hope that the boat had stuck fast on the reef, with the comparative safety of the island only a few steps away.

After a time it seemed that the wind was beginning to ease: it felt less cold about my head; and from the way it played in turn on my cheeks, ears and then the back of my neck I judged that I was travelling in a long swinging curve. The white caps appeared easier, too, though the current was stronger. I hoped the moon would give some light later on when the storm had slacked off, so that I could see if I was moving in towards a bank. I could have been near one a dozen times in the darkness without knowing it. At first I was hopeful but afterwards began to lose heart when the rain continued to sluice down. Now the wind was definitely less. I consoled myself that I mightn't be travelling miles away from Nadine but was perhaps circling about quite near her; and the thought brought me comfort for a while. I wished I had Koen's brandy. My toes felt dead when I wriggled them inside my boots. I wondered if the cramps would start there first or in my arms and whether I could do anything about lashing myself to the log when they did come.

We began to swing round more slowly and the white caps were missing. My trunk thumped into another log and then into a second one. I thought I could see other timber swirling about and reckoned we must have struck an eddy and consequently could be close to the bank. I didn't do anything to guide the log but let it pick up its own momentum again. I considered that the direction from which came the least thrust of current would be the shore. When I thought I had established this I paddled and thrashed but it was a poor effort as I was so cold and stiff. I knew that should I be swept out again into mid-stream I wouldn't be able to hang on much longer.

I fought the water and pushed at the log and then felt thorns across my face. I ducked to keep my eyes clear and at the same time reached up and found a firm branch. It was rough and solid and I realized I was ashore. But I was too weak to pull myself out of the water and hung at full stretch with a sensation of nausea in my stomach and pains in my chest. I rested, then began to vomit sour water. My feet were still hanging into the water; but when I felt strong enough I pulled myself hand over hand along the branch and at last my feet touched ground. I could no longer feel my toes and lower legs and my hands were being torn on the thorny branch. But I went on until I banged into the trunk of the tree itself, standing firm and upright in the water. I pushed on until I was quite clear of the river and fell down among some wet grass and bushes.

I lay there until the ache in my chest and arms subsided then sat up to take off my boots and get the blood flowing again in my feet. This wasn't easy: the leather seemed to have shrunk and the laces were impossible. As I sat fumbling with them the rain became colder and changed to a flurry of graupel or soft hail pellets. I crammed a handful of it into my mouth and the sweet taste washed away the sourness which had stuck like a wad at the back of my throat. I managed to get the boots off at last, emptying them of water; but as my exposed feet now felt even colder I put them on again.

The sound of water was everywhere. I tried to make out where it *wasn't* coming from, arguing that in that direction would be solid land; but I couldn't manage to pinpoint it. I explored, and found water near by, on every side: my island was about the size of two tennis courts. I found my way back to my original starting point, which I recognized from a scatter of the same tussocky grass I had encountered when first I'd cut the fence surrounding The Hill. When I lay down in the grass my imagination began to play tricks, and I fancied it was Nadine's drowned hair that I held between my fingers. The cold and fatigue made me lose control and I buried my face in the wet grass and wept, finally passing into a nightmare

177

between waking and sleeping.

It rained all night.

I lost all count of time and must have really slept because I remember jerking awake at the roaring. It was the flood and it seemed much nearer to me in the dark than it had been when I first landed. I thought the water lapping at me was rain, but when I crawled a little way away from the tussocky patch I found it was the river and that very soon my refuge would be under water.

I stood up and knew daylight was near because there was a grey smudge in one part of the sky. The wind was down and the downpour had changed to a drizzle. I decided to stay in my safe place amongst the grass and wait for the day. I stood there while the sky changed to a pale shade between brick and rose and the water level reached my ankles and then my shins. There was the extra cold which always comes with the dawn. When it was light enough I faced east and could make out in the distance a kind of flattening-out of the low hills on the northern bank which I guessed must be Rhodesia. Between me and the visible shore line was an apparently endless expanse of bucking dirty water. It was too dark to see the other side. I guessed from the geography that I was about six or seven miles down-river from The Hill.

There was no sign of the boat.

I realized I would have to vacate my perch and decided to select the best log that came floating past. When the water was nearly up to my knees I got a big one. It was only after I'd grabbed it that I was struck by the significance of the direction in which it was travelling. I was facing east, down-river, in the same direction as a flood might be expected to flow. But the way the log came was *from* the east – in other words, it was travelling west, upriver. I hadn't time to speculate because the water was about to sweep me off my feet. I was dead tired and frozen and dreaded another log journey because I didn't think I could hang on. The growing light showed nothing but that faraway shoreline.

The sun showed rosier through the hazy rain and the great lake looked soft in its light. I propped myself up by the armpits on a fork of my log and pushed off When the current took strong hold and swung me away from the east I knew my previous hunch had been right. I was being carried *west* on the current. I could scarcely credit it at first but when my direction stayed I knew that it was so. I lost sight of the shore and after a while the waves began to steepen and slap.

The rain let up a little but the air was still so full of moisture it was soggy as a wet towel. The glow in the east became more brick-red and visibility lengthened. I tried to counteract the physical effects of the cold by concentrating my mind on the puzzle of the current. I was losing feeling in the entire lower half of my body and the skin on my hands was taking on a puckered look from the water. Then I sighted and positively identified a hilltop which I knew was a few miles down-river from The Hill itself, and the solution came to me.

I wasn't suffering from hallucinations. I was being carried in the opposite direction to the normal run of the current – back towards The Hill. The answer was that I was caught up in a situation similar to that of two rivers I'd heard about in the adjacent territory of Botswana, where, in its northern part, there is an odd geographical feature known as the Selinda Spillway. Two great rivers, the Zambezi and the Chobe, converge at this point as do the Limpopo and Shashi at The Hill. The gradient of the Chobe's bed is shallow and that of the Zambezi's steep. Under heavy flooding the Chobe reverses its course when the bigger Zambezi takes over and forces its water up the shallow-sloping Chobe bed and as a result great areas of the countryside are swamped. In my case the Limpopo, in full flood, was taking me back towards the Shashi channel and consequently The Hill.

The solution gave me a momentary shot in the arm but it was short-lived. The pale sun filtering through the fine rain had no warmth in it. I became frightened of losing my grip, so I struggled out of the poncho and tied myself to the trunk with it. Soon I was glad I had done so because the waves became sharper and started splashing into my face.

Because of this I kept my eyes closed for long periods while trying to fight off my growing lassitude and sleepiness. As a result I was almost swept past the boat without seeing it.

I thought I was dreaming when I saw it riding near an island behind a little enclosure of debris which had banked up against a reef. I shouted but my voice was so weak that I knew that even if she were still alive she wouldn't hear me above the sound of the rushing water. The deck was deserted.

As I came closer I saw, from the way the other timber was being carried, that I should miss the island. I thought of swimming but knew I couldn't make it. I slipped free of the poncho and, pushing the tree-trunk end-on, thrashed and paddled until a blue haze came across my vision from the effort. I didn't see the whole tree floating on the current before it had crashed into me. The bump sent my log off into a kind of cannon towards the boat. At the end of its impetus and before the river caught it again I let go and splashed a few strokes to the debris piled over the reef. I went from log to log until I reached the boat and then fell into the water just short of it, but I managed to get a hand over the gunnel and started to knock feebly at the hull.

I knew no more until I found myself lying, stripped, on a blanket on the cabin floor with Nadine bending over me, massaging my chest and throat with warm oil.

'I came back,' I said.

She didn't stop rubbing but switched her fingers lightly to my mouth and face.

'My darling – my poor, poor, stupid darling!'

Her eyes were misty and I knew the drops on my chest were tears: they were warmer than the oil.

I reached up to kiss her but everything span round and the effort brought on an uncontrollable convulsive tremor in my frozen muscles.

'Lie quiet,' she murmured. 'Quiet, with me. Not alone. Not like all last night. That long, long night.'

She took off her clothes and put her warm breasts against my chest and her body over me and her lips against mine as if she were reviving a drowning person until the rigors died down. I thawed and her warmth drew the sweet smell of oil from our skins. Then all at once I wanted to cry and stay like that forever and I tried to tell her so but it was she who did the comforting, with those warm breasts of hers bringing the life back into me.

A bump on the hull brought us back to the reality of the flood danger.

'We must get out of here fast,' I said. 'Your island's being submerged, as mine was. All the stuff is starting to break away from the reef and soon this little cove will disappear. Then we'll be at the mercy of the current. I don't like the look of the waves either – they seem to be getting steeper. My guess is too that they'll get worse when we approach The Hill . . .'

'*The Hill?*'

'You'll understand when I tell you how I got here . . .'

She sat up and her slim body looked very lovely in the pinky sunrise showing through the porthole.

'Not a word before you have something hot inside you.'

'I'll disobey orders, however attractive they may be,' I grinned back. 'We're not out of the wood yet and when the current switches back to normal we'll never stand a chance of getting near The Hill.'

Briefly I explained the phenomenon of the back-flowing current while we dressed and I ate a hasty breakfast, which included good hot coffee made by Nadine.

'Bless the crazy current,' she said when I had finished. 'Bless it because it brought you back to me.'

'That current is also our golden opportunity. We can ride with it right to The Hill. Then if we are lucky we can finish exploring the *isifuba* board where we left off. The whole situation's playing clean into our hands.'

Her eyes were full of lovely things. 'I've still got the "King's Messenger" safe.'

'Splendid. And don't forget about Praeger. If he's marooned in Rankin's cave we can investigate safely and get away before he can do anything about it. On the other hand, if we don't take a chance we could wait days or weeks until the water goes down and then Praeger will be back in the game. Have you seen the lake that has formed?'

We went on deck. The rain had almost stopped and it was quite still. The redness had gone out of the east and visibility was a mile or more. We were alone in a sea of muddy water. I started the engine because the island was becoming more and more submerged; soon, too, the barrier of debris which had built up on the reef would disappear entirely on the rising water.

'There'll soon be enough depth over the reef to break out,' I said. 'What happened last night when she jumped over it?'

'There were several heavy bumps, then she rode free. I didn't pay much attention: I'd lost you and the rest didn't matter.'

In the stronger light the evidence of her ordeal showed

plainly on her face and eyes. After waiting a while we decided to risk the attempt to get clear. There wasn't much room for manoeuvre and I was afraid of damage to the screw if it caught in the reef, but I took it gently and she pulled nicely into the current. I brought her head round and we headed in the direction of The Hill.

Our hearts lifted with the morning and the thrust of screw and current combined to send the boat along at a spanking clip. She was light and rode easily though I had to watch carefully the water racing up from astern, to prevent her being pooped. There was no damage to the hull that I could discover. The sky lightened for a while behind the fine drizzle and we could make out the broken country on the approaches to The Hill. It was impossible to gauge the extent of the great shallow lake but it was grand and impressive and dotted with little islands; and in the shallower parts the tops of large trees still stuck out above the waves.

When we neared our objective we spotted a long headland jutting out with the current sweeping round its base. I recognized it immediately.

'K2!' I exclaimed. 'I'm damned if I thought I'd ever see it looking like that!'

'The water can't be very deep, Guy.'

'Twenty feet, maybe – what does it matter? It's enough to keep von Praeger bottled up.'

'If he's at the cave.'

'If he's not, I could almost feel sorry for him. Something came floating belly-up past me in the night. It could have been him, or Koen, or a dead croc.'

'Or Dika.'

I pulled her close. 'I couldn't bear it. I kept telling myself it wasn't you. But I couldn't be sure. Each hour after that was its own private hell.'

'I tried to draw your face with the "King's Messenger" but I couldn't remember how you looked. I couldn't remember! I went round touching all your things to try and bring you back. Are you warm now, darling?'

'Splendid. A little stiff.'

I pointed. 'There it is. The Hill.'

'The Hill – and our future.'

We were coming in fast from the east, a quarter from

which we couldn't spot the crevasse. The Hill looked gaunt and muddy but apparently the same, standing up out of the surrounding water which wasn't much higher than the foot of the secret stairway.

'This will be tricky,' I said. 'The current's wrong for us on this side of The Hill. It must be pretty rough too where the terrace used to be.'

The Hill was perhaps a mile and a half away by this time and the drizzle seemed to be more concentrated in its vicinity.

'There's certain to be a lee with slack water near the crevasse where we came down, Nadine.'

'We can probably walk up comfortably.'

'Then we'll try there for a start.'

The surroundings looked odd, being partially submerged; and where the wadi began the current split, one half sweeping through between K2 and The Hill and the other round the extremity of The Hill itself. The waves there looked dangerous against the rocks and I couldn't prevent the boat from being carried close in but we skidded past successfully and managed a sharp turn around this point which took us into calmer water. I kept the boat close in against the cliffs and the engine's noise echoed off them. We came in sight of the fatal wedge-shaped crevasse only when we rounded another small point and were almost upon it. The underlying rock had been swept virtually free of soil by the storm and an easy gradient ran from the water's edge to the tabletop.

We were heading towards a landing spit here when an aircraft engine started up.

Our eyes naturally went to the sky and so I lost valuable moments holding my course – and by the time I'd jammed the rudder hard over to make a break for open water it was too late.

A prop rider – a twin-hulled, shallow draught boat driven by an airscrew rigged on deck – shot into sight from behind The Hill and came creaming across the water straight at us.

'Oh God! It's Praeger!'

Nadine was right. He was wearing bright yellow oilskins and a sou'wester. He stood steering the craft from a forward cockpit and the propeller spun in a kind of enclosed wire cage astern. Too late I realized that this is what I'd seen on the river; not an aircraft propeller turning in the wind.

183

I yanked the throttle wide open and tried to reach broken water where the light-hulled skimmer would have to reduce speed in the waves but von Praeger anticipated my move and swept in a wide circle, effectively cutting off the escape.

'Duck, Nadine!'

I pushed her down before he fired: I only heard the report of the shot and didn't see where it went.

'Guy, Guy! He'll go for you, not me . . . !'

'He'll be a marvel if he can shoot straight from a bucking boat!'

I gave the boat full helm towards another escape route – the one we'd used to approach The Hill from the east – but the current was against us and cut the boat's speed and a bullet thumped into the hull somewhere for'ard.

We were caught like rats in a trap, but the trap had one opening left: the crevasse. I swung and headed for it and hoped it would not prove impossible. Praeger followed and as we found the entrance another shot ricocheted off the rocks flanking it. Once I felt the strength of the current sweeping through I knew we had lost. The boat slowed and Praeger guessed he had us because he didn't shoot again but came up stream gunning the airscrew in short bursts, the Mauser held ready until he should catch up with us.

Both boats were hanging against the current and in the confined space the racket from the engines was deafening. As a last resort I was about to cut my motor and let the boat crash stern-first into von Praeger's in the hope of damaging his craft's fragile hull, when he pulled out his automatic and held it on me. It was the look in his eyes which made me obey his gesture to kill my engine and make fast to the shore. They seemed sightless, as I imagined an executioner's eyes would look.

I jumped ashore and tied up the boat. Praeger then brought the prop-rider close astern and signalled me to secure it to us because the crevasse was too narrow for two boats alongside each other and the current race was very strong.

Dika was next to him in the cockpit and after he cut his engine we four stood and faced one another until the prop stopped spinning and it was possible to hear again.

His voice was harsher and higher pitched than before.

'I'm coming aboard! Dika!'

While he held the pistol on us the hyena jumped lumpishly on to our decked-in stern and stood there snarling.

Praeger followed.

'Where is the hyena's blanket?'

His eyes were blank and remote and terrifying. He then glanced involuntarily down at his hands the way he had done before he had tortured Rankin and I knew that he meant to kill me.

'You haven't got long, Bowker. I knew you'd come back to The Hill, that's why I waited.'

'See here, Praeger . . .'

'When you're out of the way I'll make the girl tell. Take your choice.'

I knew he wasn't bluffing. Nadine held on to me.

'Show him the "King's Messenger", Nadine.'

'No, Guy – never! It's ours, ours!'

Von Praeger's mild animation at the mention of it made him look slightly less inhuman.

'Ours? Ours?'

'Rankin gave it to us.'

'No, Guy! No!'

'Rankin did, eh?'

'We saw what you did to him, you bastard!'

'Then you know what to expect. You can make it easy for the girl and yourself. Come clean, and I'll be quick.' He gestured with the pistol.

'Show him, Nadine. We don't know any more.'

She still hesitated but when he aimed the gun at my head she pulled the great bead from her pocket and held it out to him.

He looked at it and us contemptuously. 'Don't try and bluff me that that's The Great Star of Africa! It isn't even a diamond!'

'Damn your great diamond, Praeger! And blast your bloody stupid crazy notion!'

'Get up forward out of the way, Bowker, and stay there. We'll soon see if you won't talk!' He rounded on Nadine. 'Come here! Get your clothes off! *Schmell!'*

I was already on the foredeck and he was too far away for me to jump him.

'Praeger!'

'Guy – please!'

'It always works,' he sneered. 'You've given yourself away. There's more to come, that's clear. Get it out!'

I sketched our discovery of the *isifuba* board and my belief that the 'King's Messenger' was a key in a kind of primitive combination lock.

He still looked wary and unconvinced.

I pointed. 'It's all up there at the top. It's not far if you want to check up. You can't get anything more out of us by torture or shooting or anything else because there simply isn't anything else to tell.'

Nadine was tense and her voice shaky. 'Guy's right. That's all. We didn't have time to see if the "King's Messenger" worked.'

'We'll soon find out,' he retorted. 'If you're lying, you'll pay for it, both of you. If you aren't, I'll make the end quick once I have The Great Star. You can't buy your way out. All you can do is make it easy for yourselves.'

The hulls of the two boats rasped together and the current gurgled past. Nadine turned from von Praeger and looked up into my face. I saw in her eyes everything I'd ever wanted to know.

'Let's go, then. It's scarcely a climb any more.'

Nadine led the way up the easy gradient of sloping rock and outdistanced von Praeger and myself to the top.

'Guy – it's *him*!'

Even Praeger, I think, discounted the possibility of a double-cross from her genuine astonishment. She gestured through the gaping roof of the underground chamber to its interior.

I thought at first that the copper-coloured face lying in a grave hewn in the solid floor was a mummy's but when I went nearer I saw that it was a perfect replica of a human countenance made of gold. The likeness to a living face was uncanny: it was mature, strong and sensitive, the lips full, the nostrils slightly flared, the eyes big under full brows.

There was no doubt, it was the king.

We had been right in our guess that the *isifuba* board was a slab of removable rock. It had been thrown aside by the up-heaval and the slotted ivory and gold combination groups were visible on its reverse side. The 'King's Messenger' was the masterkey but where Rankin had got that curious name, smacking of a court chamberlain whose function was to open doors to a throne room, we would never know. The slab had, in fact, formed a kind of solid window above the king's head and chest.

It was also clear from the outline of debris that he had lain in a narrow wooden boat before it had crumbled to dust. We knew when we went close that it was not a coffin because a miniature replica of this craft carved out of soapstone had been placed by the head – the king's phantom or spirit boat which ancients believed carried the souls of the dead to the next world. At its tiny tiller was an eighteen-inch high carving of a man in a golden toga and its likeness to the features of the golden mask was unmistakable. The tiller-head proper was a fish-eagle, pilot for the spectral voyage.

It wasn't only these superb examples of the goldsmith's art which took our breath away. The king's chest was encased in a short jacket of golden chain-mail and laced to it through rings at each corner was the most extraordinary and beautiful object I have ever seen. It resembled a second breastplate over the chainmail, but it was made of ivory, like the ceremonial *fou* which ancient Chinese courtiers held before the heart for an audience with their emperor. In its centre was a chased socket, also of gold, with ornate clasps.

Where the code of the hyena's blanket had originated was plain after a glance at what the clasps held, without having to refer to Dika for comparison.

It was a huge uncut diamond with the characteristic oily look and it was mottled like a hyena's hide with a number of small whitish blotches. One side seemed to have been chipped a lot and it gleamed, unlike the dull appearance of the rest of the stone.

It did not occupy the whole container and the size of the unfilled space, that of a man's clenched fist, matched the Cullinan. The corresponding cleavage face which had caused so much speculation was clear on The Great Star.

Mounted cross-wise below it was a hexagonally-shaped gold tube which was clearly meant to house the old diamond pencil.

The sight left us speechless. Not all of the body was there: the grave had been damaged by a minor fissure in the rock and the lower half was missing. An outline of thousands of tiny gold beads round the head and shoulders could have fallen from a decayed shroud.

Our wonderment, however, evaporated at von Praeger's harsh voice as he waved his pistol at us.

'Stand back! Don't touch it! I understand now what your grandfather was up to. He could have financed half a dozen exiled governments with that!'

I realized that he must also have spun Asscher some yarn about where the diamond pencil came from because I didn't see a man of Asscher's reputation being involved in such a set-up. Moreover, how the original Great Star of Africa had been crudely cleaved was beyond my confused senses at that moment.

I tried to get my breath back. 'Praeger,' I began.

His retort was high-pitched and jarring. 'Shut up! No wonder Kettler held out on me even with the rope round his neck!'

'You've got everything now you want and more, Doctor von Praeger.' Nadine's voice was fluttery and strained.

His eyes had that sightless, killer look.

'I'm going to keep my side of our bargain – right away! Get down on your knees, both of you, by that crack in the rock. It's a nice ready-made grave and will save me the trouble of disposing of your bodies. The shot'll be through the back of the head. You won't know it's coming.'

We looked at the stony face and then at one another and we came together and kissed each other full on the lips. We turned away to do as he said and Nadine interlocked her fingers in mine. Then I saw a fragile ray of hope and disengaged mine to have my hands free.

I held my voice as steady as I could. 'You've seen a lot of men bound for the gallows granted a last-minute wish, von Praeger. I'd like to make one.'

'What is it?'

'To see the king as my father did first – complete, with the diamond pencil in position.'

'It makes no difference to me,' he answered in the same tone of voice. 'In fact, you can crawl to me as your last gesture.' He pulled out the instrument and dropped it at his feet. 'Come and get it and put it in position yourself: Get down, you swine!'

I prayed he wouldn't see the purpose in my eyes and I went

on hands and knees to him. He laughed when I got close.

'Very good, Bowker! You can crawl to Dika too!'

I pretended to obey but snatched up the diamond pencil instead, palmed it into a throwing position and flicked it like a dart at him and screwed my body aside from the pistol all in one movement.

It was meant for his throat and found its target and stuck out like a barb. His gun hand seemed to freeze but he kept the weapon aimed at me and with the other he plucked the pencil out and the blood gushed over his front.

As it spurted, I felt the hyena stiffen and leap.

'Shoot, Praeger! For Christ's sake, man, shoot it!'

But he didn't, although he had time. Perhaps the gurgle he gave was an order which was choked by the blood in his windpipe. The brute's jaws clamped round his throat and he dropped the automatic and staggered backwards under the impact though he remained on his feet. He clutched and clutched at the animal's head and the place was full of dreadful sounds from both of them as they went farther backwards towards where the excavation shaft had been broken off short by the crevasse. I picked up the pistol with the idea of attempting a shot even at the risk of wounding von Praeger but before I could do so the two of them lurched a few more paces and disappeared over the cliff and we heard the splash of their bodies in the water far below.

I don't know how long we stood there while I held her. We didn't look over the edge because we knew that the current racing through would have done its work.

The sun was out and the clouds were breaking up and everything was bright and clean-looking.

'We can't leave him for someone else, can we, Guy?'

She scarcely had need to say it for we felt the same way.

'No, my darling. He belongs to the queen.'

'She started him on his voyage . . . do you think she's waiting for him?'

'I would have waited for you.'

'And I for you.'

And so we knew what we had to do, but before we moved the king I washed the diamond pencil clean and put it back in the socket where it belonged. There were some small diamond chips lying next to The Great Star and I collected them as

189

evidence for myself. Nadine gathered up the king's phantom boat and I picked up the king and cradled him in my arms. He was lighter than I thought because there was nothing underneath and all that remained was a little pile of dust in the middle of the outline of golden beads.

We made a little procession down the slope, Nadine in the lead carrying the phantom boat. When I laid the king on the cockpit gratings of our boat she stood on the rock to which it was moored and fingered the fish-eagle tiller of the king's phantom boat, her eyes full of unknowable thoughts. When I had made him secure with a rock at his head and his waist she came aboard and laid her ring against his lips for a moment. She took his phantom boat back ashore with her and I fired a couple of shots through the buoyancy tanks and opened the stopcocks, started the engine and locked the rudder so that the boat would head straight out into the lake.

I jumped ashore and we stood together, watching.

'Guy, didn't Charlie Furstenberg have a special way of saying goodbye?'

'Yes. It was meant for diamonds, but I can't remember the words. Something about good luck and prosperity.'

'I'll say that now.'

'I'll say it too.'

The boat ran true on the current and where it met the main stream in the lake at the entrance to the crevasse it was caught in an eddy and swung round so that the king looked back at us and The Hill. It hung on the eddy as if it couldn't let go but then the main current caught it and we watched it go farther out and lower and lower among the brown waves until we couldn't see it any more.

Geoffrey Jenkins

Geoffrey Jenkins writes of adventure on land and at sea in some of the most exciting thrillers ever written. 'Geoffrey Jenkins has the touch that creates villains and heroes – and even icy heroines – with a few vivid words.' *Liverpool Post* 'A style which combines the best of Nevil Shute and Ian Fleming.' *Books and Bookmen*

A Cleft of Stars

A Grue of Ice

Hunter-Killer

The River of Diamonds

Scend of the Sea

A Twist of Sand

The Watering Place of Good Peace

 *Fontana Books*

Printed in Great Britain
by Amazon.co.uk, Ltd.,
Marston Gate.